## *Accolades for* Edge of Redfish Lake

"A terrific thriller and the most vivid, intimate and captivating look at the Alaskan fishing industry I've ever read."

Jack Dolan, Journalist and Pulitzer Prize finalist
*The Los Angeles Times*

"Conrad Jungmann Jr. crafts a fascinating look at the euphoric highs and tragic lows of the commercial fishing industry and the men and women who keep coming back... with a backdrop of a complicated murder mystery stretching from Alaska to Washington. A gripping read."

Chris Cocoles, Editor
*Alaska Sporting Journal* and *California Sportsman* magazines

"Packed with the kind of twists and turns that thrill-seeking readers and fast-moving journalists will love."

Randy Picht, Executive Director
Donald W. Reynolds Journalism Institute

"Filled with raw authenticity, this literary suspense novel mirrors the sometimes calm, often deadly, waters of Alaska and the Pacific Northwest."

Avanti Centrae, International Award-winning Author

"A carefully crafted tale of suspense written with rich detail. Abundant twists and turns make you doubt and reconsider what you think you know."

Brian Steffens, Educator/ Journalist/ Editor
Missouri School of Journalism

"A serial killer and the rigors of the commercial fishing industry come together in a tale of murder and revenge against the backdrop of the Pacific Northwest. "Edge of Redfish Lake" hits all the right notes."

Tom Towslee, Author

# EDGE OF REDFISH LAKE

*Puget Sound Press*

Mountlake Terrace, WA.

## A Killer Lurks in the Salmon Fisheries of Alaska

Alaska's salmon fisheries have long been the origin of adventure, intrigue, hard-earned money, danger, mystery, and tragedy. In 1988, as journalist Julian Hopkins tried to make sense of his best friend's drowning, he found out the fatally-beautiful Bristol Bay was also the lair of a killer ... an angered one who at season's end would follow him home and drag him into the heart of Seattle's most notorious unsolved serial murder case.

In his debut novel, Conrad Jungmann Jr. takes us on a suspenseful crime-legal drama, from rough-and-rugged Alaska to the edge of loyalty, loss, love, jealousy, justice, and vengeance. Full of hidden undertones and powerful epiphanies, EDGE OF REDFISH LAKE is the author's ode to the Alaska commercial fisheries, old-school journalism, the Green River Killer investigation, DNA forensic science, and plight of Pacific salmon.

# EDGE OF REDFISH LAKE

A NOVEL

CONRAD JUNGMANN JR.

EDGE OF REDFISH LAKE

# CONTENTS

For Mom and Dad and Jennifer

# ACKNOWLEDGMENTS

For six summers beginning when I was twenty, I was blessed with the opportunity to work in the commercial salmon fisheries and witness Alaska through a young man's lens. Those experiences molded me, inspired me, sometimes haunted me, as I forged ahead to future adventures in family, journalism, and advertising. Somewhere on my journey a story idea was planted. Its seed, fertilized by the fleeting tales of the Bristol Bay of yesterday, grew steadily in my mind. I vowed to someday cultivate and share it.

The process of writing the novel and screenplay, EDGE OF REDFISH LAKE took more than two years. Certainly, this couldn't have occurred without great support, belief, and love from those who are closest. During that time no one was more patient and understanding than my wife, Jennifer and my three wonderful children: Lucas, Maya, and Gabe. For giving me a chance to chase this dream, I am perpetually grateful.

I'm beyond thankful for the ongoing feedback and critique from the best listener and writing coach I know, my mother, Joyce Daniels and proofreading from BettyAnn Tyson and Alicia Dean. Hats off to Donna Pudick at Parkeast Literary Agency and Black Opal Books.

The early readers who suffered through my roughest of drafts deserve a heartfelt thanks for offering me candid feedback and enough encouragement to keep pressing forward: Conrad Jungmann Sr., Rosemary Jungmann, William Parkins, Tom Laughnan, Danielle Jungmann-Weems, Todd Maugans, Nola Morrison, and Sheila Owens.

Finally, I'd be remiss if I didn't recognize some of those who adventured around Alaska with me during the late-eighties and early-nineties living and witnessing scenes similar to those found in the pages of this story: Stephen Clark, Jon Freck, Shannon Roberts, JZ Sturm, Tom Olmsted, Darren Miller, Kent Johnson, Kyle Wright, John Miller, Charlie Lipsey, Jim Standard, Scotty Sexton, 'Wild Bill' Lancaster, and the rest of you crazies. You know who you are.

# CHAPTER 1

# THE TURN

June 3rd was the Turn in 1988 but hardly anyone knew it. Afterall, that Friday in Western Washington seemed so—ordinary. But if one had paused and consciously attuned, they might have sensed something unnerving, a hint of uncertainty, a low-lingering moon, a subtle moment of change rooted in waterways all along the Pacific coast. For on that day, deep in the water, an annual migration was triggered. And in an instant, aimless journey pivoted to a determined obligation to get home.

Acting as the catalysts for this sudden reversal, rivers, swollen with melted snow and spring rain, pressed their upper banks, gained momentum, and with each passing mile rolled longer and stronger downstream. As they clashed with saltwater, their volume, force, and silt unsettled ocean currents. Salmon, from the far depths of the Pacific felt it, the soundless drumbeat, the turbulent marriage of salinities. Unable to resist the pull or ignore its invitation, instinct took over. Now was their time. The Turn. They were at long last being beckoned from the sea.

Powerful enough to fully capitulate the elusive schools and draw them back to spawn and die in the rivers that had given them life, this magnetism was one of nature's most mysterious forces, invisible. It had no sound, smell, or taste. But as was sometimes the case, the primordial energy of this phenomenon set in motion peripheral events, and an altering of paths, for a few *people* unintended.

❧

Jesiree Vallesteros gave the candy-red elastic band one final cinch sideways to announce to her older sister she had finished braiding her hair. Now they matched. And not just by their jet-black braids so intricately woven the way their mother had taught them. They also sported identical jackets, jeans, and pearl-white tennis shoes too.

"There you go. Now the morning is simply full of wonder," she sat back in her seat and giggled her approval. "And we're on our way to Alaska."

When her sister didn't respond, she leaned back in. "Oh, c'mon Dari. Everything will be just fine."

Things in fact, were not just fine, and hadn't been from almost the moment they left their home, the day before, seven-thousand miles away in the Philippines. Amidst a panic caused by too many last second hugs spread across a large and loving family, they had missed their flight by minutes and had been re-routed to San Francisco rather than their intended destination, Seattle. The change and explanation delayed them in Customs for hours, leaving them with only one option they could afford. Racing to the other side of the beautiful foreign city, in a taxi, they barely made it to the station in time to catch the last Greyhound bus of the night. Dari had chosen seats three rows back from the driver, close enough for him to hear if they needed something, yet far enough away to make them feel like they were on their own. The sun, now fully risen on a less hectic day, found them tired, hungry, and nervous, but oh, so excited at the same time. They had finally done it. They had finally left home!

"Jesi, I hope Father called Mr. del Prado to tell him what happened," Dari finally blustered in an accusing voice. Always punctual and precise to the point where it was often a problem, she still hadn't forgiven her sister for making them late in Manila. After all, Venju del Prado had made it crystal clear when he hired them on the phone, a month before, if they weren't at the company's corporate headquarters in Everett, Washington *that night,* he would give their jobs to someone else. *Didn't she realize that?*

"Oh, lighten up, Dari please. I know you haven't slept but do chill out. We'll be there in a few hours with plenty of time to spare. And once we arrive, he won't care what airport we flew into." Jesi crossed her eyes and twisted her mouth into a contorted face that always made her sister laugh. It didn't work this time. "Oh, c'mon. We don't even need to tell him if you're afraid of what he'll say. Sure, he sounded tough, but all bosses do. Plus, he's old friends with our Father. He and his crew won't leave without us. I promise."

The Vallesteros sisters were not the only ones traveling north that day. Tens of thousands of people made the trek each summer to Alaska, flocking to canneries, processors, and fishing boats all along the six-thousand-mile coastline. Attracted by money, adventure, and more often than not, necessity, these seasonal jobs were perfectly timed to entice college students on summer break, ski bums clinging to memories of fresh powder, migrant laborers stalled between West Coast fruit harvests, and ex-convicts seeking work with only winks for background checks.

Dari tried to flush the negative thoughts out of her mind, but a portent feeling of dread wouldn't leave her alone. She took solace beyond the smudged pane of her window, where freshly cut farmland and mature cedars intermingled, and kept trying to convince herself that her younger sister was right. There was nothing to fret about. Soon they would meet the rest of their crew at the company bunkhouse, eat a good meal, and stretch out in a warm bed. None of them would care that they had missed their flight in Manila or that they'd been forced to take a detour through San Francisco. Tomorrow the whole team would fly out together for the final leg of their journey to the Bristol Bay in the great state of Alaska, a place she'd been dreaming about since she was a schoolgirl. They'd make lots of money and send some of it home to their family. Maybe they'd have enough time to travel around the country when the season was over. Perhaps they'd see a bear. Everything was going to be okay. *It was.*

As she marveled at dark-pine forests blanketing mountains that seemed to touch both water and sky, she played nervously with a salmon charm on a thin gold chain around her neck. Earlier that week, their spiritual mother had blessed from evil spirits two matching necklaces, before ceremoniously presenting, one-by-one, to each of her daughters with a whisper.

"To the Native people of the land you are travelling, these totems are Nerka. They symbolize abundance, kindred, and renewal. Use its courage to aid you on your long journey. Draw on its determination to lead you safely home."

While Jesi wore hers hidden next to her heart, Dari's hands were inexplicably drawn to hers. As if it were a delicate piece of fuzzy yarn, she rolled the almond-sized pendant over and around until its two sparkling diamond eyes, and intricate hand-etched scales, were covered with a consistent blanket of link. When the amulet wouldn't tighten any more, she gave it one final upward pinch, let go, and set it free. Like a tiny-lively bait on a string, it pirouetted into a bouncing, spinning freefall and disappeared inside her loose shirt.

"Dari, please stop that! You've been doing that for hours now and it's driving me nuts."

Eyes still glued on the rich cedar scenery sliding by outside, Dari smirked and began the tedious process of twisting the little golden salmon charm back up again, pretending not to hear another word her sister had to say.

⌦⌫

Downtown on the Seattle waterfront, Julian Hopkins nervously bounced his leg in a lobby chair outside the office of Francis Bernard, editor-in-chief of the *Seattle Post-Register*. Blown-up, black-and-white photos of major news events past and present covered every wall. Hanging prominently by the door, two framed Pulitzer prizes confirmed the paper's ongoing commitment to excellence, fairness, and credibility. Julian was grateful one of his professors had called in a favor and set up this job interview for him. In a window overlooking the vibrant harbor below, he did a double-take as his focus shifted from a distant white-and-green Washington ferry to his own reflection a foot away. Neither tie nor borrowed sport coat fit him naturally. Creases on his obviously brand-new white shirt were still visible from the package he had opened earlier that morning. Inhaling sharply, he tried to wipe the imperfections away but quickly gave up and shrugged. Ever since rolling into town the night before he had been uncharacteristically nervous, but now that anticipation had caught up with real time, his anxiety was waning.

Soon, a smartly dressed and bow-tied newsman appeared—silver hair groomed as meticulous as his mannerisms—and led him into an expensively furnished walnut room. "Julian, I've reviewed your resume and read your portfolio. And I must say, your writing has a spirited sense of energy mixed with thought-provoking style."

For over two decades, Bernard had been recognized by both the community and his peers as a thought leader who set the very highest of standards of journalistic quality and integrity. Under his guidance a generation of trust had been established between the paper and its readers. Through the years he had trained his eye to discover fresh talent and he took great pride in his approach. Seattle was a two-newspaper town and most of the hiring managers he knew at his giant competitor down the street sought only seasoned writers. Bernard preferred to hire the young and hungry. Smart grads without bad habits who he could easily mold into his image. Writers he could cross-train to handle both breaking news and researched investigations. Ones who were quick, nimble, efficient, and willing. Just the way he liked it.

"Your professors speak highly of you and no doubt your accomplishments in college are impressive. So, tell me why you want to move to Seattle from Colorado and work for us here at the P-R?"

"To be honest with you, I've been moving around my whole life," Julian grinned and drew Bernard in with his deep voice and confident tone. "I was born here locally, but we moved to California when I was four. I went to college in Colorado, and each year, to get to my summer job in Alaska, I've traveled to this area often. And for some strange reason, Seattle always feels like home. Coming back here is kind of a calling, if you will."

Bernard shot him a questioning look. "So, you like to keep air under your wings?"

Julian reassured him. "Mr. Bernard, I'm ready to start my career. Sink some roots."

Satisfied, Bernard asked Julian to walk him through his routine when he was the editor of his college newspaper. He wanted him to describe the thought process and steps he had taken when he had free-lanced an award-winning feature story for the *Rocky Mountain News*. The news manager directed the interview with fair but tough questions that challenged the new grad to think quickly. At times he pushed him out of his comfort zone before gently ushering him back in.

"Julian, a lot of good writers want to work here. Why should I hire you?"

"Mr. Bernard, in j-school we spent as much time talking about advancements in new technology as we did on fundamentals. Everything we did was on a computer. I know how to use them, I can help others, and I'm convinced that's where journalism is heading."

Bernard smiled and shifted the conversation light. As it turned out, both men shared the same sarcastic sense of humor and they both loved fishing. Julian mystified him with epic tales of wild Alaska. At the end of the hour Bernard's phone rang. He didn't answer it but rather looked at his watch regretfully.

"I'll be honest with you, Julian. I took this meeting more as a favor to your journalism professor than anything else. But now that I've gotten to know you, I can easily picture you on our team. I can tell you're a man of integrity and I like your outside points of view. And I especially appreciate your grasp of computers, emerging tech, and science. Different perspectives keep everyone on their toes, and Lord knows some of the ongoing investigations we have in this area could sure use a fresh set of eyes," he pointed to a black-and-white photo of two detectives, one in mutton chops, carrying what appeared to be a dead woman out of a river. "And a new set of tools to get them solved."

Julian nodded with the newsman even though he didn't know what event the photo depicted.

"Jobs don't open up here often and unfortunately I won't have one available until the end of the summer. One of my best reporters has announced her retirement and we've already set the date. Of course, we're sorry to see her go, but as I always say, dark voids are made to be replaced with bright lights. Her desk is yours, if you can wait until then."

Julian needed no time to contemplate and made up his mind before he even heard what the job paid. It didn't matter. This was the break he'd been dreaming about. "Mr. Bernard, that works perfectly for me. Dragline Fisheries wants me back for a fourth summer in Alaska. It's only an eight-week season, so I'll easily be back from Dillingham by the time your position is ready for me. If that timing works for you, I gratefully accept your offer."

Bernard held out his hand, "Splendid. Should we plan on August fifteenth?"

Julian shook it, "August fifteenth it is."

⌘

Detective Nick Nizzi drove the slow way home. He dreaded the conversation, and guaranteed confrontation, he was about to have with his wife. For the past four years, as part of a special forty-member team formed by the King County Police to crack the country's most notorious unsolved homicide case, he had worked both days and nights, weekends and holidays. While investigating leads that always petered into nothing, he'd immersed himself into the city's underbelly of prostitutes and pimps, delivering heart-wrenching news to families of victims, all the while tracking his activities on a brand new computer system neither he nor anyone else knew how to use. And now, just like that, it was over.

Somehow still stuck in the 70's but not giving a shit, Nick had long, signature, Elvis-like mutton chops and rumpled black hair. He wasn't tall, or short, or handsome, or homely. People came to him when they needed to hear the truth and avoided him when they wanted to brawl. Except for his wife. She picked a fight with him every chance she got. From his back pocket he tugged out a pair of black-callused leather gloves and tossed them into a banker's box on the passenger seat full of newspaper clippings and other items he'd swept off his desk. The sight of his handcuffs made him grimace. Once shiny, determined, and polished, the cuffs were now faded, weary, and worn. He'd snapped their heavy-dull steel over the wrists of thieves, abusers, druggies, and drunks. But not on the killer who had left three dozen women in his wake. Not on the one who had littered the southern woods and hillsides with bodies. Not on the one who lurked in the shadows just beyond his reach. Not on the Green River Killer.

At a stoplight he slammed his forearms against the steering wheel. Goddam bureaucrats. Goddam city budgets. Goddam mayor. Goddam media. *Goddam it.* The investigation had gone cold. The serial murderer had stopped killing and the Task Force was now being slimmed down to a skeleton crew. Only the handful of detectives who had started it in 1982, the originals who had suffered through every one of the tough and painful early years, would remain. Nick Nizzi was not one of them. At thirty-two, he was suddenly off the case and being forced to choose where he wanted to be reassigned.

Even though he had joined the team later than some, a full two years after the first bodies were found in the river, the hunt for Him had still turned to obsession. No vacation he had ever taken was far enough away, and no hobby or diversion had ever allowed him to replace the unaccomplished feeling in his mind and in his life. As much as he tried, he had never been able to capture even a few minutes of peace. His first wife had left him because he hadn't been able to give her the attention she deserved. There was a good chance his second one would soon leave him too—probably less than ten minutes after he told her his news.

"Christ, the killer is still out there," he murmured. "Would I realistically be able to move a few desks down and swap homicide for regular police work? Until he is caught, no matter where I am, will I ever be able to think of anything else?"

He sat in his driveway for almost an hour before making his mind up for certain. He'd take the transfer to Everett, twenty miles to the north where he'd still be a homicide detective. At least a part-time one. Very few murders occurred there, maybe one or two a year, and the small suburb was generally sheltered from the problems of the big city. He swallowed the knot in his throat and trudged slowly to his front door. *Did I really lose my job before I could finish it?* Whether his wife liked it or not, he

was moving to Everett. With or without her. As far aw፤
River Killer as he could reasonably get.

❧

As late afternoon turned to evening, the predator smoked in the shadows across the street from the Everett station: watching, waiting, wishing, wanting. From a steady stream of buses, he sized up each departing passenger like the elk and deer he had been hunting in the mountains his whole life. His adrenaline spiked each time a new carrier pulled up, but to anyone on the street passing by him he seemed plain, calm, quiet, unassuming. They paid him no heed. Always using the same proven techniques for luring, culling, and hiding his prey, he had lurked in places like this many times before. Practice had taught him how to detect vulnerabilities and single out his victims. The passing of time had taught him how to mask his inner pain. Deceptively intelligent, he had trained himself through the years to blend in so well with his surroundings that when he left a room people usually didn't remember he'd been there. On the exterior there was nothing to warn them of his deep-rooted hatred for humanity. His lack of empathy. No hint of the burning rage that had been simmering inside him since he was a child.

Earlier that day when he first pulled into town, he was anguished to learn the Mexican work crew, that he had been a part of the year before, hadn't yet arrived. They were still harvesting down south and might be delayed for weeks. *Damn his bad luck.* Broke and hungry after a seemingly endless winter during which he had run out of both meat and fish, those were weeks he did not have. As he waited in the hall for the janitor to come and issue him a bunkhouse key, Venju del Prado popped out of a door, yelling at someone back inside.

"Damn those two sisters," the Filipino boss bellowed. "They're late! They should have been here long before now!"

A Filipino voice from inside responded, "Calm down. I'll call the Seattle airport to see if they even got on their flight."

"I bet they changed their minds and stayed in Manila," said another. "This happens every year with young women."

"Damn them," stomped del Prado. "They could have at least called. If they're not here soon, I'll have to give their jobs to someone else. I have no choice. We leave in the morning!"

The predator remembered some overseas workers the year before had flown to San Francisco before riding a bus north. He snatched a key from a nail on the wall and snuck out without being seen, eyes sharpened with a hint of hope. Tonight, he'd hunt with a purpose. Premeditated and desperate, a kill would land him an immediate cash job for the summer at Dragline.

A bus pulled up. Nothing. Then another. His heart raced. There they were. He watched them skip down the steps. Sisters. It had to be them. He flicked his burning Salem Menthol onto the sidewalk where it landed next to eight others just like it and opened his door.

Like a phantom with slicked-back, oily, charcoal hair disguised by a deliberate, meek demeanor he stalked across the street and melted into the melee of pickups and drop-offs. One girl carried a backpack sporting a patch that read: "Far Eastern University, Manila." He trailed his marks closely. Venju couldn't know they were here. No one else could either. The killer's instincts felt right. The glisten in his eye turned to glazed intent. When the taller of the two asked an attendant for directions, he craned towards her foreign accent from three feet away. Satisfied, he rushed back to his truck and calmly pulled up beside them as they skipped away from the station. With a trusting smile he rolled down his window, tapped his wrist, and shook his head with feigned dismay.

"You're late," he slavishly grinned. "I'm your ride to Dragline Fisheries. Venju and the whole team is waiting for you to arrive. Hop in."

"Sorry we're late. We missed our Seattle flight and got rerouted," confessed Dari.

"To lovely San Francisco!" quipped Jesiree. "See, I told you everything would be okay." She reached around and pinched her sister's butt. They both giggled as Dari tried to return the gesture, forgiving her in the process. Relief replaced worry in the older one's eyes. Lulled into complacency by his contrived and well-rehearsed pleasant personality, the girls had no reason to be alarmed. They smiled as he lifted their heavy packs into the back of his truck and sweetly thanked him as he opened their side passenger door. The commotion of other passengers filled the air. No one had any reason to look their way.

As he eyed a stone club strapped behind the seat, and slammed his door shut, he felt no love or kindness. No empathy or remorse. No sadness or regret. For him, murder had always been a prideful game, unspeakably mean, cruel, quick, and calculated. He killed when he got angry. He killed when someone did him wrong. He killed to steal or when killing benefited him in any way. Throughout his adult life he killed anytime and anyplace he had an opportunity, and about his heinous crimes he had never whispered a word. Indifferent to age, sex, race, and religion, sometimes he killed simply to kill.

Hours later, when he pulled back into the gravel lot and parked behind the Dragline bunkhouse, he didn't notice Jesiree's small backpack fall out and roll under his truck. His eyes were too mesmerized by Dari's salmon charm necklace, erratically swaying from his rear-view mirror, lost, —like a gasping fish—freshly jerked from the water.

# CHAPTER 2

# JULIAN HOPKINS

The one-hour flight west to Dillingham from Anchorage was Julian's favorite leg of the journey and on this day featured the rare thrill of a drizzly morning burning off into a magically clear afternoon. Smoking volcanoes passed by in jagged rows to the south. Creeks sliced through the magnificent vastness like nonuniform wrinkles in an ancient face. Julian let his eyelids softly touch, mentally preparing himself for the work-challenge marathon he'd face the moment he stepped off the plane.

Soon the faded white *PenAir* puddle jumper approached a sea-sized lake. Dramatic, unnamed, snow-capped mountains lined one shore. Virgin tundra hiding the region's mineral lifeblood—undisturbed by bucket or shovel—stretched north and west for as far as the eye could see.

"We're crossing over Iliamna," the pilot announced. "It's the nursery for the world's largest run of Sockeye."

The boat captain whose bony knees kept pushing into the back of Julian's seat educated the greenhorn beside him, "Unlike other salmon species, Reds must pass through a lake before they can spawn. They're already on the way. And when they get here, those streams you see down there will turn crimson, like arteries in a cadaver. It's a marvel to see millions of Redfish all together in one place."

14

To the other passengers crammed in around him, Julian looked older than his years. His cheeks, aligned with a strong sloping nose, were slightly lifted and perpetually poised for a smile. His charismatic hazel eyes carried an air of educated alertness and during conversations were quick to connect with others. Broad of shoulder, he was of average height, healthy weight, and had sable brown hair that he preferred to wear longer than short. Even though he had shaved before his job interview three days earlier, a consistent layer of whiskers now covered his tough-square chin. He felt perfectly at ease in his faded jeans, hiking boots, and a plain white tee buried beneath a thick red-and-black checkered wool shirt.

Ever since his meeting with Francis Bernard, Julian had been suppressing a genuine grin, one he'd been flashing more often than normal, even at complete strangers. He couldn't wait to tell his college roommate, Boone Davis, and his best friend since childhood, Dave Stevens the good news. Both knew how his dream to be a journalist had driven him through college. Both knew he had his sights set on a big market on the West Coast. At twenty-five, Dave was a year older, and had been Julian's confidante since they were little kids growing up across the street from each other in California. Even during the summers, when Dave was in Alaska fishing with his grandfather, they would write letters and at the end of the season, pick up right where they left off. Four years earlier, it had been Dave who had lined up this summer job for him when Julian announced he was moving, to Colorado, to attend journalism school.

Julian inhaled deeply. To get a job for a paper like the *Post-Register* right out of college was amazing enough, but to have the chance to come up here, make some quick money, and spend another summer with his best friends before he started? Loudly exhaling, Julian grinned at his grateful reflection in the window.

As they approached the west end of the massive lake, they entered the ancestral land of the Yup'ik. Rivers flowed quicker here. Trees became scarce. Soon, a cluster of buildings materialized, nestled at the confluence of two mighty rivers. For the Native people of the area, the village was Curyuk, named long before Russian fur traders arrived a century before or the white men who incorporated it into Dillingham after they left. Here, in the surrounding waters of the Bristol Bay each summer throughout millennia, massive schools of Sockeye formed, waiting for powerful tides to push them far upstream to their natal waters so they could spawn in the exact gravel of their birth. Their annual return was the largest on earth and each season sparked an international billion-dollar industry. During a good year, commercial seiners and gillnetters harvested thirty million fish. In the heat of the frenzy, significant fortunes were made, missed, stolen, saved, and spent.

Right on time the aircraft touched down, throwing sprays of gravel with each bounce until it grabbed wet ground and powered across a pothole-laced runway. The pilot revved both engines, then let them sputter to a rainy, breezy, cool silence. Fresh budding alders lined a ravine to the east. Green, white, and red blooms of early summer burrowed through the tundra beyond. Julian tucked a wild strand of long hair over his left ear and squinted down the runway as nineteen working men, all bred from the same hard school of labor, pushed past him to light smokes. Other than a treacherous multi-day voyage by boat across the Gulf of Alaska and through False Pass in the Aleutians, this desolate airport was the only way in. And the only way out.

On the side of a beat-up old shed the locals claimed was a terminal, a man in a lime-green Dragline Fisheries ball cap motioned him over. Julian and two commercial fishermen about his age made their way in his direction and climbed into a hard-ridden, dust-caked Chevy van. In the distance they could see hurried movement on the town's main dock a mile below. A forklift offloading freight from a large ship disappeared through the tall doors of a brightly lit warehouse. In the marina Julian counted twenty, twenty-five, thirty fishing boats loosely tied up, ready to fish at a moment's notice.

"Won't be long," one of the ruffians in the back seat pointed, breaking the awkward silence.

The driver nodded. "You're right about that. Won't be long, indeed. So, tell me what's going on down south? I'm dying for news. I haven't seen a paper from the lower forty-eight in over two weeks. Yesterday I picked up the Filipino laundry crew and only two of them spoke English I could understand. The boss, Venju, he was talkative enough, but he didn't know much either. The other dude—Christ he was a prick. When I prodded him for headlines, he just glared at me. He's a real piece of art, that one."

One of the fishermen laughed. "What an asshat."

The other shrugged. "Somebody needs to put a boot up his crack."

"Maybe. The son of a bitch pushed me out of the way when I tried to help him with his duffels. I know we get all kinds up here, but that guy sure seemed angry about something. I'm not turning my back on *him* this summer, not even for a second."

Julian raised his brow and took mental note. Being so far out in the bush of Alaska, news from the rest of the world trickled in slowly to Dillingham, and mostly, not at all.

"The Lakers are on a roll again," bragged one of the men in the back seat, finally answering the question. "I think they're gonna win it all this year."

"Nah. The Pistons are the true NBA champs," the other sat up tall as if posturing for a fight. "You watch, Isaiah Thomas will end the Magic in tinsel town."

"It will be a good series for sure. Game one tip-off is tonight," Julian added to the conversation as it quickly escalated into passionate debate.

Forty yards ahead, as they rounded a wide bend in the road, the pulsating yellow and red neon sign of the Blue Spruce flickered "Open." Julian smiled at the irony. Between June and September, the bar *never* closed. A half-mile past that, beyond the blue-domed Russian Orthodox church, the family home site of the close-knit Chiklak subsistence fishing clan came into view. Weathered and old, the large main house was carved into a bluff overlooking a Mississippi-wide muddy river. On clear days it had a bird's eye view of distant mountains that glowed deep amethyst. Four or five smaller houses spread haphazardly out around it, as if someone wearing a blindfold had thrown stones left-handed to mark where to build. In front of each dwelling sat a shiny new snow machine, flat bottom boat, and pickup truck. In a clearing overgrown with weeds was a rusty line of older models now used for parts.

"Look. They've got slabs hanging already," the driver pointed.

On the crest of a breezy rise, the men's eyes were all drawn to the bright crimson and silver contrast of split salmon sides spread inside-out over aged alder racks. Generations of Chiklaks had been drying salmon on those arbors in traditional Yup'ik technique for as far back as local memory could recall.

Suddenly the driver fishtailed down a gravel incline and came to a sliding halt in front of a massive gray corrugated sheet-metal warehouse with a Mediterranean blue roof. Even though eighty-mile an hour winds swept in regularly from the Bering Sea and slammed it full force, the facility had never lost a panel. A man-sized, hand-painted red salmon holding a net and wearing a crown was centered above a tall roll-up door. Twenty feet off the ground, spanning from one end to the other, in black-block, hand-traced letters were the words: 'Dragline Fisheries Dillingham'.

"Honey, we're home," the driver guffawed in a fabricated, high-pitched voice to no one in particular. He honked twice and disappeared around the side of the plant. The two fishermen followed. Julian watched them melt into the yard where dozens of fishing vessels, varied in shape and age, were laced in haphazard lines leading to a towering wooden dock that reached far out into the slow-moving, yet powerfully dragging river. Nets were strung between boats like gargantuan cobwebs. The smell of diesel fuel, paint, and hot metal overpowered the humid air. The shrill scream of aluminum being ripped by a grinder provided a blistering beat for hard-working men: welding, ratcheting, painting, inspecting, loading.

With a crash, the heavy-steel side door of the plant flew open and a bearded man with ripped jeans and a blue-and-white checkered flannel draped over a black *Ski Telluride* T-shirt swaggered through. He lit the bent Marlboro Red that had been tucked over his ear and grinned. His eyes were cobalt-blue and jovial. Shoulder-length blond hair streamed from under a red bandana tied snugly around his head. He strutted over to Julian, gave him a strong smack hug, and threw one of his packs on his shoulder with the strength, prowess, and poise of a rodeo cowboy.

"Well, look what the damn dog dragged up. I'm glad you made it up here before the fish arrived, Jules. Dang dude. It's June seventh already.

But I think I have a pretty good idea of where you've been and why you're late. Let's go drop off your shit so you can tell me all about it."

As they crisscrossed through the maze of boats, Julian stopped to soak in the estranged surroundings of the fish camp, unchanged by the passing of an icy winter, sitting exactly where he'd last seen them. Realizing their apparent foreignness was caused by his own altered lens, he mentally readjusted his focus and by doing so, tempted the problems, pressures and people from back home to slowly fade away. He wouldn't have to deal with any of that for a while. Up here he could focus solely on work.

"Where's Dave?"

"You know him, he's already got his boat in the water," Boone laughed. "I'm sure he's out. Scouting for fish. Exploring. He brought up a greenhorn deckhand this year. His younger cousin, Charlie."

A mosquito landed on Julian's neck. He artfully smacked it dead and glanced at his palm.

"Jesus, it doesn't take long to get bloody up here."

Boone grinned jocosely, "Nope. Not long at all."

# CHAPTER 3

# DRAGLINE FISHERIES

Two hundred feet south of Dragline's main processing plant—plenty close enough to catch a foul whiff of fish every time the wind blew downriver—sat the bunkhouse, mess hall, and laundry. Rooms were reserved for select early arrivals, single women, and key employees who had boarded the last plane home the season before. Bright blue trademark paint melded the prefab pieces together into one large unified dwelling. On each side of a well-traveled center hall a dozen doors opened to dimly lit but warm, dry rooms. Each one featured two open closets, one electric heating vent, and a pair of wooden bunks stacked tightly to the walls on each side. Other than a beat-up old cassette player and a handful of homemade mixed-fruit tapes, the only other entertainment was reading. Like most, Julian brought with him two books and by the end of the season each would be traded and read by at least thirty others. A two-by-three-foot window allowed one to peer out at a permanently saturated greenish-orange treeless tidal flat, blanketed with cotton grass, for as far as the eye could see. Because twenty hours of midnight sun throughout the season blended the days into weeks, these small windows generally stayed tacked over with army-green, wool blankets. Bent sixteen-penny nails hammered in uneven rows outside each door accommodated coats and raingear. Every time there was a shift change, people were awakened by the angry yells of, "Hey dumbass. Leave your boots and raingear in the hall!"

Boone plopped down on a short stool. "So, did you get the Seattle newspaper job, Jules?"

With an affirmative nod, Julian tossed his sleeping bag onto his reserved top bunk and stuffed his duffel of clothes into the dark cavern beside it. Farthest away from the bathrooms, this den was Dragline's best sanctuary for sleep. A fish-free zone in a fish-full camp. A pair of two-by-four steps provided a thin layer of protection from needy factory workers and meddling thieves. He traced his fingers through the letters he had carved the season before deep in his bed's wood crossbeam, SAVE THE SALMON. As one who helped dismember over a million fish a year, he never tired of the dry irony and sometimes yelled it at the top of his lungs as a whimsical motivational mantra when his tired crew needed a boost during the grind.

"Yeah, I did," Julian took a seat on the bottom bunk. "They're expecting me to start right after the season, which unfortunately means I won't be adventuring through Denali with you this year, buddy."

Before Boone could complain there was a single loud knock and the door burst open. A short man with sharp-chiseled cheeks, pronounced chin, reddish-blond mullet, crooked nose, and a beard resembling a goatee stomped in. He wore a Metallica T-shirt without sleeves to show off his bulging biceps.

"Oh, hey Jules, I didn't know you were here yet. I'm heading to the galley for sup. You guys ready to eat?"

Like Julian and Boone, Chris Fitzpatrick was one of the returning foremen at Dragline and had taken the room across the hall.

"Let's do it, Jules. I missed lunch," Boone stood up and smacked Julian's shoulder in a teasing manner. "Some of us show up on time and still work for a living around here. I'm starvin'."

At the far end of the hall was a well-worn door that led to an all-you-can-eat buffet served every six hours. During the peak of the season the mess hall was so crowded that crews had to be split in two half-hour shifts. But until the main mass of seasonal workers arrived, everyone ate together in one big family-style setting. As they got in line, Julian waved at Pete the Cook whose famous buffet accommodated every work shift and featured breakfast, lunch, and dinner with military precision. Six, noon, six, midnight. Loads of potatoes. Lots of meat. Add your own salt and pepper. If you put it on your plate, eat it. "Well fed men work harder. I'll do my part. You boys do yours," Pete frequently bellowed.

Lined up single file down the south entrance stairs, hungry fishermen with large strong appetites waited impatiently. "I heard they're gonna let us start fishing at Ekok early," one of them announced.

Men turned to size up the voice. Accurate information was as important to remote coastal Alaska survival as water, food, fire, and shelter. Unlike other places, the truth here was rarely exaggerated or purposefully distorted. Liars were resented, rumors usually fact. Men were judged and respected by the accuracy of their word in this rough and rugged land. Apparently deciding the guy's information matched his reputation, the line shuffled forward a little bit quicker and with a heightened sense of urgency.

As Julian picked up a steaming-hot plate, he scanned the seated rows of men, many hiding under green company hats, for faces he knew. A fisherman flashed a peace sign from the far side of the room. A pair of grease-covered engineers who looked like they had been there all winter nodded. Four Japanese roe techs he remembered from the year before said something in their native tongue, laughed, and waved. A brown-eyed girl with a bunny on her sweatshirt looked up from wiping a recently vacated table. Her shy, vulnerable eyes lit up and her ponytail bounced with each step as she made her way toward him.

"Well hello there, Hannah," Julian voiced with genuine surprise. "I didn't think I'd see you back for another season."

Plain, pleasant, and gullible, nineteen-year-old Hannah Miller had flown to Dillingham for the first time the season before, a few days after graduating from high school. The middle girl in a family of five, Hannah had rarely been the center of attention growing up. She wasn't uncomfortable when people looked her in the eye and talked to her directly, she just wasn't used to it. But once she warmed up, her laugh was infectious and genuine.

"Pete talked me into returning," she explained, dropping her gaze to the floor. "He knew I needed money for college and promised me I wouldn't have to touch any fish if I came back."

Pete had raised his family in the same suburb of Anchorage as Hannah's. He was good friends with her father and always protective.

"That's awesome. I'm happy you listened to him."

Julian's words gave her enough courage to give him a hug tighter than he expected, his surprised look was as awkward as the loose squeeze he returned. Farther back in line, Chris cleared his throat. Like many others in the male-dominated camp, Chris had an obvious crush on Hannah but denied it when asked. Julian ignored him and continued to scan the room. In the back corner, close to Venju del Prado and a table full of Filipino workers, sat a man with slicked-back, oily, charcoal hair. Other than piercing burnt-russet eyes, his facial features were unremarkable. His complexion was weathered and dark like a deep suntan and he blended in well with his crew. Julian didn't recognize him at first, but when their eyes connected a second time, he did.

"Well, I'll be damned. It's Lev Warrens," Julian gave him a friendly nod.

Lev forced a tepid grin before darting his eyes quickly away.

Julian studied him closely before sitting down with his friends. "There's something changed about that guy, but I can't quite put my finger on it. He looks different somehow. I almost didn't recognize him. Wasn't his hair lighter last year?"

"Yeah, he dyed and grew it," Hannah concluded almost in a whisper. "Last season it was short brown."

"Yeah, that must be it."

"I bet he's trying to look Filipino," Chris quipped.

Noticing the confused expression on Julian's face, Boone explained, "Lev flew up here from Everett over the weekend with the Filipino laundry crew. Venju hired him when a couple of his female workers didn't show up from Manila. He'll help us process fish until the rest of our gang gets up here, then he'll move to laundry duty full time."

"Well, he doesn't look Filipino to me," Chris sneered. "Except for his new jet-black hair. And I can tell you right now he's not working for me again."

Boone grunted, "here we go again."

"C'mon dude. You know he was a drag on my crew last year. Big time. I had to show him how to do everything two or three times and it seemed like he could never keep up no matter where I put him. He's a royal pain in the ass. I won't take him back. No fucking way."

The year before, Lev had come up with the Mexican crew and as one of the oldest men in camp, struggled at times to keep pace. Julian glanced again at Lev's dyed hair and felt sorry for him. He released a sigh and turned to Chris. "Cut the guy some slack, man. I'll take him. He'll do just fine. I can teach anyone how to slime."

Hannah turned to Julian, and with her smile, revealed the crush on him she had kindled at the end of last season and had steadily grown in her imagination over the winter. Just then, someone from behind put a hand on Julian's shoulder. Startled on both fronts, he whipped around to see a thin figure with black-wire glasses hovering over him. Both men laughed at his reaction.

"Oh shit, Mike. I wasn't expecting anyone to do that. How in the hell are you?"

Julian stood and gave the plant manager a strong, vigorous hand-shake. Mike Matthews was in his late thirties, and like a taller Alaskan version of Napoleon, had been the undisputed leader of the Dillingham plant since the day it opened a decade before. Born and raised in a heritage commercial fishing family, he could organize the intricate moving parts of the Bristol Bay fishery better than a Swiss watchmaker could assemble a timepiece. Through the years he had mastered the ability to squeeze more production out of his small facility than most of the larger fish factories down the coast. No plant manager in the state had more inside information than Mike, after all, two of his cousins worked for the Alaska Department of Fish and Game. Mike knew when the openers were coming long before they were announced. Not even the know-it-all corporate money men back at company headquarters, in Everett, dared tell Mike how to do his job differently.

"Glad to have you back, Julian," Mike ripped a napkin from the dispenser. "I got a call from corporate this morning letting me know you were on your way."

He took off his glasses, breathed on them twice, and wiped them clean before putting them back on. In a voice loud enough for surrounding tables to hear he disclosed, "They also mentioned you landed a job as a reporter for the Seattle P-R. That's a big-time gig. Congrats Mr. Hopkins. When do you start?"

"Hey, congrats Jules!" Hannah cooed.

"Awesome dude," Chris added.

Julian told them about his interview, the job he'd accepted on the paper's combined breaking news and investigations team, and how he would need to rush out of Dillingham to make it there by August fifteenth.

"As the time gets closer, let's talk," invited Mike. "I may be able to help you. I used to spend so much time down there that I bought a nice old house in Everett. It's in a great neighborhood on Kromer Street. The upstairs is already rented, but not the downstairs efficiency apartment. I'll hold it open for you if you're interested."

"Interested? Heck yeah, I am. That would be frickin' awesome. I haven't had a chance yet to think about where I'm going to live. Thanks, Mike."

Mike excused himself and walked to the front of the mess hall before he turned to the crowd. Men grew quiet and put down their forks. Some shushed those across the table as they craned their ears in his direction. They all knew Mike Matthews wouldn't be here if he didn't have something important to say.

"Everyone listen-up. There's an early season opening up and we're not even close to being ready for it. Half the boats aren't yet in the water, we're short staffed, and if we don't get the production lines tuned up better than they are now, this will be a shit show. Dock crew, you might as well plan on working all night. Get all the totes stacked and cleaned. Engineers fire up the freezers. Eat up quickly folks. There's a whole hell of a lot we need to do."

The glare of Mike's glasses accentuated his narrowed eyes, which darted from table-to-table, issuing silent challenges—unvoiced accusations felt by everyone. Every summer the fish season began like a wintered garden hose that when turned on starts, sputters, and stops before finally filling up and spouting out in a strong-steady stream. This season the spigot was being opened a week earlier than expected. Without waiting for questions, Mike disappeared out the side door. He always ate by himself in his office—his version of a ship captain's wheelhouse, where he was an arm's length away from a radio tuned to the frequency of the fleet, the plant's only phone, and a pair of oversized marine binoculars he constantly trained on the river out his big bay window.

Men throughout the galley murmured. Raising both brows, Boone sucked in a deep breath and slowly let it escape between his teeth in a shrill whistle.

"So much for slowly getting acclimated to my new surroundings," Julian laughed. "This season is already on like Donkey Kong. I haven't unpacked yet and it's already time to slime."

For an instant his eyes caught Lev's, who once again turned away. Julian frowned. Had the man been listening to his whole conversation with Mike? Of course, he had, and for some reason, that thought made him uneasy.

∽✕∾

After supper, as the mess hall emptied out, it was Hannah's job to wipe down each table and make sure the napkin holders and salt-and-pepper shakers were full. She had mastered the art of holding a funnel into the small openings with her left hand and pouring with her right by propping up her hip as a stabilizer for the heavy paper bag containing bulk salt. It was amusing to watch her, and sometimes fishermen snickered. But she didn't care. No longer did she need help like she did her first few try's. She could now almost make it down an entire line of tables without spilling any grains. Lev lingered in a seat by the window, hands wrapped around a cup of coffee, one eye on her, the other on an arrow-shaped band of white geese, sporting tangerine beaks, that had landed near the boat yard. Hannah finished straightening up all the tables but his, almost said something, but instead turned and began wiping down spots she had already finished.

"Would you like for me to move?" he finally asked, softened by her shyness.

Her neck reddened and she acted surprised, but in a quiet-awkward voice she nodded, "I guess so."

Lev got up with a sardonic grin and moved one table down.

"By the way, I like your hair," she said timidly. "It makes you look younger."

Lev paused, fumbling for words. "Thanks. I ... I like your yellow bunny shirt."

Hannah beamed.

# CHAPTER 4

# FIRST FISH

As the commercial fishing opener at Ekok Beach loomed, Dave Stevens gave his greenhorn cousin a crash course he called Deckhand 101. Dave was twenty-five, four inches taller than six feet, muscular and fit, tanned and toned, a stereotypical California surfer dude. He sported shoulder-length curly-blond hair and almost always tinted his sea-blue eyes with hip designer shades. He wore sweatpants instead of jeans, and those he usually pulled over obnoxiously colored Bermuda shorts. When he wasn't working, he wore flip-flops. You could hear him coming from a mile away. Tough, cool, and unbreakable as hundred-pound braid line, Dave had been coming to Alaska with his legendary grandfather since he was ten. When the old man passed away seven years before, Dave skipped college and took over the operation without missing a beat. The family boat, *Proud Mary*, remained a high liner on the Bristol Bay fleet just as it had for the past thirty years. Dave Stevens, it was rumored, could catch fish anywhere he wanted, even in an empty bathtub if he chose.

"The most important rule, Charlie—is keep your blade on you at all times."

Dave had presented his younger cousin a double-edged deckhand knife before they came up together from Sacramento, along with a new pair of brown XTRATUF boots and orange Grundéns rubber work bibs, standard issue for experienced Bristol Bay fishermen. One side of the blade was serrated, the other was straight and sharp like a shave razor. Knowing his cousin was prone to losing just about everything, he had etched the initials C.S. into the red plastic handle with a wood burning tool. It fit snugly in a plastic scabbard connected securely to Charlie's raingear chest straps.

"Working with net on a boat, you'll need your knife every single day, guaranteed. So, don't ever board Proud Mary without it, okay? Treat that blade as an extension of your hand. And always do exactly what I tell you, when I tell you to do it. Charlie! Charlie, are you fucking listenin' to me? Hey, pay the fuck attention!"

Charlie was a thick six-foot-two, hard-working, and weight-room strong. He had wide sloping shoulders that he usually pulled together with a slouch. Growing up, football coaches fought to have the big kid on their team, even though Charlie's poor grades usually kept him on the sidelines on game day. Ever since high school, he had begged Dave to bring him to Alaska. But right now, he was so overwhelmed trying on the gifts from his cousin, he could barely focus on anything else.

∽∾

Ekok Beach was just a few miles downstream from the Dragline plant. Past town. Past the mouth of the Nushagak, around the bend, and on the opposite side of the Wood River. As captains muscled their boats the next morning into the designated fishing zone, they were greeted by calm seas and overcast skies. The short six-hour opening covered just one tidal change, and everyone was determined to maximize that short window to produce a fat early paycheck. Tight boundaries were set and would be monitored from helicopters and small planes circling above. Boats caught out of bounds would receive a hefty fine or be shut down altogether. A magnificent bright-orange and white Coast Guard cutter prowled farther out in the bay.

The fish did their part. A large school of Sockeye had moved in over-night and was now congregating in the river's mouth. Captains gunned

their motors in tight circles or zigzagging lines, searching for the schools
as they eagerly waited for the radio to officially announce it was time to
drop their nets and start the season. Flocks of gulls, terns, and cormorants
circled over waters they knew would soon erupt in chaos to feed them.
The smell of decayed mud being churned up by boat props, tilling the
river bottom, permeated the fresh air. A black bank of clouds threatening
wet weather was moving in from the west.

As "Time" was announced on Channel 7 of the VHF radio, the
hundred-strong fleet of thirty-two-foot boats quickly fanned out,
dropping behind them long lines of heavy monofilament gillnet where
they hoped the valuable schools of salmon would pass. Even though
everyone knew it already, KDLG radio broke their programming every
ten minutes to announce to the townsfolk a commercial fishing opener
was now underway.

As they searched, Dave explained to Charlie how salmon were caught
in the specially designed mesh held to the surface with a string of buoys.
"Up here Sockeye are the big money makers. They're worth far more than
Kings, Pinks, Silvers, or Chum."

Lead weights on the bottom suspended the gillnet in the water. Fish
could push their heads in but could not pull them back out. The pair
raced into the melee, hunting for Sockeye far enough from the other sets,
yet close enough to intersect the darting schools before they swam into
their competitor's formation.

"Charlie. Release the net. NOW!" A shimmering shadow flashed
underneath, dodging to the left. The mass broke in a circle and raced
back to the right. *Proud Mary* was dangerously close to the boundary,
but Dave knew the current would push them back the other way. Charlie
released the roller and the net quickly spread wide to greet the incoming
tide.

"Now we wait for them to swim in. Hopefully the school turns back
this way. And hopefully it won't take them long to find us."

Suddenly, as if they were beckoned by a shepherd's flute, the congregation of Sockeye veered straight toward them. Fish hit the net, erupting
geysers of spray each time they realized they were snared.

"There's one, there's another, and another," Charlie yelled, hopping up and down like an excited kid at the circus.

Corks all down the line bobbed violently from the thrashing fish. Before long, there was so much weight pulling it down some of the corks disappeared under the surface.

"Hot damn, we nailed 'em big time Charlie! Let's haul it in."

Dave flipped the switch on the hydraulic roller mounted in the middle of the back deck. The wheel strained and popped at first but slowly began a steady click as the heavy net was retrieved. The first fish appeared, a ten-pound Sockeye that powerfully shook as it saw the boat, thrashing to release its head.

"Shake 'em out. Pull them out. Rip 'em out," Dave yelled as the angry Red came in the boat and flopped across the deck. "Do whatever you need to do to get them out fast. We don't ever want to stop the wheel if we can help it. Keep it movin'."

Charlie grabbed the mono on each side of an entangled fish head and pushed-and-pulled and pulled-and-pushed until its armor-plated gills finally snapped free. With plenty of opportunities to practice coming just seconds after the first, he quickly caught the hang of it as fish after fish slapped down on the weathered-wood surface. Salmon and shaved ice, red from blood and fish slime, was soon brimming out the holds and onto the deck on each side.

"Pick 'em out as fast as you can. Don't lose any, Charlie. We hit the mother lode! Keep pickin'!"

Eventually, they hauled their entire bounty into the boat and muscled their net back on the roller. As they prepared to move, Dave looked out across the fleet. It was mayhem. One boat had crossed nets with another. Men on both rails screamed furious blame with clenched fists and profane insults. One of the captains flashed a pistol, assuring himself a violent brawl on the beach for later that night. Several other boats in the distance, painted the same Mediterranean blue with black stripes, had worked together to corral a large school. The nets in between their boats looked like they were in boiling water. They had scored BIG.

"Let's deliver and do it again, Charlie. There's plenty of Redfish here today for everyone."

Dave guided his plugged boat toward a towering tender ship anchored, a quarter mile away, in the middle of the river's deep-water channel. Off to their left, Fish and Game sped toward a drifting vessel intent on pulling in a tangled net, clearly over the out of bounds line.

"Look around. Amazing, isn't it?"

Dave gave his cousin a powerful high five that splashed fish juice across the deck with a messy pop. His tongue rejoiced at the salt spray on his cracked lips as a marine gust blew spray on his sunglasses.

"You did awesome. *Proud Mary* did awesome. WE did awesome, Charlie!"

He turned to embrace the breeze coming off the Bristol Bay, shook his head so his long blond mane could catch sail in the wind and screamed as loud as he could bellow, "I fuckin' LOVE this life!"

Ten minutes later they slid up next to the tender, one of the first boats to plug and off-load. Just like many others in the fish carrier fleet, the *M/V Kasilof* was a commercial crabbing boat specially fitted to suction, refrigerate, and haul salmon in their off-season. During the winter months, it faced unfathomable Bering Sea storms in an icy battle with Mother Nature to snatch crab from the depths. During months of maintenance it moored at the Seattle shipyard in Ballard. It stretched one-hundred and twenty feet long and rose from the water a wheelhouse almost three stories high. Inside were showers and free hot dogs to entice gillnetters with full loads to bring them their fish for sale. A lanky man in ripped jeans and arms covered with tattoos appeared at the rail and motioned them to the front of the line on the starboard side. Even though his eyes were shielded by dark aviator glasses, deep wind-burnt wrinkles—acquired from squinting at thousands of miles of coastline—spread visibly out from each side.

"Hey, Hey Clint! How ya' doin'?" Dave hollered. "I wasn't sure if you were coming back for another season or not. Last year I thought you were talking about moving to Australia."

Clint Allen had been a deckhand on the *Kasilof* for years. He frequently came to shore to drink, try to find a girlfriend, and eat in the Dragline mess hall whenever he got sick of leftover hotdogs and boat food.

"Looks like you were the first to find the school again, Dave," he applauded as he lowered a large mesh brailer bag connected to a mechanical boom and giant scale. "I didn't make it Down Under this year. Maybe next, I'm hoping. Let's get these weighed so you can get back out there and score some more. It's a good day to be out on the water."

One bag, two bags, six brimming bags of fish came off the boat. As Charlie pitched the last salmon into the cargo netting, Dave boarded the *Kasilof* to get a fish ticket from the captain which Mike would later trade for cash in the Dragline office. On his way out, he grabbed four hot dogs in foil bags and slipped them into his coat pocket.

"Hot damn, Charlie." Dave jumped back in the boat. "Fifty-seven hundred pounds at two ten a pound—we just made twelve thousand bucks. Booyah! Let's go do it again!"

"Hey, Dave, try the west boundary," Clint shouted. "From the sounds on the radio, they're catchin' the shit out of 'em over there."

Dave took Clint's advice and motored west but was immediately smothered by the crowd of the fleet. As he jockeyed between two parallel boats, each pulling in nets, the current shifted unexpectedly causing a large-jagged tree stump to pop up in the channel right in front of them. Dave threw it in neutral and rolled hard on the wheel to steer around it.

"There's fish all through here, Charlie, but don't release the net 'til I tell you," Dave warned as he turned and focused on the log jam. *Clunkk. ZZipp. Whizzz.* The net raced off the wheel out the back of the boat.

Dave whipped around. "Charlie, stop! What the fuck are you doing?"

But it was too late. The net unfurled out of the stern like a fishhook drawn to a large magnet and sunk deep into the menacing root-balled deadhead. Dave could not remember ever screaming as loud as he did at that moment. Certainly not at his cousin Charlie. He swore until his voice cracked. He punched his hand repeatedly as they spent the next two hours trying to free the mess from the snarl. Right before the Ekok opener closed, Dave looked at this watch.

"Gaddammit, we have to cut the fucker. Fish and Game won't take any excuses for us having a net in the water after it's over. They'll fine the shit out of us for everything we made today and then some. We have no choice. Grab your knife and start cutting."

Both men unsheathed their blades and began sawing the woven monofilament leaving angry, shredded gashes in the net. With every slash, Dave made up a new swear word. Fifteen minutes after they were through, Charlie broke his scared silence.

"I'm sorry, Dave. I thought I heard you say, 'throw the net' and I got excited. I didn't mean to let it out into the log jam. I didn't mean to screw things up. I didn't mean to ruin it. I'm sorry, Dave. If you want to fly me back home, I'll understand. I know this was my fault."

Dave was still securing the tatters and preparing his boat to motor up the river to the plant. The day that had started out with so much promise was now ending in bitter defeat. *And that was a brand-new fucking net too!* During their battle with the stump, the cousins watched as other experienced crews dropped, pulled, and delivered two or three times. Dave and Charlie had cashed in just once. Dave took a deep breath, put himself into his grandfather's shoes, and finally gritted a response. "Charlie, it's okay. That's fishing sometimes. You made a greenhorn mistake, but shit happens out here. Learn from this. Be ready for anything when we're out on the water. And most importantly, fucking *listen to me!*"

He had indeed pondered the idea of sending his cousin home, but with his usual deckhand laid up with a broken arm, and the season already upon them, he didn't have much of a choice. As he calmed down, his mind wandered to his family and the house he had recently bought with his wife. His boys were only two and four, but someday he'd bring them up and teach them everything he knew. They'd probably become Bristol Bay high liners. The best of the best, the cream of the crop. Living legends. Maybe he'd buy them each a boat and let them compete. Or maybe he'd let them take over *Proud Mary* together. But that was many years away. Right now, Dave needed his thick-skulled cousin to pull his head out of his ass, bounce back, and learn from his mistake. He took a calming breath and shook it off.

"Hey … we caught a heavy load with our first haul, and you did great with that, Charlie. And we *did* make twelve thousand bucks. Every greenhorn is allowed one big screw-up, Charlie, and the good news is you got yours out of the way on day one."

Charlie sucked in a full chest of thick, muddy air and stared in silence at the birds dive-bombing the glassy bay.

"Charlie!" Dave yelled, making his cousin turn around and look him in the eye.

"No more fuckin' screw-ups. Okay?"

"Yep. I got it, Dave. I won't screw up no more. I promise."

"And listen to what I say."

"I will, Dave."

"You got your knife?"

Charlie eyes brimmed with panic as he reached down, felt the knife securely tucked in its scabbard, and let out a big sigh of relief.

CHAPTER 5

# PRODUCTION

Each summer Dragline Fisheries produced fresh and meticulously
frozen salmon as fast as the plant would allow. After a week of
set-up in early June, full production ran frenzied around the clock
and transformed five million pounds of freshly caught fish into head-
ed-gutted rounds and artistically marked boxes of salted fish eggs. From
net to freezer, each Sockeye was handled at least a dozen times as it passed
through a series of precise machines. While gadgets made the madness
methodical, the soul of the industry was brute force labor.

As the *Kasilof* pushed up the Wood River toward the Dragline dock,
Boone and his veteran crew bounced in excitement, ready to finally get
their gloves on fish after weeks of anticipation and preparation. Even
though it had only been a short opener, enough fish were caught at Ekok
to work kinks out of machines and train inexperienced workers how to
do their new jobs.

"Archie, flip the switch," Boone yelled as two men hopped from the
dock to the ship and lowered a twelve-inch suction hose into the boat's
first holding tank. A gigantic electric pump, nicknamed *Big Bertha* by
the crew, roared to life with four-hundred and forty volts of deafening
ferocity.

"That thang could suck a bowling ball through a fifty-foot garden hose," Archie Deacon said lovingly in his often attempted yet rarely successfully imitated Texan panhandle drawl. At six-foot six and weighing two eighty, Archie towered over most of the other men in camp. Back home in Amarillo, he worked as a mechanic in a motorcycle shop and he had carried those skills with him to Alaska. Within a week after arriving his first season, he was unanimously promoted after he took the regulators off Dragline's forklifts, juiced up their motors, and doubled their top-end speed. Archie liked to drink and fight but rarely found anyone dumb enough to take him on. He had a dry, sarcastic sense of humor that provided comedic relief for both those who sought it and those who didn't. There was nothing in the world Archie loved more than Harley Davidsons. Most of the tattoos on his arms, shoulders and back proved that was true.

Suddenly, the greasy-yellow forklift Archie had named *Fat Cat* whizzed in and began catching fish that were being jettisoned out the other side of the pump. *Thump.* The first salmon of the season came off the boat and hit the bottom of a thousand-pound capacity, white-plastic tote. *Thump, thump, thump.* Bloody water and shaved ice splashed in all directions. Water and fish slime soon spread over the dock. *Thump, thump, thump, thump, thump, thump, thump.*

With great glee Archie whooped, "Look at *Big Bertha* now. She's shakin' like a robin shittin' peach seeds in bob cherry season!"

The driver twisted *Fat Cat* into a brisk two-point turn and raced down the dock with a full-sloshing tote towards a tall and wide rolled-up door on the back side of the plant. Without letting *Big Bertha* miss a beat, a second forklift swept in, this one more faded yellow than the first. Uneven black hand-written block letters spelling *Hell Cat* covered its sides. Its driver sped in, just in time, to take *Fat Cat's* place at the pump before a single Red could hit the ground. *Thump, thump, thump.* A second deep-laden tender ship appeared in the distance and dropped anchor downriver, waiting for its turn to off-load.

With two quick pounds on the horn, *bleep, bleep, Fat Cat* and its rider came whirring through the foot-wide, FDA approved, plastic strips covering the back door of the plant. The forklift drivers considered them a matador's game, smashing into them at full speed with each delivery. Raising the fish-filled tote to almost the full height of the lift, the driver inched forward to the fifteen-foot-tall aluminum holding tank and poured the iced fish cocktail in with a loud *sloosh*.

As the forklift reversed out of the plant, its safety siren blared *honng, honng, honng* adding another layer of sound to the growing wall of industrial music. With another well-rehearsed two-point reverse pivot, the driver lowered the now empty tote and whipped *Fat Cat* through the plastic strips and barreled back down the dock, barely reaching *Big Bertha* in time to intersect its steady stream of fish as *Hell Cat* pulled out full. The dock crew was under intense pressure to get the first tender ship emptied as quickly as possible so the second one could make it up the river to take advantage of the flooded tide. Occasionally, if a driver lost track of the amount of fish in the hopper, or if he had to stop to fill his forklift with gas, the fish line crew inside would chant "More Fish! More Fish! More Fish!"

Whenever that happened, Archie sounded off with frantically animated waving arms near his post at the pump. "Move faster you moron! Don't stand there gawking at me with a face that looks like a bulldog licking piss off a nettle."

If a stunned driver tried to retaliate, he'd quip, "You're so dumb I bet you sit on the TV at home and watch the sofa."

During the only four hours of darkness each night, blazing hanging halogen lights lit up the dock, and the well-choreographed dance of the forklifts continued in tandem until the last tender was off-loaded and the final tote of salmon disappeared into the tall aluminum production hopper inside. As Boone's dock workers and Archie's high-octane gang of forklift drivers greased their synchronized rhythm, the production crew anxiously awaited inside the processing plant.

"Does anyone know what time it is?" Julian yelled to his green crew as the first tote of fish rained into the towering aluminum hopper. *Sloosh*. Excited "Wups" and "Wooees" erupted from the slime crew. "It's time to Save the Salmon!"

Someone pushed play on a boom box tucked in a dry corner by the restrooms, volume full blast. Bon Scott and a big AC/DC bass beat added percussion to the symphony of the salmon. A manual door at the bottom of each side of the hopper allowed two sorters to control the speed of the fish coming out.

"Roll open the hatches," Julian commanded.

The rookie fish sorter, on each side, raised a small hopper door and jumped back as a pile of fish and bloody ice avalanched out. One tried to hold the barrage back, but it was too late. Several fish smacked down hard on the cement floor.

"Don't ever let a fish hit the floor!" Julian barked. "That's cardinal rule number one. Control the doors like this."

He finessed the door open. Three fish slid out. Julian effortlessly flopped them over, so their backs faced the hopper and pectoral fins saluted the sky. "Line them up like this. Five at a time. Every single time. And don't ever make the header wait for a fish."

Julian crooked his thumb toward the next two men in line, on each side, who were standing in front of menacing machines that resembled a pair of miniature v-shaped guillotines. "You two headers set the pace of the whole operation. If you stop, everyone else stops. So, don't stop. Ever! That's rule number two, don't *ever* stop the lines!"

"The six of you," Julian narrowed his eyelids and pointed at the first three men on each side of the line, "must not ever miss a beat. Start a continuous stream and move together as a team. If you can't do it, I'll find someone who can. You don't have to like each other, but you *do* have to work together."

The head of the line jobs were coveted positions. Newcomers on the slime line, desperate to get there, waged a constant and vicious psychological battle with everyone around them in hopes of attracting the attention of any factory boss willing to give them a shot to be promoted. Like the star quarterback of a high school football team, an experienced header who played his cards right could go to the bar and get handed free beers all night. A fast header commanded respect, a slow one, ridicule, immediately followed by demotion. Julian turned his attention to the guillotines. Eyes intensifying, he yanked one of the men off the line by his suspender straps and stepped up in his place.

"Rule number three. Never, and I mean NEVER, reach your hand in there."

He pushed his foot down on a high-pressure air pedal inside a protective box on the floor and pointed as the razor-sharp blade of the header machine dry fired with a swift, powerful *psthunk*. Every year up and down the Alaska coast there were tales of people losing thumbs, fingers, even hands in header machines. "That thing will cut your hand off at the wrist without missing a beat. So, respect it. Fear it. Have nightmares about it. And make every cut perfect by holding the fish at this angle."

Julian grabbed a large Sockeye, pushed it to an invisible mark only hours of experience could reveal and pressed the foot pedal in one fluid motion. The blade dropped from its chamber above and decapitated the salmon ... *psChunk*. The fish head dropped into a white tote below. "By the end of this shift you should be doing thirty fish a minute," Julian challenged as he slid the headless fish to the next person in line. "Sixty fish a minute within a week."

*Bleep. Bleep. Hell Cat* raced in and dumped another thousand pounds of fish into the hopper. *Sloosh*. The AC/DC marathon continued to reverberate through the rafters. *Honng, honng, honng.*

"You need to pick up the pace down there," Mike yelled from a balcony that ran along the second story of the plant outside his glass office. The perch served as both a viewing area of the production facility and an entryway to six private rooms used by Mike and corporate visitors or fish buyers who visited during peak season. "We have two more tenders waiting to off-load out there and they can't miss the tide. Pick it up!"

"Hey, you—you're a gutter," Julian proclaimed as he moved down the line one spot and turned to a wide-eyed man who was wrapped head to toe in banana-yellow rubber raingear. "Grab the fish by the tail, roll them belly down and slide them into this thigamarocker."

The entrance to the gutter machine looked like an elevated one-way cat door with the sound of whizzing Armageddon on the other side. Under the enclosure, a conveyor latched on to each fish and guided it over a series of long razor knives and brushes that sliced open its belly and ripped out its innards before flopping it in a water-filled tank on the other side. *psChunk*. Fish-by-fish both headers gained confidence, breathed life to their machines, and began to pop them with uncertain hesitation. *psChunk. psChunk. psChunk.*

"And you guys—are slimers," Julian slid around the gutter machine to where the sliced fish had just plopped out the other side. *Sploshh.* He reached in to grab it from a wash table that held six inches of frigid water. A line of short garden hoses hung from a suspended bar down the center and emitted a steady stream of ice-cold water. Twelve people stood around each wash table, six to a side in a single file line. Like the loader on line one, they looked like rubber bananas wearing thick orange rubber gloves duct-taped over cotton liners.

"You guys get the fun job," Julian lied. In reality, being a slimer was the worst job in the plant. Wet and messy, sliming was a dreadful activity reserved for newbies and laggards at the bottom of the factory totem pole. While no job at Dragline could be considered cushy, or borderline respectable for that matter, workers on the slime line were continuously exposed to near freezing bloody water and guts that could cause bacterial poisoning through cuts on unprotected hands. Repetitive and monotonous work aside, slimers were required to stand in gutty-bloody water for an entire sixteen-hour shift. As the ceaseless season wore on, a worker's status at Dragline was defined by how far away their job was from the slime line and how long it had taken for them to be promoted. Bon Scott stopped singing. Someone walked over and clicked in another cassette. The assembly line chorus continued, *psChunk. psChunk, psChunk.* Robert Plant wailed a ballad with his Led Zeppelin ensemble. *Bleep. Bleep. Sloosh. Sploshh. Sploshh. Sploshh.*

"When the fish come out, scrape their guts out with this." Julian held up a strangely shaped serrated object that resembled a deformed ice-cream scoop. "This is not a spoon. This is not a knife. It's a—spife."

The new members of the slime line let out a nervous laugh. Even Lev Warrens who had sourly filled a spot at the slime table grinned for a second. Julian looked around at the naivety in their faces, mentally capturing snapshots of smiles he knew he might never see again. The next six weeks would undoubtedly prove to be the most physically and psychologically demanding times of their lives. He gazed into faces one at a time and wondered how many of them would have made the journey all the way out to Dillingham if they had known that intense throbbing in their hands and feet, pain that would not go away for the duration of the season, would be their welcome.

Julian turned to Lev standing beside him and whispered, "You doin' alright?"

Lev nodded and Julian moved away, readdressing his crew. "And take special care of these."

Julian pulled out two foot-long, bright red skeins of salmon eggs and held them high. "Don't toss them or drop them. Don't throw them in with the guts. Don't rip them in half. Handle these like a mama holding her baby."

Julian gently laid the roe skeins in a blue plastic container that resembled a miniature laundry basket. A Japanese egg technician nodded with overdone animation from the sidelines. Salmon roe was handled away from the fish in a secluded building located between the plant and the dock. The Japanese company that purchased the Dragline egg contract each season sent their own specially trained team of Hokkaido technicians to salt and pack eggs into highly coveted Sujiko. Japanese egg techs rarely interacted with the other processing crews, but they were known to promptly hire almost all the pretty women who came to Dragline each season. Fish prices paid to fishermen had fluctuated around two dollars per pound for the past several seasons. Sujiko prices in the Tokyo Tsukiji market peaked at over twenty. Corporate managers reminded plant bosses that salmon eggs paid all the bills, fish meat provided the profit. The Japanese egg crew at Dragline shipped out an average of twenty tons of Sujiko in artistically packaged wood boxes each year. After looking around to make sure all eyes were focused on Julian and not him, Lev dropped two skeins on the floor and smashed them with his boot.

"Keep sliding fish down the tank until they're thoroughly washed. By the time they get here," Julian had side-stepped to the far end of the wash tank, scraping, washing, and dunking the salmon as he taught, "it should have no guts, no eggs, no blood line and no slime." He proudly held up the glistening Redfish like a professional boxer showing off a championship belt.

"And now these guys," he jerked his head over at four workers standing in front of brand new shiny digital scales. "They set the Dragline price for the buyers. They're our graders."

The grader's job was to weigh each and every fish before separating them into three different piles. The higher the grade, the more buyers paid. A group of Japanese inspectors watched their every move and sometimes argued with Dragline graders as they scribbled down notes on waterproof paper.

"The cold crew will take them from here," Julian clapped his hands to imitate a magician that had made a rabbit disappear, "and will usher them to the freezers."

On cue a man dressed in insulated coveralls appeared and grabbed the cleaned and graded Sockeye Julian had just finished. He walked over and stacked the Red uniformly on a square rack propped up by a rickety-or-ange hydraulic hand truck. Behind him four ammonia blast freezers built into the back wall were the heart of the Dragline facility. Operating at full tilt, each one could turn thirty-three thousand pounds of fresh fish into frozen solid—*break your toe if you drop one on it*—product in six hours. As general manager, Mike managed fleet deliveries and fish purchases to match the capacity and pace of the freezers. During peak production, the freezers never stopped, the lines never slowed, and fish never aged more than three days from the moment they were caught. If any one of the blast freezers broke down or slipped in its ammonia intake, it could stop the line and strand thousands of pounds of salmon out on the dock and all the way out to the tender fleet on the grounds. The ripple effect of such an event was immediate and catastrophic.

As soon as the Sockeye were frozen to at least negative ten degrees at their core, Chris and his team of glazers took over. The first two on the glazer crew heaved the stacks of frozen racks out of the freezer and wheeled them over, with a hand lift, to a large cement block. Racks were stacked ten high. A man on each side—*the taller and stronger the better*—lifted a rack off the stack and dropped it on the concrete riser emitting a gunshot-loud *crack*. In one unified motion, they dumped the frozen fish into a dunk tank, which instantly formed a thin layer of ice glaze around each one. These were immediately pulled out by eight people wearing shoulder high rubber gloves and slipped in individual plastic sleeves sporting a Dragline Fisheries logo.

"Weigh the boxes perfectly," Chris repeated over and over. "Fifty pounds means fifty pounds. Not an ounce more. Not an ounce less."

After getting zipped with plastic straps, the boxes were loaded in a line of refrigerated cargo containers which got hauled down, when they were full, to the deep-water pier in town by a fleet of semis. People in high-end fish markets and fancy restaurants across the globe licked their lips as Dragline filled orders, fifty thousand pounds at a time, and shipped them to Seattle, London, Paris, Shanghai, Berlin and Oslo. Most went to Japan.

For eight grueling weeks, paychecks were ground out hour-by-hour, shift-by-shift, ache-by-ache, for seven days a week, until the last Sockeye of the season was slid into its final plastic sleeve sporting the logo of a crowned red salmon holding a long net.

❧

When Pete opened the mess hall at six the next morning, Julian and Boone had just wrapped up their shifts. Always dependent on the cycle of the freezers, Chris would be done around noon. Mike walked in with company owner Bob Clayton and a couple of potential fish buyers—there observing from Washington, seated them at an adjoining table, and approached the two foremen.

"You guys need to move some people around," he feigned exasperation. "And find a left-handed header." Mike was putting on a show for the company big wigs, but Julian knew he was secretly pleased with the one hundred and twenty-six thousand pounds they had processed with a green crew in fifteen hours.

"I'm hitting the showers then my bunk," Julian announced after he left. "With a frosty can of beer. And when I wake up, I'm gonna drink some more—at the Blue Spruce."

"Oh, hell ya. I'm in," Boone volunteered. He loved wild nights out at the bar just as much as anyone, and even more than most.

From behind, Dave Stevens flip-flopped up. Julian heard him coming and greeted him with a bear hug. "Hey Dave. Good to finally see you brother! I heard you had quite the opening day."

Dave scoffed, let it go, and grinned, "I don't want to talk about that. But I do want to talk about sportfishing. You guys wanna go? Tomorrow I'm teaching Charlie to mend net, but we can go after that. There won't be another opener for a few days, I'm told. If we leave at first light, we can make it up to the Agulowak for a full day of fishing and be back by nightfall."

"Damn right we do," Julian pounced.

"That's like asking an itch if it wants a scratch," added Boone.

High-fives all around. "And count Chris in too. He can't stop talking about that blue spotted rainbow he caught up there last year."

## CHAPTER 6

# THE BLUE SPRUCE

The Blue Spruce Bar was a stereotypical working man's watering hole, a Native Alaskan hangout, and the only always-open drinking establishment in Dillingham. Sawdust floors and low-sagging ceilings provided protection from the ever-present mud and rain outside. Two smoke-smudged Budweiser mirrors, one on each wall, offered sparse decor. Backroom entertainment featured a not quite level pool table and a dart board three inches lower than regulation height. For anyone carrying an extra quarter, a jukebox stood willing to trade for any one of its eleven good songs. While destitute of luxury, the Blue Spruce was the perfect congregation spot for wild and restless fishermen who spent each day working and cussing, and each night one beer away from a senseless and violent brawl.

By the time the Dragline crew entered the joint, it was already packed. Big Al nodded at them in familiar fashion. Pool balls cracked like whips through the dense and lurid gloom. A group of fishermen who didn't care that they hadn't showered in days were throwing darts, drunkenly singing "Take it to the Limit" with the Eagles for the third time that night. The men's eyes were immediately drawn to a shapely woman clearing empty glasses and wiping down a round table near the bar. Her loose-fitting sweatshirt hung over tight jeans. She had her hair pulled back and she too was crooning to the chorus.

"Well, they weren't kidding about the new waitress," Boone swallowed. "In a jar full of old pennies, she's a shiny new dime."

Finally, she achieved the sheen she was seeking, looked up, and gave them a welcoming smile. Acting as if he had never seen a pretty girl before, Chris froze, unable to twist his lips into a coherent response. Josie Vance would control a man's attention in any dive bar in the country, her presence mellowed this one like the taste of a sugar cube dropped in a tart glass of lemonade. Boone took off his hat and approached her, eyes wide and glistening, much like those of a prospector who has discovered a gold nugget in a stream, but unsure if the claim already taken.

"I'm Boone," he said, reaching out his hand. "And you are …?"

"Josie." She beamed and reached for his shake. "You guys want this table?"

"Josie," Boone repeated. "Now there's a name I like saying."

Smiling, Josie brushed off the compliment and turned to the others who were draping their coats on the backs of chairs, marveling at Boone's moxie.

"Round of beers?"

She noticed they were all moving slow from aches and pains she guessed could only have been born from the bowels of hard labor or a fight where the opponent had gotten the upper hand.

"Looks like you guys could all use something cold."

She gave each a confident handshake and asked their names as they sat.

"Boone from Colorado, I got that one. Chris from Burien, south of Seattle. Jules also from Colorado but soon moving to Seattle. Okay. I think I can remember. Nice to meet y'all." She laughed and headed back to the bar. "I'm Josie. And I'll be right back."

"And three Captain Morgan shots!" Chris bellowed with a blossoming grin and a burning Marlboro Light held high between two fingers. He took a shot of air with an imaginary glass. Ash dropped on the floor.

"Three beers and three shots of rum. Got it."

"So, it's going to be one of *those* nights?" Julian groaned as he took his eyes off Josie for the first time and glared at his friend. "Let's not jump overboard, Chris. Remember, Dave wants to leave early for the lake."

When Chris was drinking, both his best and worst nature came out, and it was impossible to predict which one you'd get. On good nights, he'd buy anyone a drink who would listen to him ramble meaningless stories, in minute detail, for hours. But his bad nights almost always ended with a fight where violence had no bounds.

Chris grinned. "Yeah, but we're not fishing until the day after tomorrow. Plenty of time to create cobwebs and clear them. Tonight, we have lots of catching up to do. Besides, it's always one of *those* nights at the Spruce."

Back by the pool table, two men started arguing. Their slurred voices escalated and finally erupted into a pushing-and-shoving match. Big Al quickly ushered them out the front door. Julian, sensing Boone's growing attraction for Josie and possibly her interest to him, decided to play wing man. Each time Josie brought a round when Boone was present, Julian peppered her with a barrage of questions. Boone's eyes stayed pinned on the pretty barmaid as he strained to hear every word. Chris couldn't take his eyes off her either. She was from New Mexico. She had never skied before, but always wanted to learn. She liked her job at the Spruce but hated the violence that sometimes erupted.

"She's perfect for you Boone," Julian remarked as she walked away. "But you might have to fight Chris for her."

Chris snapped out of his hypnosis. "Nah. I've got my eye on someone else."

Julian winked at Boone. "If it's Hannah you're after, I think she's already taken."

In a teasing tone, Boone added, "Yeah, I saw her talking to Lev Warrens this morning. It looked to me like the start of something special—a budding romance."

"No fucking way. You can't be serious. There's not a snowball's chance in hell she'd fall for an old guy like that. Could she? Are you being fucking serious?"

More rounds. More beers. More tequila. More smokes.

Late in the evening two wet and muddy Yup'ik men sauntered in and dropped exhausted onto tall stools. One covered his head with his arms as if he were sheltering himself from rain and dropped his broad forehead on the bar.

"We lost them," he lamented. "They're—they're gone."

His brother reached over and put his hand on his shoulder. They both shook their heads with distant, watery eyes.

"What's wrong, Henry?" Josie leaned in with a whisper from the other side of the bar.

Henry Chiklak lived a mile down the road on the knoll overlooking the Dragline plant. She waved at him each day on her morning jog. In return, he frequently dropped in for hot coffee at the Inn she tended for Big Al. One morning she had even stopped, at his house, so he could show her how he dried salmon in the summer breeze on ancient alder racks and bury 'stinky-heads' in the tundra.

Henry collected himself only long enough to look up at her. Deep sorrow and pain bled from tired eyes. "Eddie ... and Thomas ... are gone. They went out in the skiff last night and didn't come back. Eddie's girlfriend broke up with him ... they wouldn't listen."

His voice drifted into darkness, got lost, and didn't return.

"We found their skiff upside down in Nushagak Bay," his brother continued for him. "There was no plug in the boat. Why was there no plug in the boat? Eddie always keeps the plug in his boat." He too, turned inward.

Big Al shuffled over prompting Henry's composure to briefly resurface. "We looked for them all day. Both sides of the river. We found Thomas washed up on a beach far downstream. But there was no sign of Eddie. He probably drifted ..." unable to finish, the grieving father conceded to teary moans.

His brother took off his hat and carved his fingers through wet, matted, black hair. "Eddie knew to always keep the plug in his skiff. He knew how cold the water is out there and how strong the tides can be. When it started seeping in, they couldn't make it back. He knew ... by now he's probably been carried far out to sea."

A sobering hush swept through the crowded bar. The pool tables went still. Someone yanked the jukebox's cord from the wall. Everyone from town knew Henry's youngest son Eddie and his best friend Thomas. Eddie was bright, funny, and always the prankster. Sometimes too quick to tease a stranger, his mischief was genuinely playful. Always in jest. Thomas was quiet, yet game to laugh at any witty joke Eddie could muster. Both eighteen-year-olds had graduated from high school less than a month before.

There wasn't a fisherman there who didn't know the summer tides in this part of Alaska were some of the largest on earth. The natural shape of the Bristol Bay acted like a funnel for a massive movement of water each twelve-hour cycle. Propelled by the phase of the moon and rotation of the earth, the difference between high and low tide was sometimes as tall as a three-story building. For centuries, seafarers had struggled with the Bay's extreme water movements and treacherous nautical complexities. Every local mariner feared the northern summer tides, especially in this part of Alaska.

"I'm so sorry, Henry," Josie whispered, placing her hand gently on the heartbroken man's arm. She too knew what sudden personal loss felt like. It took every ounce of her strength to hold back her own tears.

"I don't know how I'm going to tell his mother."

Big Al's eyes connected with Henry's and in the split of a second voiced volumes. In silence, he pushed aside some bottles on the top shelf and blew the dust off a decanter of Metaxa, a flagon he reserved only for moments like this. He carefully brimmed two glasses and placed the half-empty bottle on the bar. Julian, Boone, and Chris filed out with the rest in silence, leaving the Chiklak men to contend with their anguish alone. The party that night at the Blue Spruce was over. The icy water and ripping tides of the Nushagak had claimed the first two souls of the season.

# CHAPTER 7

# THE AGULOWAK

Tragic news travels fast in remote Alaska villages, sweeping from dwelling-to-dwelling, camp-to-camp like a fever, leaving no one unaffected. Before breakfast could even be served everyone within fifty miles knew two Native teens had drowned and one of their bodies had not yet been recovered. At lunch Mike addressed the mess hall crowd and requested a moment of silence for the dead boys. Then he put his hat back on and cleared his throat.

"Listen up everyone. Spawning escapement goals are way ahead of schedule, so Fish and Game is opening up commercial fishing three days from now in every area. It's time. The run is upon us. We need to get this plant cleaned up and ready for peak season production."

Fishermen whooped and cheered, a stark reversal from the somber silence they'd been sharing. To ensure long-term sustainability and to withhold upriver tribal treaty promises, each year Bristol Bay marine biologists allowed the first waves of returning salmon safe passage upstream before they allowed commercial fishing nets to drop. Only during seasons of record fish runs did escapement goals get met this quickly.

"About a hundred more workers will arrive this Sunday. If you're going to get any sleep before we go balls to the wall, tomorrow is the day. If you want to get any sportfishing in before we shut down in August, better do it now. From the sound of things, I don't think we'll get another break until it's all said and done."

An avid sport fisherman himself, Mike understood the draw trophy fishing had on his key men. A tantalizing hour upstream loomed the legendary Wood River lakes system. All five species of salmon and six other types of trophy sport fish could be caught there on any given cast. The series of lakes connected by wild short rivers provided extraordinary diversity, size, and abundance found nowhere else on earth. Mike was convinced it was the primary reason the core of his key workers came back to Dillingham each year, rather than go work in other parts of Alaska.

Dave Stevens was quick to inform Mike he'd already taken the bait. Everyone knew he'd frequently run up the Wood before the season, after the season, and any rare chance he got in between. "I'm going. You guys still joining Charlie and me?"

"Fuck ya, we are!" Julian, Boone, and Chris said in unison.

"I'll get my Whaler in the water tonight. You guys gather up food and drinks so we can roll out early tomorrow morning. Charlie and I will meet you here in the mess hall at six."

Some jobs in the fish business were repulsive for the soberest soul, but when nursing a hangover, they could curdle milk stored in an armored stomach. Coupled with the tragic news from the night before, the afternoon passed by painfully slow for the three friends. Tubs were scrubbed and filled with ice shavings. Forklifts got topped off with fuel. Dozens of fifty-pound boxes were folded together and stacked in impressive cardboard pyramids. Hidden chunks of fish guts were squeezed out of cracks as machines got hosed down and deep cleaned.

"It will just be the four of us today," Dave announced the next morning as he filled a large green thermos with coffee. "Charlie's sicker than opossum shit and it's not alcohol related. He really wants to come but I made him stay in bed. I need him healthy for Monday's opener. So, that leaves one open spot in the boat."

"Can I go?"

The men all whipped their heads around. Seated across from Hannah, Lev managed a smile. To the surprise of many, and chagrin of Chris, the lonely girl and awkward man had recently become friends and were often seen hanging out together.

Chris groaned and in a jealous tone snarled, "Do you know how to fish, Lev? Do you own a fishing pole? Or any gear?"

"Uh, well, no… maybe I kin borrow some'n from Mike. He 'uh … Mike might loan me some'n to use."

"I don't think Mike will loan anyone his gear," Chris lied, and without thinking said, "Plus, the boat won't fit five."

"Then how was Charlie gonna'…" Lev's chest deflated as he realized Chris was lying, hope flushed from his face. Julian was startled by the flash of deep-rooted anger in his eyes, but he couldn't blame the guy. Chris was being a jealous asshole.

Dave made eye contact with Julian and without words they agreed on a plan. "Lev, if you want to go, you can use some of my gear. We have plenty of room in the boat."

"And I've got tons of lures," Julian added.

Chris gasped and shook his head in disbelief. Lev looked up at Dave and Julian to see if they were being serious and confirming they were— aided by a comforting smile from Hannah—slowly nodded. His pupils burned hatred at Chris.

"All right then," Dave decided. "We've got a full boat. Let's go fishing."

The twenty-foot outboard Dave kept at Dragline for the sole purpose of sportfishing was tied to a floating platform at the end of the dock. Because it moved up and down the height of a two-story house each tidal change, the dock crew had hoisted the Boston Whaler over the previous night when the tide was high. In just a few hours the river would flood, raising the platform to be even with the top once again. Under the dock, steel crossbeams and angled wood planks crisscrossed in layers for one hundred and fifty feet back toward the plant. Pigeons and gulls shrieked and shrilled as they flew beam-to-beam picking barnacles and pieces of dead fish from exposed pilings. As he climbed down the rickety-steel ladder, Lev began to point something out to Julian in the labyrinth of support under the dock, then didn't.

"You guys all got blades on ya?" Dave confirmed as they boarded. They all nodded, even Lev. Dave manned the Whaler upstream with confident captainship. He was more at ease behind the wheel of a boat than a car. After all, he had spent a lifetime of summers learning from his legendary grandfather. As they meandered upstream past alluvial shores of silt, sand, and gravel, the men marveled at the river's inherent beauty and placid serenity. Misty veils of fog wafted over the water in quilted complexity like rolling layers of cigarette smoke in the Blue Spruce. They spotted a bull moose shredding off his velvet in the willows of curvy Arcana Creek. Swans, ducks, and geese rose in noisy processions from the braided sedge, cotton grass, moss, and white lichen landscape. The wind whispered an ancient verse as it rustled through waist-deep river grass.

An hour later, around a corner in Lake Aleknagik, they heard it, rushing like a rumor through walls of head-high alder, its icy spray splashing across large boulders—the Agulowak. Sun rays slanted toward the glacial peaks of the Wood Mountains, filtered in places by spruce, poplar, aspen, and birch on upland benches. The fabled fishing oasis consisted of a narrow, fast-moving river just a few miles long that funneled a million migrating fish up to the next lake in the chain, Nerka. Layers upon layers of Sockeye were now stacked at its mouth regaining the energy they'd need to master the fast-moving water and next strenuous leg of their journey.

Dave slid his boat up on a small sandy beach. "Tie us to that log, Lev. We most certainly have arrived."

Chris jumped out with his fly rod and popped his shoulder into Lev as he passed, almost knocking the man down. "I know where I'm heading. And don't even think about following me."

At the end of the previous season, Chris had caught a unique strain of blue-shadowed rainbow trout and an enormous Dolly Varden in a gentle secluded pool downstream near the lake. Without waiting for a response, he bolted. Boone and Dave grabbed their gear and raced each other upriver to another famous spot, leaving Julian and Lev suddenly alone. The soulful cry of a loon added to the stillness.

"What do you like to fish with, Lev?" Julian asked. "You can use anything you want in my tackle box."

Lev examined several different lures and put each one back.

"I dunno," he finally sputtered. "I've, 'uh ... I've never bin here b'fore. This place is different from the lake my Pa took me to in ... 'uh ... the mountains back home."

Julian laughed and motioned with a full sweep of his arm. "I know what you mean, man. There's no place like this one. It's the best fishing spot on earth. And look at all the beauty around us."

Julian used the tip of his rod to point out a bald eagle landing in a large pine. "What did you and your Pa fish for at your lake in the mountains back home?"

"Uh, wild Redfish. I git 'em every year when they come back to the lake. I take 'em back to my cabin and smoke 'em. The lake is 'uh ... close to my cabin in the mountains. On the Reservation."

"You from Alaska?"

Lev shook his head and looked away. "Nah."

Sockeye? Really? Swallowing his frown, Julian focused on Lev to see if he was kidding. He had been expecting him to say trout. Other than Alaska there weren't too many high mountain lakes that still had wild runs of Sockeye salmon. Few that he knew of, anyway. Reservation? Lev was an Indian? Who was this guy? Was he pulling his leg?

"Well, you should know what you're doing then."

Julian pointed out a school of yardstick long, bright-crimson fish with cedar green heads and hooked jaws muscling upstream through the clear alpine water.

"What do you catch Redfish with there? At your lake in the mountains by your cabin on the Reservation?"

"Spears ... or nets."

"Spears. Ah. I got ya," Julian chuckled.

So, Lev was a joker. A wild storyteller. A bullshitter extraordinaire. Might as well play along. He reached in his tackle box and jiggled out a shiny gold spoon with a dazzling pink center and dimples that refracted the morning sunlight like a kaleidoscope.

"Well, I didn't bring any spears with me, Lev, but I do have this Pixie. It will catch anything here. In fact, it's probably the deadliest lure in the whole state of Alaska. And *I* make it even deadlier."

When he was six, Julian's favorite uncle had taken him fishing for the first time. On a lure with a black permanent marker his uncle had drawn two dots. "Big monster fish like to eat things that can see them do it. So, I make sure my lures have eyes," he had explained. A mesmerized little Julian caught two fish that outing, and from that day forward, always drew eyes on his lures. It had become his unique trademark to constantly remind him of his uncle.

Lev caressed the lure in his palm, seemingly spellbound by Julian's explanation.

"Cast it in that pool, Lev, right below those rocks. Let it bounce downstream across the gravel and watch what happens."

The Pixie plunked in the river. As it started to flutter to the bottom, a live red torpedo flashed up and aggressively snatched it, before jettisoning downstream and nearly jerking the pole from Lev's grip. He leaned back and fought the fish like it was a dog on a long leash, up and down the strong current, until it finally grew tired and glided into a shallow pool. Julian splashed in and firmly latched on to the Sockeye's gill plates.

"Oh hell, yeah. That's a dandy, Lev!" Julian proclaimed, and in the thrill of the moment they were united. "First cast too. I told you monster fish like eyes. This one's got to be over twelve pounds. What a beauty!"

The older man picked up the quivering fish and examined it head to tail. It was a bruiser buck with hooked jaws and ice pick teeth. Julian rejoiced and fumbled through his day pack for his camera.

"Smile, Lev. This picture will make you famous. You might even make the cover of *Field and Stream* magazine!"

"No. No pictures," Lev shrieked, turning his back, tossing the fish back in the water, and effectively snuffing out any potential bond between them.

Bothered and confused by the man's abrupt reaction, Julian stuffed the camera back in the bag and readied his own fishing pole. Slightly frustrated, and more than a little perturbed, he calmed himself down and changed the subject.

"It's a real tragedy what happened to those Chiklak boys, don't you think, Lev? Poor kids. They were so young. I saw the father at the Blue

Spruce the other night and the man was devastated. He could barely hold it together. He kept talking about the plug not being in their boat."

Lev stared out across the river. "I dunno."

Julian bristled and turned, eyes locking on Lev.

"You don't know what? What the fuck does that mean? Why would two eighteen-year-old kids deserve to die like that?"

Lev absently shrugged, making Julian's face flush red. "Lev, that boy's father was heartbroken. He lost his son. How would you feel if it was your kid?"

Lev kept his back to Julian and shrugged again. Julian's hands began to shake, and he unconsciously stilled them by pulling them into fists.

"Lev how would *your* parents feel if it was *you*?"

Lev whipped around and glared, eyes transformed to cold-rusty steel. "I don't remember my Ma. She's dead. My Pa..." Lev paused. After the eternity of a few moments, he continued in a chilling tone. "My Pa didn't like us Injuns."

Without waiting for a response, the older man stomped upstream to fish alone. Lev's revelation rippled through Julian like a deep shiver, one he couldn't easily shake, so he kept a wary eye on him. Lev spent the morning sitting on a boulder staring into the current, refusing to join the group for lunch, preferring to remain motionless—a silhouette without a line in the water. Late in the afternoon, as Julian and Dave were packing the boat, Lev approached.

"Here's your lure back, Julian. Thanks for lettin' me use it." Lev unhooked the special pink Pixie from his pole and placed it back in Julian's tackle box. Then he lowered his voice to almost a whisper and turned his back away from Chris who was walking up the bank their way. "I 'uh ... I wanna thank you for takin' me fishin'. I've 'uh... never had friends b'fore."

A sense of admission released from Lev's eyes, like he had confessed a secret he'd been harboring for a long time. The loneliness of his tone made Julian again feel sorry for him, but then he remembered their earlier exchange about the Chiklak boys. It had been bothering him all day. His heart hardened. The only thing he could bring himself to say was a muffled, "Welcome."

"I'm glad you came, Lev," Dave set down the bag he was loading, put his arm around the man's shoulder, and gave him a playful shake. "And I hope you had fun. Jules told me you caught a trophy fish today—a real monster. Wish I would have seen that. You can come along next time too, heck, anytime you want. As long as there's room in my boat. Okay?"

Lev looked up and connected eyes with Dave. He didn't verbally respond, but his cheeks managed a slight upward lift. Dave patted him on the back and laughed.

The whole ride back, Julian's emotions were in turmoil. On one hand he had just experienced some of the most intense sportfishing of his life. Over the course of the day he had landed seven species of fish including a grayling that had to have been close to the state record. The weather had been spectacular, Agulowak perfect, and he felt an even closer bond with buddies Dave, Chris, and Boone. He appreciated Lev's sincere words of gratitude and felt pride in the way he had stuck up for him that morning and invited him to come.

But as the mudflats rolled by, Julian's chest became tight and at times he found it difficult to breathe. He was overwhelmed by a nagging feeling—an unsettling premonition—that something was seriously wrong with Lev Warrens. When he looked at the older man, he felt anxious and unnerved, a prescient foreboding he couldn't quite articulate. How could Lev have no empathy for the Chiklak boy's father? Did he somehow have something to do with it? Julian shuddered when he recalled the horror in Lev's eyes when he spoke of his Pa, the angst in his voice when he mentioned his Ma. *My Pa didn't like us Injuns.* Did Lev's father kill his mother? Was this guy bullshitting or not? Was he telling the truth about spearing wild Sockeye in a mountain lake by a Reservation not in Alaska? What did Lev mean when he said he never had friends? The barrage of unanswered questions made his head throb, dried out his throat, and turned his hands an uncomfortable, clammy cold.

Shortly before the sun completely melted into the western twilights—as the expedition rounded the last bend of the river before the Dragline dock came into view—a log popped up without warning beside the boat. Four of the five men shifted abruptly, making the vessel lurch dangerously sideways, almost tipping it over. In that instant, they had all imagined it was the body of a dead boy and breathed a collective sigh of relief when it was not. Julian's gaze shot to Lev. Why was that fucker smiling like that?

## CHAPTER 8

# TRENCH TOWN

Dragline buzzed with excitement that Sunday as the first of several large yellow buses—rented from the Dillingham school district—carrying fish crews pulled up to the plant. Julian, Boone, and Chris observed the emigration from the top of a forty-foot fuel tower that sat on the hill next to the Chiklak homestead overlooking the yard. Tediously, they had lugged up the rickety-steel ladder a twenty-dollar twelve-pack of generic beer purchased from Big Al, for the entertainment and view were as good as it got, and from a crowded Dragline school bus you never knew what you'd get.

First off was the Mexican crew. A dozen men and a handful of women climbed out hesitantly, as if unsure of their safety. As the group picked through bags being tossed out in a huge pile, their boss Reuben Martinez chattered in rapid Spanish, pointing out the plant, dock, egg house, boats, and mess hall. His team nodded confidently, but from the height of the tower Julian and his friends could see they were rattled.

"Isn't that the crew Lev was on last year?" Julian asked.

Chris quipped. "Yep. He was Mexican last year. Filipino now."

"Talk about culture shock," Boone smirked, tossing an empty beer can and watching it fall on the gravel far below. "They got it."

"That's no shit. Dillingham ain't Ensenada," Julian grinned.

The first wave of workers off bus number one were lucky for they were given the last open rooms in the bunkhouse. The rest of the settlers colonized Tent City. Since the beginning of the season, a gigantic pile of slatted-wooden pallets had been growing on a flat gravel rectangle, on the edge of the mudflats, behind the mess hall. It was so tall that even with a ladder it was a sketchy climb to the top. Next to the pallet mountain stood a heap of flattened, broken-down cardboard boxes secured to the ground with blue tarps and rectangular cinder blocks.

"Have at it," Mike rosily offered, first pointing to the mounds of raw building materials then downriver toward town. "The wind blows in from there. The mess hall is right behind you, and the bathrooms and showers inside are kept clean. You each get one garbage bag of dirty laundry cleaned for you each week. Food is free and all you can eat. Use whatever you want from any of these piles. It's all yours!"

His generous offerings did nothing to assuage the shock from the new pioneer's faces. They raised their brows in surprise and disbelief, naïve realization setting in that they were expected to spend the next two months sleeping in a tent on a rainy, treeless mudflat. Before they could voice their despair, Mike turned and split for the plant, spinning back around as he suddenly remembered something important. "Oh…there's an all-hands meeting in the processing facility after supper. Eight o'clock sharp. Get yourselves situated before then. And don't be late."

The hapless looks on long faces didn't last long. One man wearing head-to-toe camo stepped forward. Earlier in the day the group had established that he had traveled the farthest to get there, all the way from New York. He now addressed the group like he was their boss.

"I did this at the last place I worked," he preached. "It's actually not so bad. It works best if we put our claims in lines to block the wind. Start by setting your tent on a pallet to keep it off the wet ground. Then use the cardboard as padding on top of that."

Several men, clueing-in to the importance of claiming a high-dry spot, rushed to the top of the towering hoard of pallets. They began dropping them, unbroken ones first, to their companions waiting below. Over the next two hours, Tent City came to life. Some chose to set up by themselves off to one side. Others formed mini communities with symmetrically stacked layers of decking complete with walkways in between and elaborate double levels for sitting areas. Two preppy-looking dudes wearing pink and green Izod shirts staked their claim by the mess hall steps as far away from the mud as they could get. Three brothers from North Dakota, who constantly talked about going out on a crab boat after the salmon season, shared a large white-canvas hunting tent in the middle. Two tough farm kids wearing Iowa Hawkeyes football jerseys set up by themselves almost all the way out to the putrid mudflats.

When the second bus arrived, Julian and his friends climbed down from their perch and finished the rest of their beer on the mess hall steps. They offered advice as some workers pitched their tents in an outer ring and others filled in the spaces between them. Five women, who arrived on bus two, secured their living areas together with blue tarps. Boone caroused from group-to-group, answering questions, cracking jokes, and sizing up potential workers for his dock crew.

"Last year a mother brown bear and her two cubs walked out on the mudflats over there," he said, pointing downstream. "She was a behemoth. That old mamma-bear probably weighed over a thousand pounds."

"Hell, each cub probably topped five hundred. Biggest bears I've ever seen," Chris added. "They left paw prints in the mud the size of your head."

Upon hearing this, the Iowa guys pulled stakes and moved closer to the others. Chris and Boone winked at each other, turning to conceal smiles.

Dry cardboard to soften wood planks and bridge the gaps of pallets became the most sought-after commodity. Quarrels broke out as greedy campers rushed the pile for more boxes. Tent stakes didn't hold well to the tundra mud and soon the cinder blocks were gone too. Slowly yet steadily, scattered tents evolved from an encampment into a settlement, then a village, before finally blossoming into a full-blown, unified Tent City. As construction neared completion someone rolled in a fifty-gallon barrel and satisfied to have reached their final destination, wanderers huddled around a bonfire, shared stories, and forged improbable friendships.

"This place needs a flag," one camper remarked. When none was produced, he tied a white Bob Marley T-shirt to a stick and jammed it in the mud. "I hereby christen this place, Trench Town!"

As determined as everyone was to make Trench Town structurally viable, Julian knew the elements would eventually prove to be too much. Very few tents would make the return trip home. As it did every year, the endless rain and harsh Alaska climate would pull Tent City into the mud, ever so gradually, piece-by-piece-by-piece.

At eight o'clock that evening everyone crammed into the Dragline plant. It was the first and last time they would all be assembled together as a large group. Mike addressed them from his balcony. "Welcome to Dragline Fisheries Dillingham. I know most of you have traveled a long way, to get here, and no doubt you're ready to get to work and make some money. The good news is, we have plenty of work. The bad news is, we have plenty of work."

Nobody laughed but still he took a moment to chuckle at his own joke. "They're already fishing the Egegik River and out at Coffee Point, so we'll have fish here late tomorrow morning. Once production starts, I don't plan on stopping until the fish peter out in early August. There are no days off and we're not stopping the line for any reason. For those of you who are new, the foremen over there will show you what to do."

He pointed at Julian, Boone, Archie, and Chris. They put up their hands, on queue.

"From now until the end of the season, we'll run alternating sixteen-hour shifts. Each one of you will work sixteen on, eight off. Your foreman will put you where they best see fit. Show up on time. Do as you are instructed. We won't have time for any bullshit excuses."

Mike looked around at the faces in the crowd below to make sure everyone was listening. "During off hours, sleep. You can go to the bar all you want after the season, but not during. No drinking on the job. Stay off the dock. Rest. There are no rides to town. Only go to the mess hall when it's your time to be there," he hesitated then continued. "And if you get sick or hurt, you'll be sent home. The only ones allowed in this camp are the ones who are working. If you leave early for any reason, or quit, the cost of your plane ticket will be deducted from your last check."

The contract Dragline Fisheries followed for first-year seasonal workers came from a standard template used by most Alaska processors and canneries at the time. Employment started the day a worker arrived and ended when the plant shut down in August from lack of fish. Base pay was seven twenty-five an hour. Time-and-a-half was paid for everything over eight hours in a shift, or forty hours a week. Dragline paid for an airline ticket to and from Dillingham after the contract was completed.

"We've split you into random teams," Mike continued, pointing to sheets of paper containing lists of names taped to the wall. "The foremen will shuffle you up as they see fit. Make sure you have boots and gear that fits you tonight. Tomorrow it's go-time. Any questions?"

One man who had been hanging in the back by himself raised his hand. "Can I get a ride back to the airport?"

The crowd erupted with laughter. The man was serious. Mike did not think it was funny one bit. Julian and the other plant foremen spent the evening walking around and meeting new workers. The crowd was a smorgasbord of people from at least twenty different states and three or four countries. Boone needed seventeen men to round out his dock crew. Even though a few were perfectly capable, no women were allowed on the dangerous docks.

"Have you ever driven a forklift before?" he challenged as he approached a new group. "Are you familiar with ships? Do you under-stand the rhythm of the tides?"

One-by-one workers were chosen for crews, scratched-off lists, added to new ones, and told what time to report.

"Make sure every tent has a wind-up alarm clock. And use it," Chris warned. "This ain't baseball. Two strikes and you're out on my team, not three. You'll go straight to the slime line if I have to come wake you more than once."

"Who's left-handed?" Julian challenged a group of men circled around the orange-glowing burn barrel. One man shot his arm in the air almost before Julian could finish asking the question. Another looked around sheepishly before meekly raising his too.

Julian pointed to the confident one, "You're my new header on the left side."

"You," he grunted to the other, "are on the slime line."

The Mexican workers were split up into three groups. One assigned to Chris, another to Julian, and the women to the egg house. The male foremen tried to claim as many of the girls as they could for their crews, but in the end the head Japanese egg technician, just like every other year, recruited most of them.

The next morning the first tender ship appeared and chugged up to the Dragline dock. Within minutes, the musical dance of the forklifts began, and the industrial crescendo of production picked up steam. For the next forty-six days, the rhythm would continue as over five million pounds of fish were suctioned, fork-lifted, headed, gutted, cleaned, stacked, frozen, glazed, weighed, bagged, boxed, and shipped. The Dragline peak season grind had begun.

Most of the jobs were so brutally monotonous that their only saving grace came from hours of mindless conversation with the person on the left, right, and across. Most were careful not to discuss religion or politics. Others were not, and Julian frequently had to shuffle workers around before fights could erupt. Hour-after-hour, shift-after-shift workers talked, joked, and turned everything they could think of into a competition with machismo motivations. During those few precious hours away from the plant each day, when sleeping bags became one's sole personal sanctuary, most slept. Others partied whenever and wherever they could. But the only true escape from work and tedium was through endless talk.

As someone who would soon be a reporter for the *Post-Register*, Julian often quizzed people from Western Washington about local events. Oftentimes, conversation turned to the notorious Green River Killer, who police believed had killed at least thirty women several years before. It was the nation's worst unsolved serial-murder case and for the past five years had been covered continuously by every major Seattle news organization.

Most of the killer's victims were prostitutes or runaways and the first five were found in the Green River south of the city. Following those initial discoveries came twenty-nine more, all young women, all strangled, and all dumped in forested and overgrown woodlots of south King County. Rumors swirled that their bodies were found nude. And posed.

As the death toll mounted, a special task force was created to hunt the elusive predator down. Then the murders had simply stopped.

"I think the killer moved to southern California," one of the freezer rack workers said. He lived in Tacoma and had been following the story closely for years. "There's been a bunch of murders happening down there. And they started right after the killings stopped in Seattle."

"I think he relocated to Portland," one of the graders disagreed. "They found bodies down by Tigard. Some say there are still more to be discovered in the heavy woods around there."

"My parents think there's more than one killer," another slimer added. "There's no way one man could be responsible for that many dead women."

"I'd bet *my* money he's dead." Chris had joined them from the loading area. "No way did he suddenly lose his appetite to kill. My mother and sisters have been scared to be left alone ever since the first bodies were found not far from my house. Jules, did you know the Seattle region has had more serial killers than any other metro area in the country?"

Julian thought back to his job interview and the photos hanging on Francis Bernard's office wall—the one of the two detectives carrying a woman's body out of the river—and shook his head.

"It's true and it goes back a long time. You've heard of Ted Bundy. He was from Seattle, of course. But before him there was Bianchi, Dodd, Olson, Gohl, Campbell, Mak, Carnigan, Coe, Hanson, Bird, and Forrest. Charles Manson even lived in Tacoma for a while. Probably others. I know a lot about it because my uncle is a cop. He tells me details from local serial killer cases all the time."

"Why does your uncle think so many psychopaths live in Seattle?" Julian inquired.

Chris shrugged. "Maybe it's all the rain. Maybe it's because a killer can easily hide bodies in all the trees and underbrush. Maybe there's something in the water. Who knows?"

Julian's gaze froze on Lev standing outside the breakroom. Something about the guy had been unnerving him ever since their strange conversation on the Agulowak. His anxiety spiked when Hannah appeared, and the unlikely pair strolled out of the plant together.

❧

Now that the fleet was all out fishing, the vacant boat yard in between the mess hall and processing plant spooked Hannah, especially when she walked it alone during night shift. Broken totes, garbage, and discarded piles of gillnet were littered throughout in tall, random mounds. The smells made her gag, and, in the twilight, ship parts sometimes took on scary forms. More often than not, when she flinched at unfamiliar creaks, her imagination got the best of her. *Is that someone crying?* Pete finally realized what was happening and asked Lev to carry the heavy aluminum trays of baked treats over to the breakroom and accompany her three trips a day, which he heeded with Labrador-like loyalty. Hannah secretly rejoiced. No longer would she need to anticipate the worst, take flight and sprint the last leg of the meandering path, sliding back in the kitchen flushed and out of breath.

"What do you think that looks like, Lev?"

She waited for the older man trailing behind to catch up and study the twisted pile of metal on the far edge of the lot that had so often unnerved her.

"I dunno. A duck?"

"A duck?" Hannah squealed. "What kind of duck looks like that?"

"Ah ... a long necked one."

Hannah sat on the edge of a tote and laughed until warm tears streamed down her face. Lev, embarrassed at first, leaned up next to her, and eventually chuckled a bit too.

"Hannah. Someone gave me this." He pulled from his inside breast pocket a charm on a gold chain, fondling it tenderly before holding it out. "Here. You kin' have it."

"Are you sure? I mean, it looks expensive. I can't accept that, Lev. You should keep it."

"Nah, I don't wannit no more." Lev dropped the necklace in her palm and closed her fingers around it, lingering longer on their touch than he should. "You wear it."

Hannah slid it over her ponytail, gave him a friendly hug, and glowed with appreciation.

# CHAPTER 9

# THE DOCK

Every three hours, production crews rotated to take breaks in a clean-dry room at the far corner of the plant. "Mug-ups" were every worker's simple solace and mental goal line each leg of a shift. The fifteen-minute escape gave everyone a chance to peel off wet, smelly raingear mid-stream, warm up, tell a few jokes, and have a smoke. Sometimes fishermen, back from the grounds refueling, cashing in fish tickets, or picking-up supplies, took a quick time-out and mingled with the factory workers. Pete understood the importance of these community gatherings and always made sure there was a bottomless pot of strong, fresh-brewed coffee.

Boat-after-boat, tote-after-tote, salmon-after-salmon, fish churned through the production facility in what seemed like a never-ending procession. When he could manage a break, Julian typically avoided mug-ups. Instead he walked outside to have a smoke on his own, dream at the distant purple mountains, or hang with Boone and the dock crew. More and more frequently disturbing visions about Lev challenged his mind's peace. He grew uncomfortable every time he saw him with Hannah. Could he have something to do with the Chiklak boat accident? Shouldn't he, Julian, do something? But what was there to do? He had no proof of Lev's involvement with the drownings, just an uneasy feeling that would not go away. On days when these thoughts overpowered him, or when he was simply feeling exhausted and needed a boost, he sought out the king of zingers, himself. The master of comedic relief.

"How's it going, Archie?"

"Oh, hey Jules, not too good right now. It's raining like a drunk pig pissing on a flat rock."

Other times he'd say, "Pretty darn decent, we're making out like tall dogs on garbage can day."

Julian always walked away from Archie with an amused grin on his face. And some days that was all he needed to make it to the end of another shift.

One afternoon as Julian stepped out on the dock for a break-time smoke, a loud commotion from inside the plant stopped him in his tracks. He dropped his freshly lit Camel Light and sprinted back inside. To his astonishment, Lev and Charlie were fighting, circled by a ring of yelling workers. Hannah was screaming and trying to push her way into the fracas. Chris was egging it on at the top of his lungs, "Kick his ass! Kick his ass, Charlie!"

Julian muscled himself between the grappling men and was pushed backwards. A split-second later Dave leapt in and put Charlie in a head-lock. It took both Julian and Boone to hold back Lev.

"What the fuck is going on here?" yelled Dave.

Charlie's face was deeply scratched. Lev was bleeding from his nose. He pointed to the breakroom and hissed. Cookies were scattered across the floor. A large cooking tray was bent and upside down on the ground.

"Charlie tripped Lev for no reason," screamed Hannah. "He was carrying my cookies. Why did you do that, Charlie? Why?"

Without waiting for his cousin to respond, Dave slapped him solidly on the side of his face. At Chris's urging, Charlie had been antagonizing Lev ever since the Agulowak fishing trip as if it was Lev's fault Charlie had been sick and couldn't go. Dave shoved his cousin toward the door of the plant so hard they both almost fell over.

"Charlie won't be back for any more mug-ups," he growled.

Charlie could be heard saying, "I was just goofin' Dave. I didn't know he would fall like that."

Dave slapped him again. Lev did not blink or wipe the blood from his face until the two men disappeared outside.

∽✑

Several days after the fight between Charlie and Lev, Chris skidded into the breakroom gasping for breath. Crouching over with his hands-on-knees, he frantically motioned for Julian to follow him, then bolted back outside. The afternoon shift-change was underway. Rested workers were pulling on fresh gear, the tired ones already gone. Without explanation, Chris speed-walked all the way through the plant and out the rear door. His face was red as if he had just sprinted a mile. He didn't say a word. As Julian passed through the back-plastic flaps he noticed Boone's crew and a handful of off-duty workers gathered at the end of the dock. For the first time in weeks, *Big Bertha* was shut down. Forklifts were standing still. Other than the simple sound of seagulls screaming over a scrap of fish on the mud wallow below, it was eerily quiet.

"What's going on? Why are we stopped?" Julian coaxed as they approached the small group. "Is somebody hurt?"

The river was black and receding, tide almost at its lowest. Boone shook his head, gaze cemented on Archie who was straining below, oaring a flat-bottomed skiff through the shallow-murky water.

"There's a dead body under the dock," Boone finally whispered after Julian prodded him again. Julian froze, hair on the back of his neck bristling.

"A dead body?" Julian gulped. "What the hell happened? Who?"

Boone turned, and their eyes locked. A sharp inhale was his only answer. Was that fear in his eyes? Julian had never seen that in his friend before. Boone looked away in swift denial of the truth that had been unspoken.

Chris laid down on the oily-wood planks and peered one-eyed through the slats, trying to make out the figure. Archie pushed his boat firmly into the gook and pointed up with the paddle. "There it is. I can see legs dangling down and one arm. It's literally right underneath you.

It's caught in the metal crossbeams with a bunch of driftwood. There's no way to climb to it from down here."

Archie's boat lurched over as he pointed his oar directly under the group of people on the dock. They scattered backward. Several others came out of the production plant and got down on the edge of the dock on their knees, craning their necks dangerously over the side to try to catch a telling glimpse. The Japanese crew stood back a safe distance, fast chattering amongst themselves in a mournful tone. The crowd was growing.

"It's three feet straight under you," Archie called from below. "I don't recognize who it is, but it's definitely human. Lev was right, there's a dead body under the dock."

Mike marched down the dock yelling, assessing the situation with each stomp.

"A body? What the fuck? Under there? We'll have to cut a hole in the dock, dammit. And we'll have to do it quick." He pointed downstream at a full tender ship anchored in the bay. "Two hundred thousand pounds of fish will be coming in on the next tide."

Someone ran back to the engineer's room to grab a chainsaw. Mike screamed at the egg crew to stay out of the way. Relieved not to be in charge anymore, Boone jogged to the far end of the boat yard to find the boom truck. Cutting a hole in a dock with a chainsaw was neither a small nor discreet task. As an engineer started tearing into the foot-thick weathered tamarack planks, another wave of slimers—drawn to the sound like sinister flies—darted through the back-plastic flaps.

"Get back to work," Mike yelled, turning them away. "Stay inside. Process the fish in the totes. Don't stop the goddamn line."

Word traveled like telepathy and before the engineer could finish his last cut and drop a second three-foot section of plank into the mud below, the one and only Dillingham police car rolled down the hill. Neighbors and locals followed closely behind on four wheelers and in pickups. Soon over twenty people from town stood with the hodgepodge of Dragline workers in a tight-crowded group on the edge of the dock. They shifted to the side in a synchronized wave when Boone rolled through in the boom truck. As soon as the opening was revealed, a rock climber from

Arizona, one of Boone's best dock crew members, volunteered to slide through the hole. He tightly tied a red bandana around his nose and mouth and picked up the end of a thick rope.

"Wrap the line around the body three or four times," Mike instructed. "Don't let it fall. And don't fall yourself. Can you guide him, Archie?"

Archie pointed up with the oar. "Keep climbing back. Look in those crossbeams. It's over to your left."

The climber disappeared through the opening and monkeyed through the underbelly of the dock. In the group of onlookers, not one word was whispered. Eight agonizing minutes later he pulled himself back up and fell backward. He ripped the bandana off his face and gasped for clean air, arms muddy and bleeding from barnacle tears, horrified eyes blinking at the sky. His hands shook and the veins on his neck pumped visibly from holding his breath for longer than he had ever held it before.

"Did you loop it three times?" Mike asked. The man nodded. A few deep breaths later—after he was sure his heart had slowed down to the point where it wasn't going to burst—he got up and retreated down the dock without speaking or making eye contact with anyone. Afraid his nightmare might somehow get transferred to them, no one connected eyes with him either.

Boone took the other end of the rope, tied a Lariat Loop, and hooked it to the claw of the boom truck. Gradually the line became taut. With a deep breath signaling he was ready, Boone tapped on the boom lever. It strained, but nothing happened. He pulled it again with more conviction. The object on the other end resisted, then popped free. The boom truck bounced up and down. The crowd wheezed. Gulping down the urge to flee, Boone closed his eyes and waited for the bouncing to subside.

"Have you ever seen a dead body before?" Chris leaned in and whispered. "If not, you might want to leave."

Julian scanned the tense faces in the crowd. *Hannah. Where was she?* Trying to conceal from his friend that his heart was racing erratically, and he could hardly breathe, he shook his head no and with tightened lips croaked, "Have you?"

"Yeah. I have. And it ain't a pretty sight."

Slowly. Steadily. Shockingly. Stubbornly—ever so gradually, a blue and purple, bloated to three times normal size, disfigured with ghoul-like features, skin stretched as far as it could go without breaking, beastly, horrific, unhuman-looking corpse emerged from the hole. The rope was looped around its chest under its arms, digging into its flesh. Boone stopped lifting when the body dangled five feet off the ground. Its head was bowed down and crooked to the left, as if fixated on the distinctive dots tattooed on his wrists. It was young Eddie Chiklak.

From the back of the throng, Hannah screamed and broke into tears. Pete spun her around, put his arm over her, and hurried her back to the kitchen. Eddie's mother, who had arrived earlier with the officer, collapsed to her knees and began to wail the same haunting song grieving Yup'ik matriarchs had wept for thousands of years. Out of the corner of his eye, Julian saw Lev inch forward and with the tip of his longest finger, softly touch Eddie's body.

# CHAPTER 10

# THE STORM

S everal weeks after Eddie Chiklak's body was pulled out from underneath the Dragline dock, a typhoon of historical magnitude smashed into Japan and parts of coastal Russia. As the fury spiraled north and east across the Pacific, it gained momentum and made a path straight for the Bristol Bay. When waves swelled to over thirty-eight feet, National Weather Service meteorologists issued severe warnings and halted in port the steady stream of trampers set to carry thousands of containers east across international shipping lanes. Just after midnight, the eye of the storm passed Bogoslof Volcano in the Aleutians and walloped Dutch Harbor with one-hundred and forty-mile an hour hurricane force wind. The U.S. Coast Guard readied cutters and helicopters for anticipated maritime rescues. It's the "Summer Storm of the Decade" the national media decreed as they launched sensationalized live news coverage. In Hokkaido, the death toll climbed to over five thousand.

At Dragline the processing line kept going inside, as the dock crew did what they could to prepare for the approaching deluge. Boone parked three large container trailers in front of Tent City to act as shields from the wind. Mike called Trench Town campers off the line and ordered them to take down their tents. Machinery was hauled inside. Small vehicles and boats were relocated to the back of the building. Fish totes were fork-lifted off the dock and the Japanese crew abandoned the egg room. Preparing for the worst, Pete pre-cooked as many roasts and hams as he had and stuffed his freezers full of ice bags.

Fishing vessels up and down the coast bee-lined it back to port and tied together in tight formations to any available dock. Some of the most fate-tempting fishermen attempted to sleep on their boats, but most ran for high ground and rolled out sleeping bags in any dry building they could find. A few lashed themselves to tender ships that had moved into protected harbors. Stragglers in the fleet throttled for cover and anchored as far back in upriver sloughs as they could get.

As the storm bit ground and smashed full force into the Dragline plant, the crew processed until they ran out of fish. When the power finally failed, and emergency generators kicked in for the freezers, Mike told everyone to take shelter. Enough was enough. Sleeping bags were crammed side-by-side in every dry-covered nook. Few slept, however, as the monster storm flexed its might through the long, harrowing night.

Early the next morning, the worst of the weather seemed to have blown through. A few radio forecasters predicted a strong second surge, but others contradicted and declared the push had passed. Dozens of fishermen congregated outside Mike's office waiting for direction. After all, it *was* the peak of the fish run. Riding the storm, massive Sockeye schools were moving upriver fast. Time was running short. Dragline owner, Bob Clayton had been calling all morning, pressuring Mike to get more fish on the dock and start production again. There were contracts to fill and obligations that needed to be met. With such a short window to harvest, every hour shut down meant tens of thousands of dollars lost. They couldn't let the season's riches swim by them now.

"Well, I don't know what to tell you guys," Mike addressed the group. "One report says it's over. Another says there's more nastiness still on the way. There's a ton of fish pooled up out there and the season is more than half over. We can have tenders on the grounds buying fish by the time you fill your nets. I'm not telling you to go out in this, but I'm not stopping you either. Make your own decisions. Follow your own hearts."

Ever since the ripped net incident at Ekok, Dave Stevens was for the first time in recent memory not the high liner of the season. In every year but this one, he had always caught the most fish. It was a pride thing. And a money one. He was eager to go. "What do you think, Charlie? Ready to give it a shot? We came up here to fish and make some dough. We won't make a nickel standing here thinking about it."

Charlie had never been out in a boat in rough weather before. He shrugged to indicate he would do whatever Dave wanted. He'd been trying to redeem himself ever since his big screw-up on opening day and his fight with Lev. "I'm game," he resigned without giving it further thought. "You make the call, Dave."

"Okay, it's decided then. We're going. We're heading across the river to Kanulik Beach," Dave announced loud enough for everyone to hear. "It's sorta protected over there and almost within earshot of the *Kasilof* bell."

A few fishermen in the crowd took courage from his decision and began gearing up themselves. But most were leery. They talked in hushed whispers and reluctantly held back. As Dave and Charlie cinched their rain clothes tight, Julian approached. He pulled Dave to the side so Charlie couldn't hear. "Are you sure about this, Dave? That was a wicked storm. The worst I've ever seen. Hell, the worst any of us have ever seen. Some are saying it might not be over. Why don't you wait a bit and make sure this thing has blown through?"

Dave pointed out at *Proud Mary* tied to the cluster of vessels at the end of the dock. "These fish won't be here forever, Jules. We're going to wake up one morning and find out they've all disappeared. And once they're gone, they'll be gone for good."

Julian shook his head, unconvinced.

"Don't you worry about me buddy. That old wood boat of my gramps was built for big seas. You remember him. He often bragged about fishing in storms much nastier than this one. *Proud Mary* can handle it. I'm not worried one bit."

"It's not your boat that concerns me, Dave. Your grandpa always had experienced crews. You, my friend, do not."

Dave stopped pulling on his bibs and glared. "Whoa there. Charlie might not have the experience yet, but he's family. He's got my grandpa's blood running through him just like me. And the only way he's going to become salty is by getting tested. Sooner or later we all must face our fears, Jules. Today is Charlie's chance to do just that."

Julian backed off. He had an apprehensive feeling he couldn't shake but reluctantly held his tongue. Long ago he had learned not to push Dave to anger. Dave was a high liner. The one who caught fish when others could not. He knew what he was doing.

"We'll be fine, man," Dave reassured him after he finished getting ready and had a chance to cool down. "Buddy, my wife's not working right now, and I have mortgage payments to make. I *got* to fish. Charlie will do fine. Besides, my grandpa always said the only way to catch fish, is to be where the fish be. And I can tell you right now, they sure as hell aren't here on shore."

Julian started to say something but stopped and let the older boy from across the street have the last word. In silence he watched the pair walk out side-by-side and battle through arctic gusts to their boat. Troubled in a way he had never in his life felt before, he wrapped his coat tight and slogged back to the mess hall to drink coffee with Boone and the others until more fish arrived and production could start up once again.

∞⌇∞

Dave pointed *Proud Mary* into the wind and maneuvered across the wide-choppy river into the cove where he knew fish always balled up during harsh weather. His grandpa had shown him this little-known congregation place and it had served as his ace in the hole before. Charlie hid under in his raingear in the small cabin and shivered. As they let out their first net, a beam of sunlight escaped through the clouds. They both yipped as if they had just scratched winning numbers off a lottery ticket.

"Well, I'll be damned. I think the weather *is* breaking up," Dave hooted. "And look at the Redfish. They're *everywhere*! I *knew* they'd be here. This is shaping up be an epic day!"

Fish were stacked along the entire length of Kanulik Beach. The first net they set was teeming with Sockeye before it was fully extended, unquestionably their best pull of the season. Sure, the water was a bit lumpy, but they turned it into a game, whooping and hollering like cowboys on mechanical bulls as they worked. As they picked the net free, they rejoiced in the fact they were the only boat in the cove and had the whole school to themselves. *Just look at them all!*

In less than an hour they had covered their deck with salmon, boot high. They netted more Reds than Charlie had ever thought possible, more than their first pull of the season during the Ekok opener, and twice as many than any pull since. The *Kasilof* was anchored a mile away around the bend, and as *Proud Mary* off-loaded, Clint cautioned Dave to stay in protected waters. He had just spoken with another boat that had scampered up from the south coast. That fisherman was calling it quits because he was convinced more harsh weather was on the way. The skies in that direction were ominously black.

As they motored back to the hidden stretch of beach, Dave turned to Charlie. "You know, you've come a really long way this season, cousin. You're brave and strong and you're picking things up fast. Grandpa Stevens would be damn proud of *you* right now. I know he'd agree with me that the Stevens family has produced another kickass fisherman." Charlie inhaled with pride.

As the duo dropped their net a second time, without warning, they were struck by a cursed whip of wind. The temperature plummeted. Surging up waves with repeated blows, the relentless squall roiled their boat like an out of tempo trampoline. Icy rain blew sideways and stung their faces. Rising white-capped waves crashed over the sides and gushed water back and forth across the deck. It happened so fast that even Dave was caught off guard. The back edge of the storm had returned to unleash a second dose of ill-intentioned fury, far more severe than he had anticipated. Charlie's breathing got strong and short—he grew suddenly lightheaded. Burying his head in his arms, he slid to a quick sit, butt hitting the deck with a thud.

"Okay. Okay. This is getting nautical," Dave screamed above the rage. "Let's pull our net back in right now and get the hell out of here."

He took a step out of the cabin toward the hydraulic wheel. Six-foot whitecaps broke in every direction. "Hold on tight cousin. I'll cut the line and get us out of here ..."

As if it were born in the bowels of hell, a towering-jagged wave jolted *Proud Mary* broadside, slicing her bow sideways out of the foam toward the sky. The craft came down awkwardly on the backside of a cement-hard wave ridge, jerking it violently forward. Dave lost his grip and was tossed off balance. His gut hit the wheel with a vicious smack. From the opposite direction, another wave struck the rear of the boat, throwing the craft aloft and to the left. With the wind knocked out of him, Dave struggled to his feet but lost his footing again. Another surge pushed up from below. He was thrown backward into the air. His knife flipped out of his hand into the dark water. The back of his head cracked against the metal rail and his feet flew up and over the side. Charlie, who was still hiding under his raingear with his eyes sealed shut, opened them just in time to see the bottom of Dave's boots disappear into the frigid surf.

"DAVE!" he screamed.

Dave's head bobbed up. Blood poured freely from a deep gash on the back of his skull. He choked out liquid and reached his arms high.

"Charlie. Help!"

Dave's head plunged violently back under the whitewash before buoying back up again, lower this time. Still unable to catch his breath, he spat blood from his already blue-tinged mouth. Diluted red streaks streamed across his face.

In a panic Charlie staggered toward him, crashing down hard on the slippery deck. He struggled and weaved his way to Dave as the tempest threw him up and down, sideways and back. Finally, he latched on to Dave's raised arm with his right hand and locked his left around the rail.

"I've got you Dave. I won't let go. I Promise."

Pulling. Fighting. Willing. The rubber raingear was too wet. Slipping. The net was an anchor dragging Dave down. Too cold. *Nooo!* With a pop, Charlie lost his grip and was flung backwards onto the deck. Dave's head vanished under the turmoil. He was down longer this time before he reemerged. Desperately lurching out into the washboard, Charlie grabbed his cousin by the only thing he could, his hair. Dave seemed heavier. Charlie tugged. He pulled. But as hard as he strained, he could not free his cousin from his icy trap.

"I'm stuck. My leg… my leg is stuck in the net," sputtered Dave. It was an effort for him to talk now. His shivers were violent. "Charlie … Give me, give me … your knife. I think, I can … cut myself free."

Charlie unhooked his left arm and reached down for the bright-red crewman's knife Dave had told him to always keep attached to his raingear. Oh, god! He slapped his chest. His pocket. His belt. No knife. The sheath was there, but it was empty. He squinted over to where he had been crumpled near the cabin and panicked. His knife was probably laying there on the deck twelve feet away. He couldn't see it, but it had to be there. It had to be! He looked back and held Dave's eyes with his own … then glared at the sky. *Dear God, help me. What do I do?*

Sensing Charlie's agony and fearing the truth, Dave whispered, "Don't let me die, Charlie."

Buoys that had minutes before been thrashing on the surface were now underwater. The entire net was being pulled to the bottom under the weight of masses and masses of fish. In that impossible and terrifying moment, Charlie considered his choice. Should he let go, knowing Dave would certainly go under, run up to find his knife, then rush back and cut him free? Or should he keep hanging on, so Dave stayed above water where he could breathe and pray for help to arrive in time to save him?

"Don't … let … me … die, Charlie."

The words were delivered with a weak whisper. What should he do? Dave had already been in the frigid water far too long. The stream of blood from his wound was slowing, a sure sign hypothermia was setting in. But Dave was trying to remain conscious. Fighting to stay alive. Oh, Dave! DAVE! In a final act of decisive horror, Charlie watched as the red of Dave's lips turned to cruel hard blue.

"Jen … my boys. Jules. Love …"

An hour later another crew battling their own gillnetter into the wind toward the *Kasilof* spotted what looked like an empty fishing boat, barely visible above the violent surf, in the cove off Kanulik Beach. It bobbed haphazardly, like a sailboat with a broken mast sorrowfully dragging a heavy anchor through a crisscrossing reef. As they approached, they were chilled by the nightmarish sound of someone caught in a never-ending scream.

Charlie's left arm was gripped to the rail so tightly it had broken in two places. His right thumb was grotesquely dislocated and three of his fingers were snapped sideways across the top. They were all frozen in a desperate-gnarled fist, hopelessly clenching a ripped-out nest of Dave Stevens's shoulder-length curly-blond hair.

# CHAPTER 11

# YELLOW DANCING BUNNIES

Remnants of the deadly summer storm lingered for days. One hour it was calm, the next an angry squall shook the Dragline plant with unbridled ferocity. Tent City was cold, wet, miserable, and muddy. Wind snapped tarps over tents in unpredictable torrents, making restful sleep impossible. Nearly everyone grappled with the onset of extreme delirium, its severest stages manifesting in memory loss, inattention, moodiness, even hallucinations. Most ate quickly without speaking before leaving the mess hall by themselves. Conversation on the slime line grew short and eventually eroded into sad, sullen silence. The grueling work had become a cancer to thoughtful conversation, imagination, and laughter.

People who knew Dave best openly lamented his loss and recounted in hushed whispers the horrible events of that dreadful day. If only Dave wouldn't have gone out in the storm. If only Dave would have had a more experienced deckhand. If only Charlie would have cut him free. If only … if only … if only …

Charlie had been in debilitating shock since he was taken by helicopter to the hospital from Kanulik Beach. From there, he was flown to Anchorage where he underwent emergency surgeries on his arm, thumb, and fingers. Most concerning for his doctors was the fact that his eyes, when open, wouldn't blink and seemed to be focused on the sky in permanent, silent horror. Charlie Stevens never returned to Dragline again, and psyche fully shattered, forever would remain mute. Eventually he flew back home, broken, to California with his parents.

When Dave's gillnet was retrieved it was so heavy with Redfish it took the *Kasilof's* biggest boom to lift it off the bottom. Clint and the other deckhands had to shred layer upon of layer of thick monofilament and remove dozens and dozens of fish before they could even locate him to set his body free. Julian was working when Dave's father arrived and after a brief meeting with Mike, packed Dave's personal belongings. Before Julian even knew he was there, he had put a For Sale sign on *Proud Mary* and returned to Sacramento with the casket carrying his son.

A week after the accident, in the mess hall, Chris mumbled to his friends in a mollified tone, "I can't understand why Charlie didn't just cut him loose. They both carry knives on them. Dave's adamant about that."

"I don't know," Boone sighed. "Caught in a raging storm like that, people don't always think clearly."

"Maybe he just didn't have time. That net was jammed with four thousand pounds of Reds. It might have taken Dave down straight to the bottom the second he went over."

Julian had been half-listening, half-staring out the window, unable to eat. The raw emotions he felt were foreign to him. Outwardly sad, sure, but his sorrow seemed inerasable and emptiness felt self-pitying, somehow. Hollow. He fought the constant urge to lash out at those around him. So far, he had kept his temper restrained, showing anger wouldn't help anyone. But his profound pain only added to the prescient feelings of tension he had been trying to shake since the boat ride back from the Agulowak—the first day his instincts told him something was seriously wrong with Lev Warrens. He needed to speak with someone, but who? What would he even say? Without those answers, he had done nothing, avoided calling home. Let his anger build inside him. He started and finished each day, silent, sulking, and irritable.

"Neither one of them had their knives," he finally revealed. "Clint from the *Kasilof* told me he searched for them when they were towing it back. The Coast Guard noticed it too. Neither of them had a knife on *Proud Mary* at the time Dave needed one most. It doesn't make any sense."

Julian scowled when at a table across the room, Lev whispered something to Hannah, got up, laughed, and breezed out of the room.

"I've known Dave since I was four years old. We grew up together. Our Moms…" Julian paused to keep his composure. "… are like sisters. No way can I face them, not until I find out what happened out there."

"Buddy, I'm sorry," consoled Boone. "They probably dropped them in the water. Trying to save him. I don't know. Maybe Charlie will recover and be able to talk. This is all so fucked up."

⚭

One cold and windy evening, after his workday ended, Julian buried himself deep in his coat and sloshed through the rain back to his room. All day, hell, all week for that matter, he'd been in survival mode, focusing only on the immediate tasks that would get him to the end of another shift, thinking about Dave. As he kicked the mud from his boots and entered the bunkhouse, he heard Hannah sobbing. Tired, numb from concealing his emotions, and wanting nothing more than to be alone in his bed, at first, he slid past, but then stopped, paused, turned, and softly knocked. He pressed his ear to the door and heard her get out of her bunk with a thud and shuffle across the floor. Peering through the crack for only a moment, she opened it just wide enough for him to fit through and yanked him in by the arm.

Other than the dim flicker of a candle accentuating the unread pages of an open book, her room was dark and warmly insulated. Red-faced and quivering, she reached around and locked the door, as if hoping the thin layer of wood would somehow protect her from the cause of her grief.

"Jules, I am so … sad." She began to well up again. "I've never felt this way before. I can't stop thinking about Dave. About what happened out there. I can't get over it."

Instinctively, Julian stretched his arms around her to share her pain, and his as well.

"Dave was so nice," she moaned. "He was always, he was always so nice to me. He always made me laugh. He always asked how I was doing. He always made me feel important. It isn't fair what happened to him. Or Charlie, either. I can't believe Dave died like that. Jules, I want to go home."

In the glow of the dimly lit room, Julian noticed she had freed her ponytail and was wearing only an oversized T-shirt loosely concealing a pair of dandelion-yellow underwear. Smeared with tears, virtuous and innocent, she held tight to her chest a small, pink stuffed bunny.

"I really should go, Hannah."

"Please *don't. Please* don't go, Jules. I don't want to be alone. I *can't* be."

Her eyes begged him even more than her words. Embarrassed by her pleading and confused by his reluctance to stay, she grasped for something to solicit his approval.

"Look at this necklace Lev gave me."

She reached out with a thin gold chain draped across her fingers. The flicker of the candle made the soft metal glow warm and lustrous. Dangling in the center was a salmon pendant, scales intricately etched and glistening. Two small diamonds were inserted as eyes. They seemed to beckon him somehow. Beckon him like hers.

"I've been wearing it ever since. Lev says I should never take it off."

"It's nice. Probably real gold," Julian cleared his throat. "And those little diamonds look genuine too. It looks pretty on you, Hannah."

Julian exhaled. Perhaps it was the fury of the storm or their mutual mourning of his best friend. Perhaps it had been too long since he had held a woman in his arms. Perhaps it was as simple as he didn't want to be alone that night either. Whatever the reason, as he struggled to tame his own self-pity, grief, and desires, he put his arms back around her, closed his eyes, and this time held her tight.

"Okay. I'll stay for a bit," he sighed.

He shouldn't. He knew Chris was a loose cannon and had a crush on Hannah. So did Lev for that matter—that bastard. He really didn't want to lose a good friend over a girl he knew he could never love. Hannah salted her sobs with tears for a little bit longer, and eventually allowed them to subside. His inner voice told him to leave. *Leave Julian. Let the night remain lonely.*

But as she laid back on her bed, Julian noticed her dandelion-yellow underwear was covered with little dancing bunnies. He laughed for the first time since the tragedy at Kanulik. The grin felt good on his face. Then he remembered Chris's jealousy and frowned. *Get up and go now, Julian.*

Taking courage from his reaction, Hannah reached up and pulled him onto the bed on top of her. Her shy eyes disappeared as they caved to her desire for him. She leaned up and covered his lips with hers. Ignoring his sub-conscious warnings, he kissed her back and reached his hand under the back of her shirt. The wind shook the metal roof. Torrents of rain splashed against the window.

Commotion and arguing from the direction of the plant snapped him back to rational thought before he could drift off to sleep.

"Oh Jesus. What the hell have I done?" he languished in a hoarse voice. "Hannah. I'm … Chris is going freak out if he sees us together and I really don't want to deal with him right now. I need to go, Hannah. I need to leave."

"Don't leave," she whispered. "I don't like him. I mean he's a friend and all, but he's a jerk to Lev. And Lev doesn't deserve to be treated like that."

Lev? He'd been meaning to talk to her about him.

"Hannah be careful around Lev. He might not be who you think he is."

Hannah misunderstood and scrunched her cheeks. "Oh, don't be jealous. You're the one I want, silly. I came back out to Dragline this summer to be with someone I trust. Someone I love. You, Julian. You're the reason I'm here."

Her words made him bristle. He'd suspected Hannah had a crush on him but until that moment didn't realize her feelings ran so deep. His heart hardened. What had he done? He had no intention of being in a relationship with Hannah. He knew he could never love her. This had been a huge mistake. *Jesus Christ, Julian. What the hell were you thinking, man?* Deliberately avoiding eye contact, he got out of bed.

She giggled as she wiped herself off with her dandelion-yellow bunny panties, balled them up and threw them in a hamper in the corner.

"I need to go." He pulled on his jeans. "I … I don't know what to say."

Sensing he was upset but not understanding why, she stood up. Confused, she took off her necklace and placed it gently in his hand.

"Please keep this, Julian … to think of me … us. For now, it means we're friends. We'll always be friends. But think about things. We could be more. I want us to be more."

Wanting escape more than argument, Julian eased toward the door gripping the jewelry in his palm. He inched it open and peered down the hall both ways, making sure nobody was around.

"Jules," Hannah drew in a breath, let it back out. "I'll keep this a secret until you're ready. Okay? I'm good at keeping secrets."

He nodded and without saying a word, soft-stepped in his socks down the hall toward his room. Behind him, halfway down in the direction of the mess hall, a door snapped shut, its sharp intrusion shattering the damp silence. Julian swirled around and squinted, but through the stillness of shadows, saw nothing.

# CHAPTER 12

# DETECTIVES NIZZI AND HARGROVE

Two thousand four hundred and twenty-seven miles southeast of Dillingham as the gull flies, a phone rang and was answered before it could ring a second time.

"Nizzi. Homicide."

Investigations Lieutenant Nick Nizzi was working late on a Saturday, just like he had every other night since he moved to this close-knit maritime town the month before. After all, the ink wasn't yet dry on his divorce, he had nothing better to do, and privately, he was glad there was plenty of work on weekends at the Major Crimes Unit of the Everett PD. He had realized long ago that he didn't like to be alone. The detective listened to the voice, grunted, slammed down the receiver and quickly dialed another number. When no one answered, he left a message.

"Don, some kids found a woman's body near the old asphalt plant on Marine View Drive. Meet me there. Dispatch is calling it a murder. I'm leaving the station now."

In this sleepy little historic bedroom community that he had relocated to north of Seattle it was highly unusual to get an assignment like this, in fact, it was the first one he had received. Nick flipped on his squad car's red and blues. As he raced past the golf course down the hill to the waterfront, he couldn't help but think of his wife. She hadn't even paused to think before announcing she would not leave her life in Renton and move with him to his new job. What did she expect him to do after he was let go from the Green River Task Force? Stay with the Seattle PD and be miserable? Quit police work entirely? Deep down he knew that no matter what he did their marriage wouldn't have worked. For the past three years they had struggled or refused to communicate. He couldn't talk with her about his work, or the investigation that had consumed him, even when she pleaded. Through forced smiles they had let their problems seethe under the surface. Things had never quite boiled over, but it was only a matter of time before they would have. She'd never been cut out to be a policeman's wife anyway, he reasoned. *Christ. Two failed marriages before turning thirty-three. Maybe I should just get used to being alone.* He snapped out of it abruptly as he pulled up to the crime scene.

A pair of patrol cops was already there. One was stretching crime-scene tape across a well-used bike path, that separated the road from an elevated wooded hill, on the edge of the misty bay. The other had his hand on a bike to keep two teenage boys from bolting. It was overcast and drizzly, and other than the sound of sea birds, eerily quiet.

"Nizzi from the Investigations Division is here," the first young cop yelled up to the other.

Decrepit remnants of the aging asphalt plant's loading dock curled around one side of the knoll. Ancient pier posts rose broken from the shallow-brackish water like forgotten, unmarked tombstones.

"She's over there, Lieutenant," he hand-signaled, pointing to the grove of vegetation.

Nick shuddered as he took a silent moment to observe the familiarity of his surroundings. Gardner Bay Point was a popular hangout over-looking the scenic mouth of the Snohomish River. The far shore was framed by heavily wooded Whidbey Island. Young lovers were known to park here. On clear days tourists stopped to take postcard-worthy pictures. *Please not this again. Please not here.*

Across the road in a marshland, cattails shivered in the summer breeze. The unmistakable musk of a muddy Puget Sound tidal change lingered in the air. There were no large trees in the immediate area, just a patch of wind-snapped alders and a spattering of pines mixed with young cedar.

A blackberry bramble choked the underbrush together, and other than one narrow path he could see leading to a small lookout clearing on top, not even a determined dog could make it through without getting ripped apart by thorns. Nick had driven past here dozens of times before and had never stopped once. *This seems so hauntingly familiar. Has he started killing again?*

As he squeezed the snaps of his rain jacket together, his partner, Don Hargrove, pulled up in an unmarked car. Hargrove had been with the Everett PD for twenty-seven years and these days talked more and more frequently about the civilized things he and his wife were going to do in retirement. Tough and outspoken, the veteran detective had spent most of his career focused on robberies and nonviolent crimes. The two were still getting to know each. They had worked on just one illegal gambling case, as a team, since Nick arrived from the Seattle police force five weeks earlier.

"Hey, Nick. What did I miss? When you called, I was working under my car and couldn't make it to the damn phone in time. I heard your message and drove here as fast as I could."

He slid a shoulder holster over his head and felt for an edge on his oil-smudged coveralls to clip on his badge but quickly gave up and jammed it in his pocket. He was out of breath but didn't allow his partner to notice. Don Hargrove was off duty, but like Nizzi, he was always on call and always ready to go.

"I just got here myself," Nick slipped on his old-calloused gloves. "In time to hear what the boys have to say. Grab your camera bag. I don't like the looks of this."

Hargrove retrieved a notebook and hard case from his backseat, then rerouted two rubbernecking joggers coming up the bike path. Attracted to the police lights like moths, neighbors in large established houses on the bluff, two hundred yards away, peered over fences guarding their meticulously groomed backyards.

Nick threw up his hands in exasperation and mumbled, "Don't these people have better things to do? There are looky-loos everywhere in this small town."

He turned to the boys. "So, what are you doing down here? What did you find?"

"We came to see if the salmon made it to the river yet, officer," the taller teen squirmed. The scent of marijuana lingered on his clothes.

"Don't try to tell me that's *all* you were doing," Hargrove growled. "Were you two alone? Did you see anyone else?"

Both boys, visibly afraid of the detective, shook their heads. An inch over six feet, with a wide portly muscular physique, Hargrove's intensity nearly always intimidated those around him. The shorter of the two boys quivered, on the verge of tears.

"I almost stepped on her," he gasped, pointing to the trees. "I could see her bones."

Hargrove wrote down their names before motioning them to go. The three officers watched them scamper away on their bikes, before side-stepping under the yellow tape. Nick slowly picked his way into the wooded bramble, mentally comparing it to places like this he had seen before. Hargrove and the cop who had been first to arrive at the scene trailed behind.

Halfway up the hill, behind a blown-over tree and covered with cedar boughs lay the partially decayed body of a young woman. She appeared to be fully clothed and was lying face down. Her skin was cracked and had burst open in several places. New growth had sprung up around her and it was obvious she had been there for quite some time. Her jet-black hair clung loosely to her skull. She had two braids each held together with candy-red elastic bands.

Nick waited for Hargrove to take pictures from every angle before rolling her over to see her face. A rancid smell overpowered the brackish air. The young traffic cop jumped back and put his arm over his mouth and nose, swallowing the urge to vomit when he saw the maggots.

"It's hard to tell, Don, but I don't think she's Caucasian. Her skin looks dark like she's Mexican or Asian, but her face is not very recognizable, either. She might even be Native American. God dammit, look at the cut on her throat. And the back of her skull is bashed in. This girl was certainly murdered, no question about that."

Hargrove barked at the patrol cop, "Get back to your radio and get the coroner down here, right now."

From the trees, the officer stringing police tape bellowed, "Lieutenants, over here. There's another one over here!"

Hargrove turned and bull-rushed up the trail, nearly falling as blackberry thorns grabbed his clothes and ripped his hands. Nick took another long look at the first body then slowly worked his way up the broken path his partner had created. Fifty feet away, on the back side of the bluff in a small depression between two large logs on the downward side of the slope lay a second dead woman. Like the first victim, she was fully clothed and stretched out on her stomach. Her braided hair was tied with red elastic bands and she had on a green T-shirt, bra, jeans, socks, and tennis shoes. Two large cedar boughs had been pulled over her for concealment. Naturally a deep-forest green, the branches had turned brown.

"God dammit. She's dressed like the other one," Hargrove picked a thorn out of his skin. "And I'm guessing they've been hidden in plain sight right here on the edge of town for at least a month, maybe two or three. Whoever killed these girls broke those branches off in a veiled attempt to hide them. And do you know what? It worked."

He searched in his pack for another roll of film. Nick noted the back of the second victim's skull had the same circular wound as the first. He did not roll her over and correctly assumed her throat had been cut as well.

"These girls weren't killed here, Don." His teeth were clenched and the veins on his neck pulsated with anger. He took several deep breaths and paused to look out across the water. "When I was on the Green River Task Force, I saw more places like this than I care to count. Each one I can remember as vividly as if I was standing there now. This is a dumpsite. I can feel it."

"Do you think it's him? Hey, look ... what's that?" Something reflected in the forest litter near the body as Hargrove's camera flashed.

Nick moved a branch and brushed away some pine needles. Partially pressed in the mud, nearly undetectable, was a brass key. Hargrove took several close-ups before Nick picked it up. Holding it up in the sunlight, he could clearly make out the number 203 on one side and an engraved picture of a fish wearing a crown holding a net on the other. He dropped it in a plastic evidence bag and handed it to his partner.

"I've seen that logo before," Hargrove scrutinized it front and back. "It's on the sign in front of that seafood company down by the marina. It's called Dragline Fisheries. And it's less than a mile down the road."

# CHAPTER 13

# THE GRIND

Thirty-five days into production the mood at Dragline had visibly soured. Julian's frequent war cries, "Save the Salmon!" no longer got laughs. Jokes that had once been funny had now turned vulgar and mean. Conversation on the slime line grew stale, stories were repeated, agonizing stretches of uncomfortable silence made minutes quit ticking and time groan to a halt. Aches in backs that had started over a month before grew steadily worse. Overused muscles in wrists and arms burned with a constant throb. The deep-morning stiffness caused by pinched fingers and cold-wet feet served as the begrudging alarm clock for workers each morning. Most days the pain never went away. Along the way, some people got fired, others gave up. A steady stream of bandage-wrapped people was taken to the airport. Replacements were brought in when needed. Workers came and went.

Rousting folks out of bed before each shift became a constant and frustrating routine for Julian and the rest of the plant managers. Eating became a chore. Instead of lingering after meals in the mess hall laughing, most people went straight to bed and zipped themselves into their cocoon-like sleeping bags. In that brief period of gray treasured twilight, the moments before sleep when muscles could fully relax, and the mind had freedom to wander home, to the beach, to the faraway bed of a lover, many were haunted instead by images of an endless procession of dead salmon. Some were jolted awake by the vivid vision of their hand being lopped off by a header machine. A steady intake of cigarettes, chewing tobacco, and coffee became the constant crutch carrying many through another grueling day. The ones who had survived this far into the season—the rare breed who possessed the psychological fortitude, extraordinary stamina, relentless determination, and willpower required to survive—had mastered the ability to manipulate physical agony with deception tactics crafted by their minds. Those who hadn't learned those tricks, the ones weaker than the struggle to keep going, were long since gone. In their delirium, everyone was so focused on their own personal pain, on surviving the grind, they didn't realize just ten days remained in the season.

Boone's dock crew had imploded, in fact, he had never seen a team of men fall apart like his had this season. They talked incessantly about the body under the dock. How long had it been there hanging three feet under the boards where they worked? Did it wash in right before Lev found it or had it been in the crossbeams, getting picked at by seagulls, just inches away for weeks? How in the hell did Lev find it anyway? Desperate for answers, the questions consumed them. A few couldn't take it any longer, so they quit and flew home. And then Dave died. What was going on with this season? Was it cursed? Was bad karma paying them back for some unknown evil deed?

For the ones that stayed, the mental anguish of seeing the grotesquely disfigured body coupled with the dire conditions of camp life pushed their fragile mental states to the limit. Edgy and exhausted, nearly every exchange ended in a yelling match or a threat to be thrown off the dock into the quicksand-like mud below. Even the good-natured Archie allowed his clever zingers to turn hostile and cold. "You're dumber than a sack of hammers," he'd yell. "If I want any shit outta' you, I'll squeeze your head. If I want your stupid opinion, I'll beat it out of you. If you were twice as smart, you'd still be way too fucking stupid."

And then things started disappearing. At first people felt the loss of trivial things, minor annoyances, items easily misplaced or lost. One worker quizzed his buddies if they had taken half a carton of his smokes. Accusations flew over a missing pair of wool socks in Trench Town. More cigarettes were reported lost, then a pocketknife. One day, Hannah divulged to Pete she couldn't find her little pink stuffed bunny. Reuben overheard, checked with his crew, and reported one of his female crew members, Carmen, was missing clothes. He was pretty sure some of his money was gone too. When he counted it again, he screamed and stormed straight to the plant manager's office.

Mike had dealt with thieves in Alaska work camps before. He had witnessed how rapidly things could escalate, especially when the stolen items belonged to female workers. That evening, one-by-one, he discreetly called all the women from their rooms to his office. One girl told Mike she was missing a bra. Hannah couldn't find one of her favorite T-shirt's or her pink stuffed bunny. Carmen was positive someone had taken her nightgown, which was marked with her name on the inside tag. She was also missing some underwear.

Mike secretly called in Reuben and Archie, gave them keys along with the list of missing items and ordered them to search every room, bunk, and tent. Without telling anyone what they were doing, they systematically went down the hall looking for the stolen goods. And it didn't take them long to find what they were looking for. In one of rooms assigned to the Filipino crew, under Lev's bottom bunk, they found a wood Japanese egg box. Inside was Carmen's nightgown along with two pairs of women's underwear, a bra, some smokes, a pocketknife, and a pair of wool socks.

Mike immediately called Lev to his office. He slammed the box down on his desk. "What the fuck is all this, Lev? And tell me why it was hidden under your bed!"

Lev tried to shrug it away past the intensity of Mike's heavy glare. "It ain't mine, Mike. It musta' been in some clothes when I brought uh' the laundry in or some'n."

Before Mike could respond, Reuben jumped up, grabbed Lev by his shirt collar and growled through clenched teeth, "You fuckin' lyin' thief. I'll cut both your hands off and rip out your eyes. Where's my money, you rotten son of a bitch?"

Coldly greeting Reuben's rage, Lev pulled back viciously. His shirt ripped. He squeezed the fingers of his right hand into a fist so tight that they popped. With his eyes he dared the Mexican boss to throw the first punch, and slowly lowered his left hand toward his boot.

Mike's face was red and indignant. "Pack your shit right fuckin' now, Lev. Get out of this camp. Stealing is not something I will tolerate. If you're not in the van to the airport in five minutes, I'm calling the Dillingham police to let them deal with this. You're not welcome back here … EVER!"

"Ah, Mike, I didn't …"

But Mike had heard enough. He bellowed his ultimatum in a thundering voice, "Archie take this lowlife piece of shit thief to the airport. Go pack your stuff, Lev Warrens. Get the hell out of my plant. Get out! NOW!"

The three watched from Mike's window as Lev ran across the boat yard and disappeared into the bunkhouse. Minutes later he reappeared with two large duffel bags, which he threw in the back of the van. Slamming the hatch so hard it almost came off its hinges, he raged back into the plant.

"Oh shit, what's he doing now? Better stop him before he hurts someone."

Mike radioed Boone on his handheld, while yelling at Archie and Reuben. "Go grab him, RIGHT NOW!"

Hannah was setting up the breakroom with coffee and snacks. She had the radio playing loud, belting out Penny Lane like a fifth Beatle. Like everyone else in camp, she had no idea that a search had happened, the stolen items found, or that Lev had been fired. Lev kicked open the door and went straight at her.

"Hannah! Hannah, you … bitch!"

Hannah dropped the coffee pot and screamed as Lev approached her like a cougar locked on prey. Except for obsidian eyes, his face had turned a clammy murderous white. Both of his hands were spread into vicious claws. Reuben burst into the room and jumped on Lev's back. Surprisingly quick, Lev gouged him in the eye and grabbed his throat. Archie blitzed in and tackled Lev hard to the ground. Lev's head snapped back as he hit the floor. Archie rolled on top and crushed Lev's bleeding face into the cement. Hannah ran out shrieking past Mike.

The production line came to a sudden halt. Chris clicked off the stereo and yelled, "What the hell is going on in there?"

Julian and Boone tore in from the dock just as Archie and Reuben were carrying Lev out of the breakroom through the production plant to the van. Lev swore and kicked the entire way. "I'm gonna' make all of you pay," he screamed.

Lev pointed at Julian, hate seeping out of every word. "Especially YOU. You'll pay *bad*, Julian Hopkins. I'm gonna make you pay ... You fuckin'..."

Archie cracked the man's head on the edge of the door. Reuben climbed in the backseat, taking with him a hissing, struggling Lev. He was shocked by how much more powerful Lev was than he looked. As he loosened his grip, Lev bit him on the arm, breaking the skin. With a full swing, Reuben punched him sharply on the side of his temple. Lev's head sunk to his chest. His body stilled. Reuben's arm bled.

"Get him to the airport and make sure he gets on the plane," Mike yelled. "Carry him on if you have to. Stay there until the plane door closes. Watch it take off."

Archie nodded and with tires spinning, peeled up the gravel hill.

"What the hell was *that* all about?" Julian asked Mike. "What the hell did *I* do to Lev?"

"You didn't do a damn thing," Mike took a deep breath to still his anger. "Lev has been stealing from lots of people in this camp and we caught him red-handed. I fired him and told him to never come back. He has no one to blame but himself."

Mike stomped back toward his office but then turned and raised his voice so everyone in the plant could hear. "Lev Warrens has been put on a flight to Anchorage. He is no longer welcome here. Not this year ... not next year. Not ever. If you see him, immediately come find me. Or better yet, call the cops. I fuckin' HATE thieves! Now everyone back to work!"

## CHAPTER 14

# DRAGLINE INVESTIGATION

The Dragline Fisheries corporate headquarters building sat in the center of Snohomish County's marine district and served as the company's business hub for the buying, selling, and shipping of millions of pounds of seafood. To keep their Alaska facilities running full capacity each year, Dragline hired close to a thousand seasonal workers and used Everett as the staging area. Supplies were easier to order on the mainland and in addition to people, a steady stream of barges and planes carrying machine parts, food, supplies, and fish traversed north and south. Have a problem with payroll? Talk to corporate. Need another box of gloves? Talk to corporate. Desperate for six, twelve, or twenty replacement workers to round out a work crew mid-season? Corporate headquarters processed everything but raw fish.

Detectives Nizzi and Hargrove arrived at the two-story wood and glass building at nine o'clock Monday morning. Ever since the bodies had been discovered two days before, they had gotten little sleep. Saturday afternoon and evening, they had interviewed neighbors in the houses on the high hill overlooking the asphalt plant. Nobody had seen anyone or heard anything unusual. For ten hours on Sunday they had scoured the entire length of the wooded knoll as an expanded team of officers cleared brush and chopped blackberry bushes. There were no other bodies.

Neither metal detectors nor dogs had uncovered any additional clues. Other than the two dead girls laying on the coroner's table, all they had to go on was the brass key engraved with a logo that matched the one on the sign out front by their police car.

"Can I help you?" asked the receptionist.

"We'd like to speak with your manager please," Nick walked up to her desk. "We left several messages over the weekend."

"Oh, I'm sorry, I haven't made it through the recordings yet. You probably want to speak with Bob Clayton. I'll let him know you're here."

She started to dial the phone, but stopped, and with an exasperated sigh of resentment, covered her ears. Across the street a locomotive smacked into a line of train cars loaded with boat parts and scrap metal, emitting a deafening boom. Trains arrived here each evening, loaded throughout the night, and rolled back out again every morning.

Within minutes, a slender man in his mid-forties who looked like he'd tipped back too many martinis the night before, with his country club friends, appeared through a door across the lobby. He was wearing a white button-down shirt and loose sport coat with no tie. Bob Clayton's father had founded Dragline Fisheries thirty years earlier, and while it was not the biggest seafood processing company in Alaska, it was certainly one of the most profitable. Bob had taken over the operation when his father retired twelve years before.

"Good morning, Officers. How may I help you?"

The receptionist tried not to show she was listening. Sensing the seriousness of their visit, Bob motioned them to follow. "Please join me in my office. It's more comfortable there."

He led them up the stairs to the second floor.

Once they were seated, Nick skipped the small talk. "Mr. Clayton, we're here investigating a homicide, two actually. We're hoping you can help."

"Help with a homicide investigation? I don't know anything about any homicides."

"On Saturday we found the bodies of two young women less than a mile up the road. They were in the trees by the asphalt plant."

"And they were brutally murdered," added Hargrove.

"Oh my god, my wife mentioned that she saw police cars stopped there, but she didn't know why. Murders? Jesus. I drive past there every day on my way to work. That is truly terrible. But I don't know anything about it."

Nick pulled the key from his pocket. The lab had been unable to dust any fingerprints. He held it out for Clayton. "Next to one of the victims we found this."

Clayton recognized it immediately and gasped. As if it was glowing hot, he refused to touch it. "That looks like one of our bunkhouse room keys. You found it at the scene? Please don't tell me you think *your* murders have anything to do with *my* company?"

"That's what we're here to determine," replied Nick.

Hargrove got up and walked to the window. A maze of warehouses, repair shops, and dry-docked marine vessels ran in both directions down the length of Marine View Drive. He gave Clayton a confused look. "Do you house people here? In a bunkhouse? Where?"

"Out back. I'll show you."

Clayton made a quick phone call and before long an old man in dark-blue one-piece coveralls appeared. His name, Elvin, was sewn with fishing line above his left breast pocket. He wore thick glasses and well-worn leather boots.

Clayton introduced him. "Officers, this is Elvin Grant, our handyman. He knows every nook and cranny in the bunkhouse. He makes those keys and hands them out to our employees when they stay here. Elvin, do you recognize this?"

Nick handed him the key. The man nodded.

"Good lord, no. I don't need this right now. Elvin can you lead us back to the bunkhouse, so the officers can look around?"

They followed Elvin down the hall and out the back door. Behind the modern office building an old, red two-story wooden structure loomed in its shadows. Beyond that, a series of short-and-wide cold storage warehouses fanned out toward a dock where barges could be loaded. Unlike most industrial yards in the area, this one was well maintained. A nearby Naval base could be seen over an eight-foot fence that surrounded the entire Dragline property. In between the buildings were long, uneven rows of parked vehicles.

"Holy shit. I had no idea this was all back here," declared Hargrove. "And I've lived in Everett for as long as I can remember. You can't see any of it from the road."

"Nope. Keeping our operation hidden from public view was the deal my dad made with the city years ago. And I think we do a pretty good job of it. All those cars and trucks belong to our workers in Alaska. Probably a third of our work force rolls through here at some point in their journey. It's pretty much non-stop between May and September. Many have completed their season already. The last of the crews will be returning when the fishing ends up there any day now. Elvin, can you take us to room 203?"

As Elvin led them up the stairs, Clayton explained there were forty rooms in the eighty-year-old bunkhouse, twenty on each floor. Workers could move through freely whenever they wanted, and other than Elvin, the complex was unsupervised. When no one answered his knock at 203, Nick used the key to open the door. Two steel beds lay empty except for a pair of thin, stained-by-age mattresses. No clothes were in the closet. Nothing was under the steel frames or in the trash can. The detectives could see no visible signs of a struggle. No blood. The room was bare, smelling faintly of bleach.

Nick turned to the men peering in from the hall, "Until I get a tech over here with Luminol, I don't want anyone else in here. Can you make sure of that?"

Both men nodded.

"The last time you cleaned this room," Hargrove's disappointment couldn't easily be concealed. "Did anything seem out of place? Was anything left behind?"

Elvin leaned against the door jam, perplexed by thought. "Nothing I can recall. People that stay here don't have much. The only things they usually leave behind is food wrappers and empty beer cans."

Nick walked to the window and gazed out at the rows of vehicles. This case felt all too familiar, yet different somehow. Both girls were killed by the same person, he was sure of that. Their throats had been slashed.

Identical strikes on the backs of their skulls at the soft spot right above the neck were too precise to be random. The attack had been planned. Premeditated. Whoever had done it had calculated the exact position for such a blow, taken aim, and delivered the fatal swings with crushing force. *One man did this. And he did it twice. He's done it before. Could it be ...?*

Nick masked his ire. "Elvin, do you have a Lost and Found? Some special place you keep things that get turned in?"

Elvin's eyes grew large. "Yeah. Hey wait. I remember something. Someone found a bag and dropped it off to me before they left for Alaska. It's in my office."

He led them back down the stairs and unlocked a door on the first floor by the main entrance. A small workspace was carved out in the middle of a mass of clutter. Tools covered shelves. A wooden rack on one wall contained forty nails, each holding keys bearing the same engraving as the one they had in evidence. Elvin peeked sheepishly at an outdated pin-up girl calendar, taped to the wrong month, and moved a basket of plumbing fittings to reveal a black backpack with a patch sewn on the side that read: 'Far Eastern University, Manila'.

"Someone found this out back in the parking lot about two months ago. I figured whoever lost it would come ask me for it on their way back through from Alaska. I didn't look inside. I just tucked it over there and forgot all about it."

He held up the bag. Tied to the zipper was a piece of candy-red elastic that looked like the same material found tied around the braids of the victims. Clayton groaned. Hargrove unzipped it, reached inside and pulled out a notebook. Several photographs fell to the floor. Nick slid on his gloves. One picture was of a large family standing in front of a house, another a school portrait of a young man. Two young dark-skinned women seemed to jump out of the third one. They had their arms around each other and were smiling as if they were in love with whoever was behind the camera. Their clothes matched and they wore the same neck-laces with what looked like fish pendants. Each had jet-black braided hair tied with candy-red elastic bands. They could only be sisters.

"That's them," Hargrove exclaimed. "It has to be them."

"Do you know these women?" Nick turned the photo around but did not let it leave his grasp. "Have either of you seen them before? Did either of you speak with them?"

After studying the photo closely Elvin shrugged. "I don't ever remember seeing them. But that doesn't mean much. Hundreds of people come through here each season. I don't write down names or keep track of room assignments. My job is to hand out keys, collect them from rooms after people leave, and hang them on those nails until they get used again."

"I don't recognize them either," concurred Clayton. "If they were here two months ago, they were too late to board our processing ship, so they probably went to one of our Alaska processing plants in either Seward or Dillingham. *If* they're even Dragline workers. Anyone could lose a backpack."

"We need a list of every one of your employees," Nick ordered, turning to Clayton. "I assume you can pull that together for us?"

Clayton grew quiet. "A list of all our employees. Yes. I should be able to get that from payroll. I'll work on it for you with my human resources manager. I think she'll be here later this afternoon. Or maybe tomorrow. I'll let you know."

Hargrove gave the man a stern look. Something about the business owner's hesitant response rubbed him the wrong way. "And I'm sending someone over to take photos of all those license plates, so I need you to make sure none of those vehicles move. Do you have a problem with locking the gate for a few hours?"

Clayton shook his head that he didn't. Elvin shrugged. On their way out, the detectives gave them each a business card and told them to call if they remembered anything else.

❧

Back at the station, Nick emptied the contents of the backpack while Hargrove read out loud the autopsy report the coroner had delivered while they were gone. It mostly confirmed information they already suspected. Both victims were in their early to mid-twenties. One was five-foot-two and weighed an estimated one hundred and ten pounds. The other, five-four, one twenty. Both had experienced blunt-force trauma to the head, but the coroner had ruled the fatal wound for each was a deeply slashed throat. The circular fractures on the base of their skulls appeared to be made by an oblong hammer or similar weapon. Both were struck in precisely the same spot. Neither victim showed evidence of sexual assault, but nonetheless, rape kits had been taken and sent to the lab. Because both victims were found fully clothed, sex did not appear to be the motive.

Hargrove took off his reading glasses and turned to his partner, "You haven't talked to me much about the Green River case, and I think it's time you should. What do you think? Is it him? Did *he* kill these girls?"

Nick taped the photos on the wall next to an oversized Snohomish County map. "Who are you?" he whispered. Then he turned and connected eyes with his partner. "You're right Don, I probably *should* talk about it. In fact, I probably should talk about it with a shrink. And I'd do it too, if I didn't think they'd lock me up and throw away the key."

Nick had meant for his jab to be funny but judging the concern in his partner's eyes he realized it wasn't taken that way. He sat down and changed his tone. "Don, the truth of the matter is, it would make sense if it was. The Green River has been dormant for two years, and if he's still alive, he's not done killing. No way, no how. These murders? I don't know. There's lots of similarities … but there's some differences too. I don't want to state that publicly yet. For now, let's keep it between ourselves."

Even though they were alone, he lowered his voice. "For my own sanity, I hope it *is* him. I hope it's him, so I can finally arrest his evil ass and put this whole thing to rest. I hope it's him, so I can finally snap these on the fucker …" From his back pocket he produced his old-weathered handcuffs and like a hypnotist pendulated them on his finger side-to-side.

"Well, *I* don't know what *you* know about the Green River Killer," Hargrove admitted after a deliberate pause. "But if it *is* him, he's been to Dragline. He didn't kill those girls there—at least not in that room with so many people around—but they were taken from there. They must have been there for them to lose their backpack, like that. Maybe they left willingly with him. Maybe he drugged them. But my hunch is they were abducted in the back-parking lot. He took them from there in a vehicle and drove them to the wooded knoll. Where they lost their key."

"Maybe," Nick had been taking pictures of the backpack while his partner talked. "But isn't it also possible it wasn't the girls staying there, but rather the killer himself? I think Elvin would have remembered if he had given those girls a key. Pretty young women kind of stand out in a bunkhouse full of men, don't you think? One man. One man dropped his own key at the crime scene. One man stole their backpack and dropped it in the Dragline parking lot. One man, still running around, who thinks he got away with it. Jesus... if this is the Green River Killer..."

"We'll see. If you're right his name will be on the employee list Bob Clayton is pulling together. And if we get lucky, we might be able to identify him from one of those license plates. Fuckin' A. The Green River Killer hiding in Alaska. That would sure be something."

Hargrove watched as Nick cataloged the contents of the pack: a thin rain jacket and a few articles of clothing, granola bars, food wrappers, a couple of sodas, a magazine, a pencil. The notebook contained writing in an Asian language neither could read. On the last page, Nick paused on an elaborate sketch of a grizzly bear.

"What did you think of Clayton, by the way? I think something's fishy with him. Yeah, pun intended. Clayton's acting like he's hiding something, don't you think?"

Nick was done speculating—daring himself to believe their Green River Killer in Alaska theory—and picked up the pack and shook it upside down. From a side pocket, several loose pieces of paper fluttered out.

"There we go. Tickets."

He held them close to his eyes and read the small print. There were two Greyhound bus tickets from San Francisco to Everett dated Friday, June third and a pair of plane tickets from Manila, Philippines to San Francisco the day before that. Stapled to the bottom were two canceled ones from Manila to Seattle.

"Dari and Jesiree Vallesteros, we found you," he whispered to the photo on the wall. "I'm so sorry you died like this so far away from home."

# CHAPTER 15

# THE BONFIRE

Driven by instinct and the obscure call only they could sense and interpret, the Redfish of the Bristol Bay sped upriver at a brisker and more frantic pace. Their time was nearly over. Their chapter almost told. It was now or never if they were going to make it back to their natal waters in time for their final semelparous obligation. Schools at the river mouth became scarce. Commercial fishermen barely pulled in enough fish each trip to cover their costs for fuel. Tenders went from a steady stream at the dock, to one per high tide, and eventually only one every other day. The Sockeye were disappearing from the Bristol Bay fishing grounds as mysteriously as they had arrived.

Starting in late July and continuing into the first few days of August, Mike had quietly been reducing the Dragline crews. The process started slowly at first, men and women with bad attitudes who constantly complained were discreetly pulled aside and driven to the airport. No replacements flew in to take their place. Like the dwindling salmon schools in the river mouth below town ... weak, hurt, or unwilling workers didn't make it to the end. Most people were still so preoccupied with their own individual pain they didn't notice how the crowd in the galley each meal was thinning out. Only the toughest were left to survive.

Talk on the production line picked up and centered around the Lev Warrens incident. Even though he had worked at Dragline almost two full seasons, very little was known of him. He'd never talked about his family or where he was from. Speculation for his current whereabouts was as diverse as tired imaginations would allow. Most were genuinely scared he would come back to hurt them or be waiting for them with harmful intentions when they returned home. At night they kept their bunkhouse doors bolted. Some slept with fillet knives by their side. His angry and violent image haunted them in their sleep.

One evening at the end of the first week of August, Mike entered the mess hall with the announcement they'd all been yearning to hear. "This season's winding down fast and it's time to cut crew. Who's ready to go home?"

Cheers erupted. Waves of joy whipped away weariness. More hands than needed flew up in the air. Mike picked the ones he wanted to fill the first plane. "Get your stuff packed tonight. A charter flight to Anchorage will be leaving at eleven tomorrow morning."

The galley echoed with excited whoops and hollers. The departing group shoveled down their last Pete-cooked supper and rushed back to pack. But not everyone wanted to go. Plenty of people still needing cash were more than willing to stay. Besides, they had been told the last to leave were the first to get hired back the following year. Julian and the other foremen walked around that evening to make sure their best workers weren't packing. In some cases, they bribed them to stay with cans of Rainier. Julian's best header needed no convincing but gladly took a free cool one. "The day I got here I told you I'd be on the last plane home. And that's still my intent. I'm staying 'til the end. I ain't leaving 'til you do."

Minutes after the buses rolled out the next morning, those who stayed moved to the bunkhouse and officially deserted Trench Town. Over the next few days, shifts became shorter. Production tapered off. The fish that *were* being sucked off the tenders by *Big Bertha* were darker in color. More Silvers, Pinks, and Chums, lesser value fish, were found in each tote. Fewer and fewer of the precious Sockeye making it to the grader's table were labeled top dollar. Overnight, the fish price on the grounds plummeted, triggering a final exodus for Bristol Bay fishermen. And once the hegira started, it happened in a flash. Within hours, all but the locals had packed up for home. Two days later, on August eighth, Mike decided it was time to call it quits for good.

"Tomorrow night we're doing the bonfire," he announced. "The morning after, a plane is coming to get the rest of you out of here, so don't get too crazy. Reuben's team and one small pack-up crew will stay for a few more days for final clean-up and closing. Thanks to you all, we processed more Sockeye this season than last. Our equipment held up. I do hope to see you all back. It was another good season."

As annual tradition demanded, the final bonfire turned out to be a night of purging, celebration, overindulgence, and closure. After a summer of non-stop Rock and Roll, the Mexican and Filipino crews took turns playing their choices of music. Boone and Archie filled the cleanest tote they could find with shaved ice and discounted cases of beer purchased from Big Al. Most burned their fish clothes. Some threw in the inferno their tattered tents and ripped sleeping bags. Combined with the broken pallets from Trench Town, it was by far the tallest bonfire of the year and twice had to be contained with a hose.

"Burn it! Let it burn!" Archie Deacon had been drinking since Mike's announcement and anytime someone contemplated whether they should burn or keep something, he yelled in his best Texan pirate voice. "Let it burn, my maties!"

He was on his way to Dutch Harbor to be a deckhand on the *Kasilof* for Red King Crab season with Clint Allen. He'd be back at Dragline next year, he announced. "Burn it, matey! Let it burn!"

Over the course of the evening, Julian caroused around, shook hands, and made a point of saying good-bye to each person individually. He wouldn't be back. Of that, he was sure. Boone talked about how he would spend the next few months metal detecting and hunting for lost treasures of the Old West. When the snow flew, he'd rejoin the ski patrol at Telluride for another season. Like Archie, he too would return next summer to Dragline. As layers of beer slowly disappeared from the tote, he recited elaborate tales of the Lost Dutchman's Mine and the missing 1863 gold cache of a crooked sheriff from Montana to anyone who would listen.

Just like every other year, Mike would do paperwork and wait for the last person to leave. He'd then lock up the plant and disappear into the Alaska wilderness for a few weeks of caribou hunting with his wife's brothers in Bethel.

Hannah announced she was heading back to Anchorage and would be attending the University of Alaska in Fairbanks in hopes of someday becoming a teacher. On several occasions since that stormy night, Hannah, clinging to the hope of long-term companionship, had collected her courage and tried to speak with Julian privately, but he always slipped away. Eventually, with pained eyes she cornered him. He let her down as gently as he could. "You need to find a man who loves you, Hannah. I'm sorry, but I'm not the one. I have a new life beginning and I came up here to close the chapter on this one. Go find yourself someone else to love. You deserve far better than me. Good-bye Hannah."

She had puzzled over his words and for a time, tried to remain friendly. But slowly her shameful feelings turned to frustration, and eventually unforgivable anger. She woke up one morning and the thought of his face made her scream. Right then and there, she decided she didn't want to speak with Julian Hopkins ever again.

Some folks were lusting for more adventure in America's final frontier and talked of traveling to Homer, Talkeetna, or Kenai. Others, still short of the monetary goals they had set for themselves when they left home, were heading to Seward to make a few last paychecks processing black cod, before heading south to pick up the vehicles they had left at the Dragline corporate lot in Everett.

Toward the end of the evening, Josie, who was heading out to stay with friends before returning to New Mexico, showed up. Throughout the season, whenever Boone made a trip to town to get needed parts for a forklift or pump, and sometimes for ones not needed at all, he had dropped in to chat with her. To avoid harassment and possibly competition, he had kept it a secret from his crew. Only Julian knew their relationship had steadily grown all summer until it eventually blossomed into something far more serious.

She turned to Boone, "So where are *you* going from here?"

"Well … without Dave we're not fishing up at the lakes, so Chris and I are renting a Jeep and going backpacking in Denali for a couple of weeks. Maybe you and your friends will join us?"

Josie smiled and grabbed his hand. "Maybe. Just maybe me and my friends will want to do just that. Here's the phone number to our apartment in Anchorage."

❧

The next morning, before the final bus arrived, Mike called Venju del Prado to his office. When the foreman knocked, Mike was busy locking things away, packing equipment in boxes—so unorganized he wouldn't be able to find anything the following year. "Venju, I just got a call from Bob Clayton at corporate. He wanted to know if you're heading back to Everett tonight."

"Yessir," Venju sat down on the only chair not buried in mounds of fish tickets. "Our whole crew is staying there in the bunkhouse for a few days before we fly home together to Manila. We might even go downtown to Seattle to see the Pike's Place Market and have a hamburger at the top of the Space Needle. Why did he ask?"

"I'm not really sure," Mike lied. "But it sounded important. He said he needs to talk to you right away. In fact, Bob himself will meet you at the Seattle airport. Please be on the lookout for him."

Puzzled, Venju nodded.

As abruptly as the Bristol Bay Sockeye season began at Dragline, it ended.

❧

When Clayton picked Venju up at the airport, their conversation was cordial but brief. Without telling the Filipino boss where they were going, the business owner drove straight to the Everett police station. Even though it was nine in the evening, the building bustled with activity.

"What the hell are we doing *here*?" asked del Prado.

"The police just want to ask you some questions," Clayton pulled his car into a visitor stall by the front door. "They're investigating a crime. It possibly has something to do with some of your workers. They're hoping you can help."

A uniformed officer led them to a room on the second floor where Nizzi and Hargrove were seated at an oval table. On a large map hanging on the wall, the Dragline Fisheries bunkhouse was circled in red marker, along with the bus station. A thick hand-drawn green line led to the wooded knoll. Two bright-yellow pin flags marked the locations where the Vallesteros sisters were discovered. As they sat down, Clayton introduced Venju as the boss of the Filipino laundry crew in Dillingham.

Nick handed him the photo from the backpack. "Mr. del Prado, do you know these women?"

Venju studied the snapshot carefully. "Nope, I've never seen them before. Why do you ask?"

"Do the names Jesiree and Dari Vallesteros ring a bell?"

Venju dropped the picture on the table. The air in his chest released like a pin-popped balloon. "Yeah. Oh, Mary, Joseph, Jesus! Those are the girls we were waiting for before we left. I never met them. I only spoke with them on the phone. I know their father back home in the Philippines. Years ago, we worked together on a ship. Those girls desperately wanted to come to America and were supposed to join our laundry crew in Dillingham. I hired them. But they never left Manila. Why? Where are they?"

"They're dead," Hargrove stood up and towered over the man. "Murdered."

Venju's hands began to tremble. "Murdered? How can that be? I called the Seattle airport and they told me they weren't on their flight. I assumed they decided not to come over to America and stayed in Manila. They never showed up at the bunkhouse. I figured they changed their minds. It happens all the time with young girls. Oh, Jesus. How are they dead?"

Nick calmly placed their tickets on the table. "That's because they didn't fly to Seattle. We spoke with Customs in San Francisco and they told us the girls got rerouted there from Manila on Thursday the second of June. They missed their Seattle flight."

Venju gasped, unable to speak.

"And they arrived in Everett after taking a twenty-two-hour ride on a Greyhound bus Friday afternoon the third," Hargrove added. "We spoke with the ticket taker at the terminal who talked with the girls when they asked for directions to Dragline Fisheries. He positively identified them from that photo."

Venju's whole body was shaking uncontrollably now. "That was the night before we left. We waited for them in the bunkhouse. They were supposed to land in Seattle. They never showed up. Oh, dear god. No."

He covered his head with his hands. "Nobody told me they were flying to San Francisco."

"Is this the room you stayed in?" Hargrove demanded. He placed the key to Room 203 on the table. "Did you or any of your men stay in that room in the Dragline bunkhouse?"

Fighting back tears, Venju looked at the key and shook his head. "Hindi Po. We all stayed in two rooms by the first-floor entrance, right by the janitor's office. We kept our doors open so we could watch for the girls and greet them when they arrived. None of us went upstairs."

"Did anyone on your crew leave or act suspicious that night?" Nick coaxed.

"No one has a car. All night we waited. We played pusoy dos. No one left. I'm sure of that."

"Is there anyone you know who would want to do them harm?"

Fighting hard to keep from crying, Venju shook his head and looked away.

Nick softened his tone. "Mr. del Prado, can you help us get in contact with the girls' parents? We know it's them because our lab positively matched the red elastic material found on their backpack to the ties in their braids. We haven't spoken with the family yet. And we really need to do that before we notify the press."

Venju nodded and thought of his friend back home, the father of the two girls. No longer able to control his emotions, he broke down and wept. The cops motioned to Clayton who escorted him out of the room.

"He seems sincere," Nick muttered. "He's not a suspect in my book. And now we know it was the killer who stayed in Room 203."

"Mine either. I'll work with the Chief and start pulling together a press conference."

"Okay. I'll notify the parents. I've had to do this before and I'm dreading it. Two daughters—dear God, please help me stay strong for this."

## CHAPTER 16

# THE SEATTLE POST-REGISTER

Mike's rental house was an upstairs-downstairs duplex halfway up a long-steep hill where no weeds peeked through tightly cut sodded yards, on Kromer Street, not far from the Dragline corporate office. At the bottom stood a tall red-brick hospital. Kitty-corner and across, just a long block away on the banks of Forgotten Creek, sat a neighborhood family market with a diverse selection of beer and wine. Within walking distance there was a pub on the waterfront and beyond that, in the harbor below, Julian could make out the distinctive shape of a Navy battleship tied up at port. Other than a neighbor's Shepherd across the street that wouldn't stop barking, he could tell right away he was going to like it here. An eighty-one-year-old lady named Ellen Brown lived upstairs.

As Julian unloaded his truck, he watched the Everett Trojan championship baseball players run to the top of the hill, touch a telephone pole, then walk down the long-brutal grade, hands on their sides, as a painful indoctrination to the team. On the verge of collapsing, two players stopped by a hedgerow and puked in the August heat. As they struggled, two other players who had been hiding in the laurels jumped out in front of them. Neither had made the grueling trek to the top, but as a coach approached, they breathed heavily and pretended they had.

"What's taking you so goddam long?" the coach screamed. "Did you touch the pole this time?"

"We did," one of the pretenders panted. The other pointed at the two pukers, "But they didn't."

The coach flew into a profanity-laced tirade. Arms waving, he ran to the heat-stroked boys. "You two. Do it again. And this time touch the mother fuckin' pole! And if you don't get it right this time, I'll make the whole team run. We can stay here all day until you two get it right. Get moving. NOW!"

Julian was tempted to interject and tell the coach who the cheaters really were, but decided it was none of his business. One of the two players who had been hiding in the bushes smirked as he walked past. The other flipped him off. Both laughed as they kicked their shoes through a pile of fresh Salem Menthol butts oddly scattered in front of Julian's house on the otherwise clean-swept sidewalk.

∽∾∽

That afternoon, Julian called the Seattle Post-Register to notify Francis Bernard he had returned from Alaska and was ready to go.

"Hopkins, I'm glad you're back. I know we agreed to have you start on Monday but I'm short-staffed and could sure use you now."

"Now? Like today?"

"Tomorrow morning would be fine. I can introduce you to the team and then you can join us at the press conference."

"Press conference?"

"A huge story is breaking, Hopkins, one we have been expecting for two years. I'll tell you all about it in the morning. Can you be here at seven?"

"See you at seven."

The editor hung up. Holy crap, Julian thought. I just got back from Dillingham. I need a haircut. And some new clothes. Tomorrow morning? Is he kidding? A huge story is breaking? This job sounds crazier than the fish business!

The next morning, Julian showed up a few minutes early at the newspaper building on Elliot Avenue. The commute to Seattle hadn't been as bad as he was expecting, probably because it was so damn early. Francis Bernard was waiting for him in the lobby.

"Welcome aboard, Hopkins. You picked quite a time to start. I have a feeling one of the biggest stories we have had in a long time is unfolding so I've got the whole group on deck. I'd like for you to attend with the rest of the breaking news and investigations team. Listen, think, and learn. Plug yourself in where you think you fit best. I always say baptism by fire is the best way to start. I'll be watching to see if that's true. The press conference is at the Everett police station."

"Everett police station?" Julian repeated. "That's where I rented a house. If I would have known that, I would have just met you there."

"Good to know. You can cut out for home directly afterward. Until you get your feet under you, I want you to observe. Contribute. Help others. Research. Make phone calls. You'll get plenty of assignments of your own if this story blows open the way I think it will."

The two men swerved through pods of cluttered desks. Every morning, as both manager and mentor of the *Seattle Post-Register* news machine, Bernard had a daily editorial meeting with his core group. They exchanged story seeds and discussed unique topic angles. Ideas were given hot life or shot down cold. Assignments and deadlines were set. At its conclusion, Bernard decided which stories were strong enough to print and whether they would appear at the top of the front page or get buried inside. Outside the glass of the conference room window, phones rang incessantly along a wall of desks. Half the cubes held typewriters; the others contained large white-clunky computers that many still did not know how to use. People scurried about with pens and notebooks. The P-R newsroom was always a beehive of activity, but for one hour each day, no one disturbed this gathering. When the two men breezed in, nine other reporters and cameramen were already assembled and sitting around an oval-walnut table.

"Everyone, this is Julian Hopkins," Bernard announced. "As I've told you, Julian produced outstanding work in college and comes highly recommended by several of his journalism professors. I'm thrilled to have him join us, especially today, as a report comes to us that another woman has been murdered and left in the woods, and rumors swirl that the Green River Killer may have struck again. Let's go around the room and introduce ourselves before we go to cover today's main event."

❧

At three o'clock sharp, the Everett PD welcomed the press in a specially prepared room by the front entrance of the station. The crowd was much larger than they had anticipated, but they should have known better because for years, every rumor possibly concerning the Green River Killer had received heightened media attention. It had taken officers over an hour to sort through equipment and check to make sure no one was carrying a weapon. The Everett PD didn't call many press conferences like this and when they did, it was usually to announce something of major importance. On this day, a news truck from each of the three major Seattle network television stations parked on the street outside. From the back of the room where he was sitting next to Francis Bernard, Julian thought the hodgepodge of colorful microphones positioned near the front podium made the room almost seem festive, but that would quickly change.

"I'm Everett Chief of Police, Bill Wagner. And these men are Detectives Nick Nizzi and Don Hargrove. As many of you already know, they are with the Major Crimes Division of the Everett Police Department, Investigations Division. Thank you all for coming. I will first read a prepared statement. Then my detectives will try to answer your questions with the understanding some of our information will be held back to protect the integrity of our active case."

With Hargrove's help, Wagner had spent hours crafting his statement to provide enough facts to generate a miracle clue that might lead them to their killer, but at the same time conceal critical details that could potentially derail their investigation. By design, many specifics like what the victims were wearing and where they worked were not included in his brief. He put on his glasses, pulled out a printed piece of paper from his breast pocket, and started reading.

"On Friday evening around seven, June third of this year, two women arrived at the Everett Greyhound Station. They had flown to San Francisco the day before from Manila, Philippines and rode the bus together through the night to get here."

He looked around the room before continuing. Reporters were scribbling frantically in their notebooks. "On Saturday, two local teens discovered a dead body in the woods near the old asphalt plant on Marine View Drive. As we examined the area, we found a second. Both had been there for at least two months. Through a combination of fingerprints and dental records received from the family, the Snohomish County Medical Examiner has positively identified them as the two young women from the bus station. They are Dari Vallesteros, twenty-three, and her younger sister Jesiree, twenty-one years old. On behalf of the entire department we would like to offer our heartfelt condolences to the family of the victims, back in the Philippines, who have already been contacted."

Several people in the crowd groaned. Rumors had been swirling that the press conference had been called to announce a murder, and they were shocked to now learn there were two.

Wagner continued reading. "The coroner has ruled both deaths homicides and the cause for each deliberate injury to the neck. Both suffered severe blunt-force trauma to the head in the same manner. We believe they were murdered the night they arrived in Everett. At this time, we have no suspects and we have no motive. But we have set up a special hot line and would appreciate assistance from the community. With that I'll turn it over for questions."

Nizzi and Hargrove joined the Chief at the podium. Hands flew up in the small crowded room.

One television reporter, more aggressive than the others, called out, "Can you tell us what kind of weapon was used?"

"I'm sorry we can't divulge that information at this time," Nick responded. "But I will tell you we haven't yet recovered any weapons used in this crime."

"Can you at least tell us if there *was* a weapon used? Or were they *strangled*?

"A weapon was used."

"What were the girls doing here? Why were they here from the Philippines?" asked another.

"Once again, we can't comment on that."

"Were these murders committed by the Green River Killer?"

Pencils stopped moving. Some didn't look up but squeezed their eyes shut, not daring to breath, waiting for the response. Hargrove conceded to Nick with a look. The pause was deafening. Finally, the detective cleared his throat, "As some of you know, I worked on the King County Special Task Force before transferring to the Everett PD. I've seen more Green River crime scenes than I care to count. This one…I don't know. We're not ruling anything out right now. There are potential similarities, but differences too. We're not discussing that at this juncture."

There were no other questions. The press had heard what they wanted to hear. Nizzi's revelation put them in a state of near hysteria, and they scrambled to break the story ahead of the competition. If the two Everett murders were indeed the work of the notorious and dreaded Green River Killer, it would be the top story for days to come, maybe even weeks. His murders had spanned a two-year period from 1982 through 1984, but no one had ever been arrested. He was presumed to be still on the loose, even though no new bodies had been discovered since 1986. Could he have resurfaced in this sleepy bedroom community, on the north side of Seattle, in 1988 and started killing again? Possibly. Very, very possibly.

Outside, reporters feverishly called their news directors from live trucks. All three networks simultaneously began airing news teasers that a huge story was breaking. *Be sure to tune in at five o'clock.* Cameramen jockeyed for live shot positions, reporters rehearsed sound bites, and news producers fine-tuned their scripts. Everyone needed more B-Roll! Each was determined not to get scooped by the others. As fierce deadline pressure mounted, they pressed for exclusive interviews with the detectives. Some set up on the hill overlooking the asphalt plant, others in front of the police station. The heat had been turned up on a media feeding frenzy and it was starting to boil over. At four-fifty-nine and a half that evening, a full twenty-seven seconds before the others, KING Television broke the story first.

"After a two-year hiatus, the Green River Killer may have once again reared his vicious head. This time in Everett," the anchor read. "As reported earlier, exclusively by us, two young women were found murdered and left in the woods along Marine View Drive."

∽✕∾

After debriefing with Bernard and the rest of his news team, Julian stayed on the north end, rather than drive back downtown with the rest. His adrenaline had been racing all day, and he considered stopping at the pub for a beer to settle his nerves. Remembering that Bernard wanted the whole team back in the newsroom early the next morning, he thought the better of it, and returned home. That damn dog across the street was barking again.

As he fumbled for his keys, almost as if she were a lioness lying in wait on a Serengeti hunt, Mrs. Brown popped up her head at the top of the stairs. "Hi there Mr. Reporter. I made you some cookies. Something to celebrate your first day at the newspaper. It's so exciting. I bet you have lots to share, Julian."

Julian sighed. As he moved in the day before, he had made the mistake of telling her he was a new reporter for the *Seattle Post-Register*, prompting her to ask a million questions and tell him her whole life's story. He felt sorry for her senility as she often repeated sentences and sometimes forget what she had recited minutes before. Her cousin's friend had been a writer once. Back before the war. Or was it her aunt's neighbor? The whole time he carried things in, she had barely left him alone. Because of this he had run out of time and stacked most of his Alaska gear in the hall outside his apartment on the ground level.

"Mrs. Brown. I appreciate your interest ... and your kindness. But if you don't mind, I really have some things I need to take care of right now."

She huffed, gave him a wounded glare, and slinked back to her kitchen. "Oh, I almost forgot. Your friend stopped by. I called for you downstairs, then remembered you were at work."

"Friend?"

"Yes, dear. He said you worked together in Alaska."

Alarms went off in Julian's head. "Mrs. Brown. None of my friends know I live here. Except for Mike. Was it, Mike?"

"No dear. It wasn't our landlord, Mike Matthews."

Julian's thoughts raced as his pores opened and he broke out in a sweat. Was it, Chris? Or Boone dropping in early from his camping trip in Denali? It had to be Chris. "What did he look like?"

"Well, I couldn't see him very well, but he had dark hair, I think. And dark eyes. He seemed older than you. When he left, he was very polite and said he'd come back to see you another time."

Julian's chest tightened. His heart thumped irregularly. He grew light-headed and choked out his words. "Did he say his name?"

"Yes dear, I believe he said it was Lev."

## Chapter 17

# On Assignment

Big news stories don't take time off, and neither do determined reporters when hard news is breaking. Normally, weekends were a chance to decompress, get some fresh air, drink at the bar, sleep in, stay far away from the action, but not this one. Ever since the press conference the day before the entire P-R news staff had been whizzing around in a bewildering blur and Julian was having a hard time keeping it all straight.

"Smart article in today's paper, Fiori. But I want to follow it up this week with much more depth. I'm not jumping on the bandwagon yet, but if they *do* determine the Green River Killer truly *did* come out of hiding, I don't want the television crews to get *all* the glory. We need team coverage!"

Bernard drew assignments and deadlines on his war board. "Harold, get on the phone and track down the family in the Philippines. We need a humanity piece on the Vallesteros sisters. Who were they visiting here? What were they doing? Even though they weren't from this country, I want our readers to get to know them like they were their own daughters. And get more photos of them if you can."

Instructions understood, veteran reporter Harold Weathers sprang up and left the room.

124

"Rodriguez get back up to the Everett police station and interview the Investigations Unit again. See if they'll share anything new. You've got our main story for the Sunday edition."

He continued to write in perfect handwriting on his white board. "Fiori talk to your source on the Green River Killer Task Force. Do *they* think the Everett murders are connected? I know they usually keep their cards pretty tight to the vest. Go off the record if you must. Write a piece on any new developments in that case, provide a historical perspective, but no speculation. We know the TV folks will give us all the speculation we can handle. Heck, it will probably go national again if it hasn't already. And take Hopkins with you."

Lindsay Fiori was a slender, full-lipped twenty-seven-year-old with raven-black hair and brown melancholy eyes. She proudly wore her cynicism on her chest, fiercely determined to use the power of her pen to serve her community. She'd been covering the Green River investigation since she started at the P-R four years earlier. Fiori was not shy about using her good looks to open doors others couldn't. In fact, she did it every chance she got.

"My gut tells me it's him," she surmised, aggressively battling down-town hills and traffic in search of a parking spot. "He's known to leave his victims in forested and overgrown areas. Just like the Vallesteros sisters. It's not much of a stretch to think he moved an hour north and started killing again."

As they entered the federal building on Second Avenue, Fiori instructed Julian to let her take the lead and ask all the questions. "I have good relationships with these guys, the ones who are left, and I want to keep it that way. Most of my contacts moved on to different departments. You watch and listen. We're fortunate they're taking the time to speak with us on a Saturday."

The idea that one killer could viciously murder thirty victims and still run free had both terrorized and captivated the entire country. People had grown dreadfully weary of the enigmatic horror hiding in their midst. Two years earlier, there had been a nationwide two-hour television special watched by an estimated thirty million viewers. When people were directed to call a toll-free number like a murder-tip telethon, over ten thousand leads flooded in. The unmanageable volume did more harm than good. It put a strangle-hold on the police investigation and crippled the resources of the Task Force for months. Shortly after that, the case went cold and most of the Task Force was disbanded.

Forty-five minutes later they were met in the lobby by a man who looked like he hadn't slept in days. Like the others on the King County Sheriff's team that had been set up to exclusively investigate the Green River Killer's gruesome murders in 1982, Detective Hank Garrity had immersed himself in the minutia to the point where he could think of little else. He and the others on his team worked endless hours and late nights to produce over a thousand pages of paperwork each month, yet they still hadn't identified the killer. As the years passed and the mystery remained unsolved, pressure had mounted from both the public and the press. Garrity was cordial but cautious when Fiori introduced Julian.

"Damn. You look terrible Hank," she quipped. "Take a vacation, will you?"

Fiori had the reputation of being straight forward. "You know why we're here. Do you believe the Everett murders are connected to the Green River killings?"

"Lindsay, we heard about those murders right before you did, and we haven't met with the Everett PD or FBI yet. One of our former team members is up there, and I haven't even connected with him. I wish you news people would be more cautious before jumping to conclusions. The last thing we need is another bottleneck in what's left of our department, from a thousand more dead-end tips."

Lindsay Fiori nodded in a conciliatory way. "That's why I came right down here, Hank. You notice I didn't put any speculation in my story this morning. We're not here to create more problems for you. We're here to help you catch this monster."

"I know. I know. You're the good guys." He exhaled and pulled out a notebook. "I'll tell you everything I can share."

Fiori turned on her tape recorder.

"The Green River Killer has followed a pretty specific *modus operandi* all along. We know he's a man. We know he strangles his victims. He targets mainly prostitutes and transient youth. Most of them are found naked and without possessions. Most show signs of sexual assault and many of his victims are left in posed positions. But keep in mind, most of the time we recover only skeletons. Scattered bones that still need to be identified. There's a whole list of missing women still unaccounted for and we know we haven't found them all yet. If he *is* killing again, he'll make a mistake. And I want to be there when he does. I want this bastard caught, more than you will ever know."

Fiori sighed and snapped off her tape recorder. The detective was reciting a well-rehearsed script. "Hank, you know I've heard all this. Give me something I can use. At least tell me if you believe the Green River Killer is still out there."

"On the record? Hard to tell. It's possible he moved away or is in prison somewhere. He might even be dead." Garrity stood up and looked at his watch. "Off the record? He's still out there, Lindsay. And these murders sound eerily familiar. Ah, hellfire, I don't know. And I better not see that printed in your newspaper tomorrow morning."

He took a step toward the elevator.

Julian looked up from taking notes. "So, does that mean you believe he killed the two women in Everett?"

Garrity turned around and glared. "That's not something I care to speculate on yet. And that's all I got."

As the two reporters left, Fiori growled. "I thought you were going to let me do all the talking?"

Before Julian could respond she interrupted, "Garrity knows something he wasn't willing to share, don't you think?"

Julian shrugged. "Yeah. He acted like it. I think he may believe the Everett murders are connected to the Green River murders, but he didn't want to tell us that. And I bet he's pretty good at poker."

"He does. And I agree," Fiori mumbled. "Maybe he'll be freer with his information after he speaks with the Everett PD. You can be damn sure I'll be waiting for him by his car the second he leaves *that* meeting."

Julian nodded. Right on. This girl was not only smart and good-looking, but tough and determined too. He liked that.

"So, tell me more about Alaska. I've been dying to go up there. Some friends of mine went last summer and they *still* can't stop talking about how beautiful it is."

"The whole state is incredible, but one of my favorite places is Denali National Park. It's quite a drive to the north, but the mountain is magical and there are moose, caribou, and bears everywhere you look. To get in, you need a reservation, and then you take an eight-hour bus ride where they drop you off in the middle of nowhere for a week. It's unbelievably cool as hell. I couldn't go this year because I had to rush back for this job, but my buddy Boone, his girlfriend, and some others are up there now. They're flying back this Friday and I'm meeting them for drinks. They'll have lots of amazing stories to share, I'm sure."

He flashed her a coy grin. "Would you be interested in joining us?"

"As a date?"

"I suppose so."

"Sure."

∽✢✄

As the two P-R reporters were interviewing Garrity downtown, detectives in Everett met with Bob Clayton and his human resources manager, Jane Ellis, pulling together a list of suspects who could have been staying in Room 203 at the time of the murders. Along with three other police officers recently recruited, they were pouring through two long lists of names. The first contained one hundred and sixty-four registered owners of the vehicles parked in the long-term lot behind the Dragline bunkhouse. After a photographer had given him pictures of each license plate, Hargrove had spent hours at the Department of Motor Vehicles office putting names to vehicles.

"There's twenty-six cars I can't match to an employee," he reported. "Probably parents or spouses own the vehicles and loaned them to whoever parked them for the summer. Hell, they might even be stolen. After this meeting, you three call the legal owners and find out what employee they loaned it to. We need every vehicle and person accounted for."

The second report was the one Jane compiled from payroll records. All told they were nine shy of seven hundred names.

"The ones with red dots are the forty-seven permanent employees who work in our corporate office," Clayton explained. "That includes Jane and me. We park out front. None of our corporate employees have permission to park out back—or go into the bunkhouse. And no one who isn't a Dragline employee can get in back there either."

Clayton continued, "Our processing ship, *Dragline Rose* left for Sitka in early May. Those two hundred and eleven onboard workers were long gone by the time the Vallesteros sisters landed here in this country. We can safely cross them off too. There's no way they could have been here that night."

Jane's fingers tapped a calculator in a whir. "That leaves four-hundred and thirty-three. But of those, three hundred and ten never stepped foot in the state of Washington. Most of them live overseas or in Alaska. Some flew straight to Anchorage from other places without stopping in Everett. I highlighted those for you."

"That leaves one hundred and twenty-three," said Nick.

"Plus, the full-time Dragline employees," Hargrove added. "And the twenty-six unaccounted for vehicles. One hundred and ninety-six is an excellent starting spot to figure out who stayed in Room 203 the night of the murders."

"I'll go back and cross-check this list with flight dates," said Jane. "Payroll dates don't always match up to the day they arrived at our Alaska facilities. But they will be close. I'll call you when I have the airline information for our short-list. We can then eliminate the ones who flew up before the girls arrived in Everett. When you have names for the drivers of the extra twenty-six cars, I'll check those too."

Hargrove turned to the team. "While she does that, let's split up the list we have and get started. We need solid alibis for everyone who could have been in Everett on June third, starting with the full-time Dragline employees. Or else they need interviewed."

Jane started to say something, but Clayton interrupted.

"Jane, it's time to go," he warned, ushering her to the door. "We'll leave you to it, detectives. Let us know if we can be of further assistance."

Hargrove gave him a quizzical look and after they left, turned to his partner. "See? I'm telling you, Nick, Bob Clayton knows something he's not saying. He's acting shifty again, like he's holding something back."

Nick ignored him and scanned through the rows of names with his finger, reaching into the deep recesses of his mind for any connection to the Green River case. Boone Davis and Chris Fitzpatrick were on the Dragline short-list. So was Julian Hopkins.

৹৵৹

The air was tense when Julian stepped in Bernard's office. Already seated—looking like he was losing the battle with a stomach illness—nodded veteran reporter Harold Weathers.

"Pull up a chair, Julian. Weathers here has learned something interesting he'd like to share."

Weathers swallowed hard to erase the apparent bad taste in his throat. "So, I finally spoke with the father of the Vallesteros sisters in Manila. He was devastated as you can imagine, but he did mail us some pictures. He's in contact with the Everett PD but voiced extreme anger toward the Filipino boss who was supposed to be taking care of his girls. He feels helpless as you can imagine. You'll never guess why the sisters were in America."

Julian shrugged.

"They were on their way to work at Dragline Fisheries for the summer. In Alaska."

Julian fell back in his chair and gasped. "You have *got* to be kidding. That's where *I* worked. Did he say which plant? They have two. One in Dillingham where I was, the other in Seward. They also run a processing ship."

"I didn't ask."

"I didn't realize there were multiple locations," interjected Bernard. "Harold let's keep this under our hats for now. Julian, can you find that out for us?"

"I think so. I'll call the owner of Dragline, Bob Clayton. He'll tell me. Two Filipino women? Jesus, this is unbelievable. If they were on their way to Dillingham, they probably would have been on Venju del Prado's laundry crew."

The second he said it, he choked. Lev Warrens. *Oh my god!* Lev had been in Everett the weekend of the murders. He'd flown up with Venju and the rest. Boone revealed he'd been added to the Filipino crew last minute because two women had not arrived. *It had to be the sisters. And if so, did Lev kill them?* His mind flashed back to the queer look on the man's face when they pulled Eddie Chiklak's body from under the dock, their strange conversation on the Agulowak, no pictures, his lack of empathy when Dave died, the violent threats Lev made as he was being carried out of camp by Archie and Reuben. Holy shit. *He came to my house looking for me?* Julian gasped for breath and put his thumbs on his temples to silence inner-ear sirens, fighting the urge to pass out.

"Julian, are you okay?"

"Yes," Julian whispered. "I'll give Bob Clayton a call."

## CHAPTER 18

# THE SECRET

Julian waited for the newsroom's weekend exodus to be over before ducking out to a phone booth down the street. The fact he wasn't making the call from his desk was proof positive he was being paranoid, but who could blame him? Ever since Weathers dropped his bombshell, his trepid feeling about Lev had bent to fear. *You'll pay bad, Julian Hopkins.* The man had shown up at his house!

No way could he divulge his suspicions to Francis Bernard, or anyone else on the news team. Not yet. Afterall, his suspicions were probably false, and he didn't have answers to any of the questions Bernard would most certainly ask. He was the new guy still trying to find his place, make a good impression, positively contribute, not draw negative attention to himself. The last thing he wanted to do was somehow insert himself into the biggest news story in town, or have his co-workers think he was nuts. What could he tell the cops? What should he say? Could he even share the information Weathers provided? Bernard had ordered them not to. Would he be fired if he did?

He looked both ways down the street before slowly dialing the Everett PD. Without identifying himself as a reporter, he asked to speak with the lead detective on the Vallesteros investigation.

"Nizzi. Homicide."

"Officer Nizzi, my name is Julian Hopkins. I have some information I think might help you solve the Vallesteros murder case."

Julian Hopkins? Recognizing the name from the Dragline list, Nick lit up and frantically motioned to Hargrove across the room.

"Oh really? And what would that be, Mr. Hopkins?"

"This summer I worked for a company called Dragline Fisheries in Dillingham, Alaska. I think one of my co-workers up there, Lev Warrens, might have something to do with it."

Nick cupped his hand over the receiver and mouthed to his partner, "Grab the Dragline employee list."

Hargrove knocked over a stack of papers as he ran to his desk to retrieve it.

"Why do you think that? Go on."

Nick put the phone on speaker.

"Lev Warrens arrived with Venju del Prado and the Filipino laundry crew a few days before I did. I was told he got the job because two women didn't show up, at the bunkhouse, in Everett. I think it was the Vallesteros sisters. It had to be."

Hargrove scanned through the list as Julian spoke. He circled Julian's name. Then Venju del Prado. He flipped the pages front-to-back, and back-to-front. Lev Warrens name was nowhere to be found.

"And that's not all. Lev Warrens showed up at my house. Looking for me. Here in Everett. I rented a room in my old boss' house when I got back from Alaska. I don't know what he wanted, he talked to the old lady living upstairs when I wasn't there, but I do know he is one violent son of a bitch. And he threatened me. I bought a pistol to protect myself. In case he comes back."

"And you think he might have been in Everett the night the girls were murdered?"

"I do. I mean I didn't *see* him, but he *had* to be. He arrived at Dragline the weekend before I did with the rest of the Filipino crew."

"What does he look like?"

"Mid-fifties, maybe. Six foot. Medium build. Long, dark, slicked-back, oily hair. I don't know. Plain."

"Do you know where we can find this person?"

"I have no idea. The last time I saw him was when he got fired back in July for stealing. Dragline would probably know."

Hargrove tapped his finger on Julian's name, circling it again and adding a star.

"Okay Mr. Hopkins, thanks for the tip. Lev Warrens. Yes, that sounds like someone we need to get off the streets, right away. We'll follow up on this, you can be sure of that. We'll probably need you to come down to the station later and give a full statement and description. Where are you now? Is there a good number I can reach you?"

"I'd rather not say."

Hargrove blurted out, "Mr. Hopkins, where were *you* that weekend?"

The phone went cold. "Ah … listen. I don't know what you're suggesting, but I just gave you the lead you need to follow. Find Lev Warrens. Before I do it myself."

Julian hung up.

Hargrove sprang to his feet. "Nick, how in the hell did Julian Hopkins know the Vallesteros sisters worked at Dragline? That's information we've been withholding!"

Nick was already dialing. "I don't know, but we need to ask Bob Clayton about him. And this Lev Warrens person. Why isn't his name on the list? Is there really somebody by that name, or did Hopkins just make him up to throw us off his own trail?"

Hargrove stopped him. "You don't think the Green River Killer has been hiding out all this time in remote coastal Alaska, do you?"

Detective Nick Nizzi didn't respond.

❧

Bob Clayton poured himself a drink and grimaced at the detectives sitting in his living room. He didn't like how they had dropped in unannounced, at nine o'clock at night no less, and their brashness rubbed him the wrong way. He resented their tone. This whole murder affair had taken up way too much of his time already. His entire staff had lost almost a full day of productivity when Hargrove and another officer came in to interview them, earlier in the week, and this was their busiest time of year. He had a flight to Anchorage to catch in the morning and really needed to be focused on selling fish. *He needed everyone to be focused on selling fish!* Containers were stacking up and more were on the way. If he could just get everyone in his company to do their damn jobs instead of focusing on police interviews and murders, this could turn out to be a very profitable year. Everett was his town, his boyhood home. His domain. *Damn these damn murders. And damn these damn cops!*

"So, tell me about some of these names, Mr. Clayton. What do you know about Julian Hopkins?"

"Julian worked for us in Dillingham for the past four years. He was a foreman up there. Well-liked. Hard worker. College kid."

"College kid? How old?"

"I don't know. Twenty-three or four."

Nizzi and Hargrove connected eyes.

"As I was saying, Julian was one of our best. I think his father was in the military and I remember Julian telling me he was born here in Everett, on the naval base, but grew up in California. He's genuinely a good guy. I saw him drive out of here in his pickup after he returned from Alaska. He rented our Dillingham plant manager's house over on Kromer Street and works for the *Seattle Post-Register* now."

"He works for the *Post-Register*? Doing what?"

"That, I'm not sure."

Hargrove raised his brow. "Do you know if Hopkins stayed in the bunkhouse the weekend the Filipino girls were murdered? The first weekend in June? Did you see him before he left? Did you talk to him?"

"I did not see Julian before he left for Dillingham this year, but I know he was in town interviewing for his newspaper job. Actually, I take that back. I did talk to him for a few minutes before he left. That's when he told me about getting hired at the *Post-Register*. Oh hell, I don't remember. I saw him up in Alaska too. It's like a circus around here that time of the year, people coming and going all the time. I'm not sure if he stayed in the bunkhouse or not that weekend. Why are you asking me about *him* of all people? You don't think *he's* a suspect, do you?"

"We're just working through this list, Bob. How about Venju del Prado? What more can you tell us about him?"

"Venju del Prado. Let me see. Venju runs our laundry crew. I really don't know much about him. Each season he comes over from Manila, gets the job done, and goes home. I've heard he is a hothead sometimes, but he seems to have the respect of his team. He and his men took a flight home right after you interviewed him. You could tell Venju was shaken. Visibly upset. Our plant manager, Mike Matthews, who lives in Bethel, could share with you more."

"How about Lev Warrens?"

Clayton pinched his eyes tight and cleared his throat. "Lev Warrens. Let's see. I don't know of a Lev Warrens."

Nick waved in the air the Dragline employee list. "So, you're saying you didn't employ anyone named Lev Warrens?"

"Not that I'm aware of," Clayton looked at his watch indicating it was time for the officers to leave. "Why? Is he on that list?"

Hargrove stared into the man's eyes. There was something hidden in his response that didn't quite resonate. Was Clayton lying? Was he concealing something? Was he not telling the full truth? But why? He couldn't quite put his finger on it, but something about the man aggravated the hell out of him.

"Listen. If you're lying, *Bob*, I don't care who you are, we'll arrest your ass for obstructing justice. I mean that. One more time, did you have an employee working for you this summer in Dillingham named Lev Warrens?"

Clayton squirmed in his chair, took a sip of his stiff drink, and calmly mouthed the word, "No."

# CHAPTER 19

# LEVON CAMEAHWAR

The United States government didn't know Levon Cameahwar existed. No one did. He had never been issued a birth certificate, driver's license, or Social Security number. He had never filed a tax return, opened a bank account, or owned a credit card. He used cash for all his purchases and his expenses were very few. He made his own rules and lived by his own law. When he took a job, he worked only for cash. Fifty-seven years before, his Shoshone mother had given him the tribal name, He Who Sees at Night. Levon Cameahwar existed off the grid, on the fringe of society. In Alaska, he used the name Lev Warrens.

Levon's drunk and abusive father raised him in a small mountain cabin on an Indian Reservation. From the beginning he made it clear the boy wasn't wanted. Painfully clear. Lev barely remembered his mother who died after being brutally beaten by his father when he was nine. She was buried in the back yard. Growing up, he never attended school, knew no other family, and was left to himself to learn right from wrong. His pernicious father instilled in him a religion based on Bible passages filled with fire and brimstone. Without anyone else living close on their mountain, he had no friends. As he entered his teenage years and finally tried to stand up for himself, his father beat him savagely.

Once or twice a year, the pair went to the Reservation store twenty miles away. To get money and to trade for staples like ammunition, coffee, and sugar they trapped beaver, muskrat, and fox. When they were hungry, they hunted and killed. Each fall before the snow came, they went to a lake in the mountains and speared Redfish that they smoked and preserved for the lean winter ahead.

The spring after his father's heart failed, Levon left his lonely mountain. He found it difficult to adapt and struggled to talk with others. People made fun of him. They ridiculed him and called him degrading names. Sometimes they hit and kicked him. He bought an old pickup truck with the remaining trapping money and kept it hidden under branches at the base of his trail. Gradually, he traveled farther and farther away, always returning. Always alone.

When the fur bearing animals eventually disappeared off his mountain for good, he worked odd jobs on local ranches for cash. He joined a Mexican fruit-picking crew and wandered from crop-to-crop throughout Washington, Oregon, California, and Idaho stealing license plates as he went. He hated working with apples, peaches, cherries, and grapes but suffered through to survive. He developed allergies to their juice and scratched the itchy welts on his hands until they bled.

One year his Mexican boss asked him to join his crew in Alaska cutting fish in a remote coastal village. He got paid in cash. Levon felt at home in the desolation up there, and he made more than enough money to last him all winter without touching the fruit he despised picking. The next summer he went to a different Alaska town with a different crew. Year after year the Mexican bosses didn't even ask him his name. They didn't care as long as they could collect Lev's weekly wage and keep some of it for themselves. Levon didn't mind. He just needed enough money to make it through the long winter by himself in his remote cabin on his childhood mountain.

Murder was introduced to Levon Cameahwar near Yakima. At the end of one long, sweaty, itchy, and painful day, as he climbed down the last ladder before quitting time, a Mexican co-worker began to yell at him. All the other migrants had left the field, they were the last two in the orchard. Lev didn't understand the Spanish words being screamed and didn't know how to respond. When the man pushed Lev's ladder over and stood over him in a drunken fighting stance, Levon lashed out like a trapped coyote and cut the man's throat with the picking knife he was holding. He was sick of being yelled at, of being treated unfairly, despised, and ridiculed. As the man staggered and held his gushing neck, Lev struck again and stabbed the man in the chest. As he watched the man gurgle, and slowly die, he felt no empathy. No remorse. No sadness. In fact, he was bewildered by the delight he took watching the man suffer and die in pain. Afraid one of his nomadic co-workers would notice the man missing, Levon dragged the man's body to a nearby irrigation ditch and covered it with mud. But none of them did. The police were never notified, and no missing person report was ever filed. Levon was amazed at how easy murder had been. He killed his second victim less than a month later to steal his wallet. And his boots.

Through the years Levon honed his craft, concealing his intelligence with a ruse. He didn't eat when he was on the hunt. He couldn't sleep. Sometimes, as a stratagem, he raised the hood of his truck and pretended to work on his engine while he watched bus stops, train stations, and bars. Other times he approached drunk women stumbling home from nightclubs alone. They fell convincingly for his well-practiced ploy and adroit-cunning tactic almost every time.

"I'm headin' home to git my kid," he'd say, pointing to a picture of a young boy, found years earlier in the pocket of one of his victims. It always worked to soften flight instincts, erase mistrust, and sooth suspicions. "Kin I give you a ride on my way?"

Levon kept a stone club hidden behind his passenger seat and had learned the precise spot to strike a knockout blow at the base of the skull, but he always finished the job with a blade. It was more personal and rewarding for him that way. Always on the lookout for heavily wooded, hillside dumpsites, he kept a pair of rubber hip waders and a thick canvas poncho in the back of his truck. Most of the time the bodies he left in his wake were never found, and if they were, by some random mushroom picker or construction worker, it was usually many years later and rarely ever identified. Sometimes Lev took trophies. Hair and clothes and souvenirs. When he took jewelry from his victims, he left it in places it could easily be found. He relished watching others wear the sparkling objects, and when they did, he relived his heinous crimes time-and-time again. Brutal. Savage. Predator.

# CHAPTER 20

# BOONE AND JOSIE

Julian's mind raced as he drove to meet his friends at a local micro-brewery in Pioneer Square. The previous two weeks had been a blur consumed by long hours at the newspaper making phone calls and researching for the news team. Strangely, Bob Clayton had been cordial but brief when Julian called him two days before. Normally, the two joked around and had long meaningful conversations. This time the man barely had time for hello. Julian pressed, but Clayton wouldn't share any information about the Vallesteros sisters, only that it was a tragedy and if he wanted to know more, he should speak with the Everett PD. When Julian mentioned Lev Warrens, Clayton hung up.

The thought of Lev had turned his senses unfamiliarly acute. He scanned crowds for his face, and unable to shake the feeling he was being watched, constantly peered back over his shoulder. It didn't surprise him Lev had found his rental house, after all, he was certain Lev had over-heard his conversation with Mike the day he arrived in the Dillingham mess hall. But what the fuck was he doing here? And what did he want? Why was he coming for him? Sick of losing sleep and feeling like helpless prey, he kept a pistol loaded at night, lying beside his bed.

Boone and Josie were already seated when Julian strolled in. Boone gave him his familiar customary smack hug. Josie gave him a peck on the cheek. Lindsay Fiori soon arrived, and he waved her over and made introductions. Over the course of the evening, Julian told them everything that had happened since he arrived in Everett … the murdered Vallesteros sisters, the Green River Killer Task Force, the press conference, and the articles he'd been researching for Lindsay and the other reporters. In front of the girls, he didn't mention Lev Warrens. In return, Boone and Josie wowed them with their account of backpacking through Denali: the moose, caribou, bears, and the majesty of the always-present mountain. Lindsay was enchanted.

Late in the evening, Julian told Boone he needed to speak with him alone.

"Your girlfriend is awesome, by the way," Boone nudged. "Smart and gorgeous too."

"Thanks. I'm glad you like her. She's not my girlfriend, but things might be moving in that direction. I hope so anyway. I really do like her, and I think it's mutual. Hey, I have something serious to tell you, buddy. Something I haven't told anyone else."

Boone gave him a look.

"Lev Warrens came to my house. The old lady who lives upstairs spoke with him when I wasn't home."

Boone had been getting ready to take a sip of beer but froze, eyes full of alarm. "Oh shit, Jules, that guy is totally fucked in the head. Remember how violent he was the day he left Dragline? We all saw the look in his eyes. Have you told anyone?"

"I tried to tell Bob Clayton, but he hung up on me."

"What about Mike?"

"Mike. Yeah. Mike's on a hunting trip. I left him a message."

"Dude be careful. That guy's a lit fucking firecracker. He was a handful for Archie and Reuben, remember? Hell, I've been nervous about him too."

"Yeah. Well it gets even worse. You know those murdered Filipino girls we were just talking about? The ones the press conference was for? They were on their way to Dragline. Probably to Dillingham. I think they might have been the women Venju was waiting for before he came up."

"Holy shit—Venju gave Lev Warrens their job because they didn't show up."

"Exactly."

Boone emptied his glass and pressed his thumb and finger into closed eyes. Finally, he whispered, "Do you think Lev killed them?"

Julian gravely nodded. "It all adds up but the 'why'. And something else has been really bothering me. Something I'm having nightmares about. Do you think it's possible Lev had something to do with Dave's death?"

Boone looked at him curiously. "I don't know how he could have, man. He was onshore with us. But ..."

Both men grew silent, staring into empty glasses, remembering Dave, minds imaging their own versions of the horror that unfolded in the raging waves off Kanulik Beach.

"Fuck man. Have you called the cops?"

"Yeah. They started asking me questions like *I'm* the suspect."

"What the fuck. What are you going to do?"

Julian signaled to the bartender another round and waved at the girls. "I'm sure as shit not going to sit around and wait for the cops to start looking for him, or for Lev to come calling on me again. Although if he does, he'll be staring down the barrel of my gun."

"You're gonna shoot him?"

"I don't know. I don't know if I have that in me. But I *am* gonna track him down. Find out what he wants. See what he can tell me about Dave. Do the cop's jobs for them."

Boone narrowed his eyes at his friend. "And how are you going to do that?"

"The day we fished the Agulowak he confessed some things to me. He talked about his father. There was some hatred there. It sounded like he was rough on Lev and his mom whom he called an Injun. He said he lives in a cabin in the mountains somewhere on an Indian Reservation. Close to a lake that has a wild Sockeye run. Not in Alaska."

"Wild Sockeye run? Reservation? He's an Indian? Damn dude, I would never have guessed that. In Washington?"

"Probably, since he left Dillingham two months ago and came to my house just last week. He can't be far. I've been checking into it. Only five rivers in Washington state still have wild Sockeye runs. Dams, habitat loss, overfishing, ocean issues, and seals have wiped out all the others—and all five of those remaining runs are dwindling fast. Lev's not at Lake Washington, it's surrounded by city, but two lakes—Ozette and Quinault, are bordered by Reservations. That's where I'll start. I'm leaving first thing in the morning while I have two days off."

"Want me to stick around and go with you?"

"I appreciate that, but no. You have a girl to take care of now and it sounds like she's really looking forward to driving with you, down that long highway, to Colorado and New Mexico. This might be a wild goose chase, but's it's all I got. I can handle myself."

Boone stole a glance at Josie. "Want me to leave you my pistol?

"Oh, I bought one. A Ruger .357."

# CHAPTER 21

# THE LIGHTHOUSE PUB

It was ten after seven on a Saturday night and Kathy Simmons was running late. She nearly slipped and fell as she rushed through the door of her second-floor apartment and threw her mail on the counter. As a single mom and full-time registered nurse who picked up extra shifts every chance she got, Kathy rarely went out. Disney movies at the theater don't count, she thought as she pulled off her floral-pattern hospital scrubs. Tonight, is mommy's night to have some fun. Shawna will be here any minute. Oh my gosh! She hadn't been this excited in years. She dashed to the shower.

Always the meticulous planner, Kathy had arranged for her nine-year-old daughter to stay at her father's house, her ex, for the weekend. She winced at the thought of him. That bastard didn't have any problems getting remarried. She never should have given him a second chance. His infidelity had devastated her, but at the time she didn't know how to let go, and for the sake of their daughter, let him stay. Deep down inside, she hadn't wanted their marriage to end. But things had been different the second time. Red with anger more at herself than him, she had thrown his belongings in the front yard and locked the door for good. Enough was enough, the cheating bastard had to go. During the ensuing ugly divorce, she learned her instincts had been right. He'd been sleeping with his new wife for years. In the months that followed, Kathy's animosity had been replaced by loneliness. But enough of that. Kathy shook the negativity away as she stepped out of the shower. Think positive. Maybe tonight things would change.

"Things *will* change tonight," she tried to convince her reflection in the mirror. "I'm thirty-two. I still got it. Tonight, *is* the night."

Her friend Shawna Owens had been surprised by Kathy's reluctance when she initially brought up the idea of a blind date.

"I know it's the first date you've been on in six months," she persuaded. "Yes, I know you don't like liars. But Kathy, you'll like this one, I know you will. Plus, it will be good for you to get out. We'll have fun. Just like we used to!"

Too proud to let her best friend know, Kathy had secretly been looking forward to it all week. On Tuesday at lunch, she went out and had her hair and nails done at an expensive salon. Just this morning she got up early before work and tried on clothes that had been hidden deep in her closet.

She grinned. "I'm bringing sexy back tonight, and it's been a long time coming."

The doorbell rang.

"Let's go, hot mama," Shawna shouted as she let herself in. "The men called and we're meeting them at the Lighthouse Pub. They're probably there already. Your date is so cute in his picture. Plus, John says he has an excellent job at Boeing, and makes lots of money. Who knows? He might just be the perfect one for you."

Money? Kathy's ex-husband didn't have money. At least none that she could find. The savings they had managed to squirrel away together had been used to pay lawyers' fees and was long since gone. Even after she had downsized into a small apartment with Meagan, she was still barely making enough to pay the bills. Maybe tonight she would find someone new, someone to love, someone to whom she could confide her deepest desires. Someone who could take care of her.

"Okay. I'm ready. Let's go meet these good-looking hunks. How do I look?"

Shawna whistled her approval.

"Well, look at you. You look amazing—a little bit slutty," Shawna giggled. "Probably too hot for the Lighthouse. The men there won't know what hit them."

They both laughed and hugged.

As the oldest continuously operating bar in Everett, the nearby Lighthouse Pub sat at the bottom of a hill near Bayside Wharf. Widely known for serving pretty decent whiskey burgers and a wide range of beer on tap, it was a stereotypical working-town dive bar that occasionally featured live local music. Its chipped brick exterior had been a pillar on the waterfront for over eighty years. Because of its location, it had for generations attracted dock workers, laborers from the massive wood mill a half mile down Marine View Drive, and occasional sailors from Naval Station Everett. Kathy's tight-black miniskirt, loose shirt, leather heeled boots and fake chinchilla fur jacket were bound to turn a few heads.

Shawna parked across the street and they entered the small-packed pub holding hands. They didn't see their dates on the top level, so they squeezed down to the lower lounge.

"I'd forgotten how much I love the ambiance down here," Kathy purred. "It reminds me so much of Pioneer Square."

"There they are!" Shawna waved to two men seated at a booth table at the furthest point away from the stage. She and John had been on two dates already and had spoken on the phone almost every evening that week. Both were trying to play matchmaker for their friends with lonely hearts. Working men in Carhartt's and ball caps were slouched across the line of bar stools like beggars holding cups in a subway station. They unabashedly whipped their heads around to admire the pair of women walk past. One man whistled a cat call.

"Good to see you again, good-looking." The taller of the two dates got up and gave Shawna a hug and kiss on the lips. He turned to Kathy. "Nice to meet *you*, Kathy. I'm John. And this here is my friend, Grant."

Kathy gave him her hand and tried not to choke. She was immediately struck by Grant's uncanny resemblance to her ex-husband, Alan. He didn't look anything like his picture. Her chest grew tight and she found it hard to breathe. To make matters worse, he wore a loud Hawaiian-print shirt that could have easily come from Alan's closet. She fought back the urge to puke.

"Nice to meet you, Grant," she stammered, then glared at Shawna.

A waitress appeared and asked for orders.

"We'll start with a pitcher of margaritas," John flaunted, already leaning lustily on Shawna. "And keep 'em flowing."

Not even with the assistance of hard alcohol could Kathy connect with her date. Every time he opened his mouth, she was reminded of the endless fighting with her ex. On the third round, John added tequila shots to the rounds of margaritas. Kathy threw hers back, and Shawna's too, but it still didn't help. She had no chemistry with Grant and couldn't get the angry image of Alan out of her mind. Fueled by alcohol, the emotions from the past year took over. She admitted she had tried to change him and had allowed herself to provoke him into fights. She got drunker and drunker, until finally she pulled Shawna aside. "I'm calling a taxi. Alan...I mean, Grant isn't for me. I can't stand to be near him. I don't want to be here anymore. I'm sorry Shawna. This isn't fun for me, but thanks for trying."

Shawna had been sitting on John's lap for much of the past hour and had already made up her mind what she was doing that night. "Are you sure? I mean ... I could go with you ..."

Kathy wrapped her coat over her shoulders. "No. No. You're fine. Have fun and say adios to Grant for me. I mean he is nice and all. I'm sure he knows I wasn't going home with him anyway. Thanks for getting me out of the house though, Shawna. Really!"

The bartender called Kathy a taxi. Needing fresh air, she hurried outside and leaned against the exterior bricks before Grant could see her leave. Raindrops tapped tin eaves as she wobbled underneath, giving her something to focus on besides her embarrassment. A pair of drunk wood-factory workers floundered out. One tried to put his arm around her, but his buddy pulled him away. Still no taxi. Kathy hadn't been out drinking in a long time and felt like she was going to pass out. Head spinning, she considered going back in the bar to ask Shawna to drive her home but remembered Grant.

"The hell with it," she said out loud. "I don't live *that* far. I'll just walk."

She stumbled through the rain, stopping to kick off her heeled boots. Two blocks up the hill she turned down a cross street toward the hospital. A pickup truck emerged and stopped beside her. After a short exchange, she smiled, thanked the driver and got in. The vehicle pulled slowly away and like a faded memory, vanished into the night.

# CHAPTER 22

# LOWELL RIVER ROAD

Real estate agent Mary Sorenson took her lunch break at Rotary Park at ten after twelve every Sunday morning. On this day, her hidden retreat was empty except for one boat trailer connected to a Blazer parked by the boat ramp leading into the lower Snohomish River. Local anglers were just starting to catch Coho salmon in the saltwater of Puget Sound, but here, two miles upriver in freshwater, good fishing was still several weeks away.

Mary loved the peaceful serenity of the river bottom and especially appreciated having a quiet place where she could get away, from showing houses, when she worked weekends. Up in the canopy of a battalion of hundred-foot cottonwoods, leaves made music in the summer breeze. A thick-wet bramble of willows, blackberries, and thorns carpeted the mud underneath. It had rained the night before and she soaked in the earthy late August smells. With closed eyes she let her nose sort through a complex mix of pine needles, hydrangea, cedar, and rhododendron. As she did every day she came here, she planned on taking a stroll down the river path that ran along the rolling current after she finished eating.

Something in the underbrush caught her eye. Behind a broken-topped pine, forty feet beyond her parked car she could see something red. She tried to ignore it as she ate her sandwich but couldn't stop wondering what it could be. Overhead, an eagle soared. She watched it circle the water and land in one of the cottonwoods at the other end of the wide-blacktop lot. A squirrel chattered from a tree to her left. Curiosity finally got the best of Mary Sorenson. She rolled down her window, put her hand horizontally across her forehead, and squinted her inquisitive eyes through the sun's glare.

"What is that?" She slowly opened her door and crept hesitantly up the trail. "Is that a mannequin?"

Mary Sorenson screamed so loud the eagle took flight and the squirrel high-tailed it into the forest. Screaming a second time, she ran back to her car and burned rubber up Lowell River Road, leaving her carefully packed lunch littered on the ground.

Rotary Park was four miles from the station and Detectives Nizzi and Hargrove were among the first on the scene. As they pulled through the open gate into the parking lot, they could clearly see a dead woman propped in a sitting position against a small tree.

"Oh, for Christ's sake. She's right there in plain sight. And she didn't die naturally, either. I can see from here her throat's cut, and she's covered in blood," Hargrove got out quickly. "Whoever killed her made no attempt to cover her up either. They wanted her to be found. Son of a bitch."

"Or they were spotted and were forced to leave in a hurry," Nick looked around to see if there were any houses nearby. There weren't. He slipped on his gloves and headed toward the body, careful not to step on the recently used trail. In doing so, he inadvertently smashed a Salem Menthol butt into the mud that had been concealed by trailside tinder. Hargrove brought his camera. The woman's eyes were shut, and even though it had turned a subtle greenish-blue, her face had settled into a peaceful look. *It almost looks like she's asleep. So similar. So comparable to the faces of the others.* She had on a white shirt and a fake chinchilla jacket.

"She's in full rigor mortis, Don. So, she hasn't been here for long, sometime last night. Brown hair. Early thirties, I'm guessing. She's been beaten on the back of her head. Just like the Filipino victims. Same spot. Now we know for certain. Three victims murdered the same way. We've got a serial killer."

The woman's black miniskirt was pulled up over her hips. She was naked from the waist down. Her legs were propped open in an unnatural sexual position, spread wide, knees bent. Both officers agreed she had been deliberately posed. Nightmares from year's past came rushing back to Nick and the chill cut deep. *Sexually assaulted and posed.*

Hargrove growled, "Something's in her mouth. Is that underwear? Jesus Christ. The evil bastard stuffed her underwear in her mouth."

Instinctively, he reached out. Nick smacked his hand down with cat-like speed. "Don't touch. Let the medical examiner remove it. This could finally be his undoing."

Hargrove scowled and motioned several other arriving vehicles to stay back. "Seal off the entrance to the park. And get those damn people out of here—except for the coroner. This is a crime scene."

"What's going on?" A man who had followed the stream of cop cars into the parking area before they barricaded it off was running toward the scene. Nearly out of breath, he wore green head-to-toe and had a Snohomish County Parks and Recreation decal sewn on the sleeve of his jacket. "I'm Larry Phillips, the park's attendant."

"There's a murder victim in there." Hargrove pointed to where Nizzi was standing. "A woman on her lunch break found her about half an hour ago. Have you seen anyone down here? Any odd vehicles?"

Phillips peered around the detective at the waxy-skinned body. "No. Holy Hell. I know she wasn't here yesterday evening. Normally I lock the gates at dark, but last night when I came through here, I left them open."

Trembling, he pointed at the Blazer with the trailer. "I figured that fisherman over there had motor problems and was late in getting back to the boat ramp. I left here around eight o'clock and didn't want to lock him in. Whenever I do that, I get my padlocks cut."

He tried to glance again at the body, but Hargrove blocked him. "I'll probably get fired for this. I never should have left the gate unlocked. This is so terrible. I deserve it."

Hargrove wrote down the man's contact information and ordered an officer to impound the Blazer. He ordered Phillips to leave and rejoined his partner.

"There's so much blood on the ground, no doubt this is where she died. Probably after being knocked unconscious. She was murdered by a solo man in boots. He parked over there, carried her here, slashed her throat, and walked from the body to the parking lot more than once. Repeated. Calm. Organized. He wasn't in a hurry. He didn't slip and fall. His tracks show no sign of panic, no wasted movements. No stopping to think. No running. They were made sometime after midnight, after it rained. And my gut instinct tells me you were right. The killer put her here where he knew she would be discovered. If he had taken ten more steps into the trees, we might not have known she was here for days or even weeks. We need someone in here to get forms made of those footprints before they disintegrate."

Hargrove hustled back to the lot and barked directives. Another officer readied a plaster kit. Nick was in the brush behind the body pointing at a shiny-gold fishing lure on the ground when Hargrove returned. "What do you make of this?"

Hargrove studied the scene. "It's a salmon lure and it looks fresh. Like it was recently dropped. It hasn't yet settled into the leaves. And it's strange considering it's not the right time to be salmon fishing in this river. It's too early for Silvers and it's an off year for Pinks. Humpies run up the Snohomish in the hundreds of thousands every other year. But not this one. When the Pinks *are* in, the riverbanks are lined shoulder-to-shoulder with fishermen and the boat ramp is a steady stream of chaos for weeks. But no fisherman who knew what he was doing would be using it now. Look around. It's Sunday. There's nobody here. That's because the salmon haven't arrived yet. That lure is out of place."

"Any chance a novice fisherman dropped it on his way from the parking lot to the water?"

"Maybe, but I doubt it. Fifty yards from the river, five feet away from the body of a dead woman is a pretty odd place to lose it, if you ask me."

"That's good enough for me. Take some photos and bag it and tag it."

After the scene was thoroughly processed and the coroner had wrapped the woman in a sterile sheet, placed her body in a bag, and carried her to his van, Nick spotted a bloody purse and pair of black leather-heeled boots in the blackberries further down the lot. Using a machete, he busted through to retrieve them. Standing waist deep in mud and thorns, he read the driver's license out loud to Hargrove. "Kathy Simmons. Age thirty-two. She lived on Pacific Avenue here in Everett."

# CHAPTER 23

# LINDSAY FIORI

For as far back as she could remember, Lindsay Fiori had been a writer. The overwhelming desire to constantly capture her thoughts on paper propelled her to carry a notebook everywhere she went, even at a young age. As an only child, Lindsay had spent most of the family dinners, of her youth, listening to her parents' banter about academics, politics, and world affairs. Both were college professors, and both encouraged their daughter to question events around her with a cynical eye. They were delighted she grew up not being content to accept things the way others told her they were. From the time she was nine, Lindsay had been telling people she would be a journalist, someday.

Soon after graduating with honors from the University of Washington, she accepted a quick offer from Francis Bernard at the Seattle P-R. He instantly became her mentor and took great delight giving her assignments that challenged her thinking and put her abilities constantly to a test. She loved it. As a result, in the years that followed, Lindsay had done little but work. As an intellectual, she preferred imaginative conversation over a bottle of wine in a quiet and relaxed atmosphere, or just spending time by herself. Too focused for the party scene, on weekends she generally avoided people outside of her family, even her handful of close, long-time friends. Her first step in a bar in over a year was when she met Julian and his friends in Pioneer Square. She knew she sometimes held herself and others to unrealistically lofty standards. And often those demands clashed with an imperfect world. It made her lonely at times. She knew that. But she expected things to be a certain way, and sometimes became aggravated when they were not. She was working on it.

Inexplicably, she was fascinated with Julian Hopkins. She'd felt an attraction towards him ever since their first conversation, but as a devout professional had kept her feelings to herself, and her interest in him out of the workplace. At twenty-four, he was a few years younger than she was, but could easily pass as older, and the two couldn't be more opposite. It made her confused … in a good way. Since the day he joined the team, she had been paying close attention to his transformation from a sometimes, rough-talking outdoorsman to a professional, genuinely curious journalist. His energy and work ethic impressed her. He had a quiet confidence about him, yet a wide-eyed exuberance at the same time. An unpolished edge that she liked. She was surprised when he asked her out so quickly and shocked to hear herself say yes. Where was he anyway? It was already ten.

"Good morning, Lindsay," Julian sauntered up with a grin. "I loved seeing you the other night. And I'm glad you got a chance to meet Boone and Josie before they rolled out on their road trip home. Did you have a good weekend?"

Lindsay stopped typing. "Nice. Relaxing for a change. I got some reading done. But I thought you were going to call."

"Yeah. I needed to get out of the city for a bit and ended up exploring the Olympic Peninsula. I drove to Lake Ozette, then down to Quinault. Saturday night I camped in an old-growth forest next to a river close to Forks. It's gorgeous. One of these days we should go out there together."

Great. He's a mountain man, she thought. I went out on a date with Grizzly Adams.

"Hey, I have something serious I need to tell you, Lindsay. Something I need to get off my chest."

Julian had spent the weekend driving as far as Taholah, interviewing people along the way. Nobody he spoke with knew Lev Warrens or even recognized the name. Starting at the ocean and following the courses of rivers upstream, he scoured the shores of inland lakes. With each unsuccessful mile, his unshakable anxiety mounted. Even at the desolate campsite he'd stayed at near Forks, he'd been jittery, constantly on the lookout, sleep assaulted by Lev's face. The more he pondered it, the more certain he was that Lev was a killer. And not just the Vallesteros sisters. As snippets replayed in his mind, he grew more and more certain that Lev was somehow responsible for Dave's death too. Short on time, his weekend search had been limited to the few miles along the rivers he could drive in his truck. Next time, he'd take hiking boots.

Julian looked around again and balked at the activity in the newsroom. "Can I take you out to lunch Lindsay? Or dinner, perhaps?"

"I'm working on deadline. Francis needs my article posted by five. Dinner works best."

"Okay, dinner it shall be. I'm buying. I'll take you wherever it is you want to go."

⌾

Nick Nizzi tightened his grip on his Smith & Wesson and used his foot to push open the door. Heart pounding and mentally prepared for the scene of a desperate-bloody struggle, he flipped on the light with his elbow. The apartment was tidy. Other than a pile of unopened mail on the counter, everything was in place. He sifted through the bills. One was in the name Alan Simmons and he set it aside. One bedroom down the hall was recently lived in and decorated for a little girl. The master, which he could tell belonged to Kathy, showed no tell-tale signs of a man. He slipped on his gloves and from one of her dresser drawers removed a dozen pairs of women's underwear. All were brightly colored: blue, red, pink, yellow, and appeared to be the same size as the pair they had found with her body.

The phone rang and startled him. He hustled back to the kitchen and picked it up. "Kathy? Kathy where the fuck *are* you? I've been trying to reach you all morning. Don't you know your daughter is here waiting for you? Kathy?"

"Mr. Simmons? Kathy's not here. This is Detective Nick Nizzi from the Everett Police Department. You better sit down."

Normally, Nick didn't deliver tragic news on the telephone, but given the circumstances, this morning he did. After his initial disbelief, Alan Simmons explained that his ex-wife had dropped their daughter off two days before, on Saturday, so she could go out with her friend Shawna Owens that night. He hadn't seen or spoken with her since and hadn't even tried, until this morning, after she didn't show up when she was supposed to. The man seemed genuinely shocked by the news of Kathy's death. He claimed to have air-tight alibis all weekend and agreed to meet later that afternoon at the station.

Shawna's story was more revealing.

"Oh my god!" she screamed. "Yes, we were together Saturday night. We went to the Lighthouse Pub on a double date, but Kathy took a cab home around eleven o'clock. She apparently didn't like the guy I set her up with. He reminded her of her ex, the asshole."

Through tears, Shawna was more than willing to give the names of their dates. Nick added them to his growing suspect list for future follow-up, even though Shawna insisted the three had closed the bar down together and left around two. After leaving a hysterical Shawna, Nick drove to the Lighthouse Pub and spoke with the manager who called his bartender in early. The man recognized her picture and recalled seeing Kathy. He remembered dialing her a taxi but amidst the busyness of the bar that night, didn't see her leave. The cab company had no record of Kathy as a passenger, but the cabbie remembered the call. He told the detective he had been delayed by another fare and when he got to the Lighthouse Pub half an hour late, Kathy Simmons was nowhere to be found.

As he drove back to the station, Nick knew. The day's conversations had been identical to hundreds of others he had experienced before. The grief, the tears, the tedious trails that all led to the same empty words, "I don't know". Kathy had been picked up by a serial killer, every one of his instincts told him that. But was it the same one he'd spent so many years seeking? The same one who slept in the shadows of his psyche? The one he couldn't catch.

At what point does obsession become madness? When the need to search outweighs the achievement of destination? When the burning desire to hunt eclipses whatever cool satisfaction a capture would eventually provide? Could the balance be corrected once it is knocked off kilter? Was he already too far gone, or would the eventual apprehension of this killer allow him to once again experience normalcy? As much as he hated to admit it, he and his partner could no longer go it alone. When he got back to the station, he called the Green River Killer Task Force. And the FBI.

# CHAPTER 24

# DATE NIGHT

For dinner, Lindsay chose a quiet little Italian restaurant on Dexter Avenue near the Space Needle. She requested a window table so she could watch the boats cruising on Lake Union toward the Ballard Locks. It was a clear summer night and the flickering lights of the city reflected playfully on tranquil waters. But Julian's attention was focused only on Lindsay Fiori. Her dark hair was pulled back in a sophisticated bun and she wore thin designer glasses over sincere and compassionate, yet subtly sad eyes. To him, her smile resembled a palace of sand—beautiful, intricate, delicate—yet easily damaged, and probably hard to rebuild. This wouldn't be easy. He had a lot to say.

"You may remember when I pulled Boone aside at the bar the other night," he began. "I shared some things with him. I need to share those things with you too. And I should probably start at the very beginning."

Julian told her about arriving in Dillingham after his job interview with Francis Bernard, how the fish season started so quickly, and how he had been thrown right into his job. He painted pictures of the people he had worked with, things they had said, places he'd seen and gone. At first, he had planned not to mention Hannah, but changed his mind mid-stream, and confessed to Lindsay the whole truth. The more he talked, the easier it became. Lindsay was enthralled, almost disbelieving, by the tales he spun of such wild-faraway places. The Agulowak, Naknek, Egegik, Aleknagik, Iliamna, Dillingham, Ekok Beach—she secretly longed to go see those places herself. She asked volumes of questions and sat spellbound as he spun his long descriptive narrative. They both laughed when he imitated Archie. But right about the time the waiter announced the kitchen was closing, Julian's mood changed.

"The summer was also full of tragedy, Lindsay. And I'm still trying to make sense of it all."

In a soft, subdued voice he told her of the drowned Yup'ik boys and how they had retrieved Eddie Chiklak's body from under the dock. He nearly broke down when he told her about Dave and Charlie. Lindsay nearly cried herself. She didn't have words to give.

"The worst part is, I don't think the fish season ended in Dillingham," he whispered. "We worked with a killer up there. I'm sure of it. And I think he followed me down here. I think he may have murdered the Vallesteros sisters ... and may have had something to do with Dave."

"What?"

"His name is Lev Warrens and he got kicked out of camp for being a thief. He made threats the day he left Dragline. Some were at me. He's a severely deranged guy, and honestly, I'm more than a little nervous thinking about what he might do next. Last week he came to my house in Everett when I wasn't home. Mrs. Brown spoke with him. I've been packing a pistol ever since."

She gasped and gripped his hand. "Oh my god. He came to your house, Julian? Jesus. What are you going to do? Have you told the police? Wait. You think he killed the Vallesteros sisters? They really need to know that."

"Yeah. I called Detective Nizzi and told him everything I know. But I don't want to say anything to Francis Bernard. Or the news team. Or anyone else. Not yet. Just you."

They sat in silence. Lindsay was quivering.

"That's the scariest thing I've ever heard. You're not going back there. To your house. You can't! Not with Lev Warrens around. He knows where you live, Julian. Jesus. I'm freaking out knowing someone like that is even out there. You can sleep on my couch until they catch him. I insist. And you do need to tell Francis."

Julian remained fixated on the boats, their lights loitering through the soothing shimmer of the glistening Seattle night. Maybe a temporary move was wise. Besides, Mrs. Brown was driving him nuts and the only halfway decent sleep he'd had since Lev's unexpected appearance was in the back of his truck out on the Olympic. Every time he entered his apartment, he expected the man to be there waiting for him, watching. His nerves were frayed.

"On your couch?"

Lindsay tried not to laugh as the worry vanished from her face.

"Well—Maybe not on my couch for long."

## CHAPTER 25

# THE FBI

When FBI Special Agent Dan Livingston and Hank Garrity
of the Green River Task Force arrived at the Everett police
station, half a dozen officers were already seated around a
large conference table. Snohomish County's Chief Medical Examiner,
Dr. Richard Johnson followed them in with his newly completed autopsy
report for Kathy Simmons. Nizzi and Garrity took seats next to each other
and it was obvious to the others they knew each other well. They had, in
fact, spent hours, days, weeks, months, and years working together on
the Duwamish River case.

Ever since graduating from Princeton's prestigious psychology
program years before, Livingston had lived at the crossroads of law
enforcement and criminal ideology. In 1972, he had been one of the first
eleven agents hired for the newly formed FBI Behavioral Science Unit
in Quantico, Virginia. Because he possessed the uncanny and instinctive
ability to accurately interpret the meaning behind offender behavior,
he was one of the first to develop criminal profiles to assist serial rape
and homicide investigations. To draft those, Livingston focused on four
aspects of behavior: manner of killing, precursory conduct, body disposal
pattern, and post-crime tendencies. He had literally written the book on
how it was done.

163

"Gentlemen, I've reviewed your reports and the coroner's autopsy notes. Today we have three major questions to answer. A. Do we indeed have a serial killer at work? B. If so, is it the Green River? And C. What are we going to do about it? I am here to help you get into the mind of the man, and our common goal needs to be that we walk out of here with consensus."

"And a firm plan to catch him," Chief Wagner inserted.

"As we share, I want you to consider the following questions: Why were his victims targeted? Were they simply in the wrong place at the wrong time, or is there another reason at play? And why is your murderer doing what he is doing? I've asked Dr. Johnson to stay so he can share with us his report and offer his insights. Garrity is here to bring us up to speed on new developments in the Green River case."

Livingston sized up the room, "Okay, first. Are we dealing with a serial killer? Did he kill three or more victims in distinctly different events with time to cool down in between? Dr. Johnson, you've examined all three bodies. Please share with us your findings."

Johnson bounced out of his chair. Two years before, an interviewing panel had unanimously chosen him for the job just as much for his willingness to utilize innovative technology as his passion for forensics. Fiercely determined to never allow any victim to carry their story to the grave, he was always testing new forensic science techniques to coax the dead into revealing their truths. He began to read his report in a loud-clear voice.

"As you already know, and we confirmed through fingerprints, your victim is indeed Kathy Simmons. She had twice the legal limit of alcohol in her blood, but no trace of narcotics. There was no skin under her fingernails and no obvious signs of a defensive struggle. Because of her stage of rigor mortis, I estimate her time of death was right around midnight on Saturday."

Nick and Hargrove nodded in agreement.

"Here's where it gets interesting. There's robust evidence to prove Kathy was killed with the same weapons and by the same person that murdered the Vallesteros sisters. Kathy was struck right at the base of her skull in a very precise manner, by a blow delivered with enough force that

I'm sure it knocked her out but didn't kill her. We found the exact same wounds on the women from the Philippines. All three back-skull fractures were measured to be the same shape and diameter. We can safely assume they were made by the same weapon. Circular like a hammer, but larger. I've never seen anything quite like it. Very unique. The fatal wound for all three was a deep cut to the throat, almost a decapitation. We got a better study on Kathy's injury, and the blade that was used is peculiar. The cut was jagged, not straight. Almost as if it was done with a serrated steak knife. Very uncommon indeed. All three were deliberate, premeditated homicides. I'm convinced this is the work of one man using the same weapons."

Garrity slammed his fist on the table making Livingston, who had been taking overly neat notes, jump. "Thank-you Dr. Johnson. Your findings are explicit. You've confirmed for us what we have all been fearing. We can safely assume we have a serial killer at work."

"I *knew* it was one man," proclaimed Nick. "I *knew* it was a serial murderer the minute I saw the first body in the trees by the asphalt plant."

"But is it the Green River?" challenged Livingston, snapping open his briefcase and pulling out a stapled report. "I'll summarize for you the twelve-page psychological profile we created for the Green River Killer, which has been revised several times since the first one we did in 1984. It's been expanded with confidential details Garrity, Nizzi, and their team collected from crime scenes through the years and new eyewitness testimony."

Agent Livingston cleared his throat and began to read, not as loud and boisterous as Johnson, but ample enough to make everyone attentive. "We believe all of the Green River killings are the work of one man, probably Caucasian. Nearly all were done south of Seattle. The closest body was discovered thirty-three miles from here. Because he's a strangler, he is most likely large and in good physical condition. We believe he's in his late-twenties to early-thirties with average or slightly higher than average intelligence. He probably has low self-esteem resulting in an 'average Joe' demeanor. We believe he is quiet by nature with strong personal feelings of inadequacy but can hide this trait from others. We feel as if he comes from a broken home. He's probably divorced or at the very least has had bad relationships with women. Most likely he was raised by a single parent. And it's very possible he was abused as a child in some way."

Livingston took a drink of water, made eye contact with Garrity, and gave sufficient pause for his words to sink in before continuing. "Almost all of the Green River victims were prostitutes and we believe the killer regularly pays for sex. His victims are diverse. He has no racial preference. This guy probably feels like he has been 'burned' or 'lied to' or 'deceived' or 'abandoned' by women one too many times. Judging from his actions, he's angry. He feels he must demonstrate power over his victims. It's possible he did not go out the first time with the intention of murder, but rather killed when he had the opportunity. And after his first taste of inflicting death, he wanted more."

Livingston looked around the room. A few of the newer detectives were noticeably upset and had closed their eyes. Others sat in numb silence.

"The killer may have a strong interest in police work and may have initiated contact with his victims by posing as a police officer. He may have a prior criminal history of assault and rape or has possibly been diagnosed with more severe psychological issues. And finally, we doubt the killer could haul bodies and do everything he has done with a car. He probably drives a van or pickup truck. Something older and unmaintained. One that blends in well with the seedy areas where he picks up his victims. We think his dumpsites in the trees down south were meticulously chosen, so he's probably familiar with that terrain. Because of that, we believe he is a hunter or fisherman or sportsman of some sort, comfortable with woods and water. I know that's a lot to digest, but can you picture this person as being your killer?"

Lost in morbid thought, nobody was quick to respond. Finally, Hargrove stood up and tapped on the flag-sized wall map. In addition to lines labeling Dragline Fisheries, the Greyhound bus station, and the location where the two Filipino girls' bodies were found, a thick blue tracing had been drawn from the Lighthouse Pub to Lowell Rotary Park. A red pin marked the exact location where they had found Kathy.

"I'll comment on that last part. I don't think our killer is familiar with the area. If he was, he'd know there are far better places to hide a body in Snohomish County than this. He's not from around here and I'll tell you why. Yesterday, I drove the straightest route from the Lighthouse Pub to Lowell Rotary Park. It took me only nine minutes. It's just two and a half miles. I think the killer picked the victim up outside the bar, took a right on Rucker Avenue and after a short drive made a left on forty-first. If he did that, he would have popped right out at Lowell Park. This isn't a well thought out dump site," —he tapped on the map again— "traveling that route, it's the first woods he would have come to. And if you drive the other direction from Dragline, the same thing is true for the wooded knoll."

Another officer chimed in. "And if the killer scouted the park on a different night, carefully choosing a dump site like you say, he would have found a locked gate. I live close by there. Those gates are almost always locked at night. If that Blazer hadn't broken down, he wouldn't have been able to drop her off there at all."

While he was on the subject, he gave a quick update. He had spoken with the owner of the Blazer in the nearby town of Monroe. When his vehicle didn't start after he finished running the river, he and his son had pulled their boat upstream from the boat ramp and tied it in the trees. The man's wife had picked them up around eight-thirty and he was adamant there were no other vehicles in the lot and no other people around.

"Then I agree the serial killer is not from around here," Garrity consented. "Neither location seems like a carefully planned out dumping ground. Not like the ones down south. It sounds like this serial killer chose these locations, hoping his victims *would* be found."

"Is it possible he lives down south, drives north to kill, and got damn lucky that gate was unlocked that night?" questioned Hargrove.

"Unlikely. But possible, I suppose. But that would require a major change in behavior," explained Livingston. "I'm more intrigued by the way these victims were murdered. As I mentioned, the Green River Killer strangles his victims, thirty-one confirmed so far, and has never used a weapon of any kind. Up here we have not one, but two weapons used, and the same weapons were used on all three victims. To me, that is most telling."

Sensing some of the men needed clarity, Agent Livingston explained, "It would be highly unusual, almost unprecedented, if a serial killer as prolific as the Green River did change his M-O. Serial killers tend to operate in well-defined geographical areas with repeated patterns of behavior. And changing murder tactics is a cataclysmic change. In this case it would be like a sushi chef getting a job at a waffle house. Is it in the realm of possibility? Sure. Is it probable?" He shrugged like he didn't buy it. "Okay. What else you got?"

"Our victims weren't prostitutes," Chief Wagner inserted.

"True," Garrity took his gaze off the wall map. "And all the Green River victims were."

"Let's talk motive." Livingston looked up from Johnson's report. "The first two Everett victims were fully clothed and left face down. That's a stark contrast to Kathy Simmons—and all the known Green River victims."

Nick breathed deeply and let out a pained sigh. Like Garrity, he'd walked into this meeting hoping the Everett victims *were* at the hands of the Green River. During their time together on the Task Force, the two men had obsessed over every piece of evidence and studied crime scenes in three states. They'd theorized, speculated, and argued. Garrity had heard from psychics and even visited Ted Bundy on death row in Florida. They both desperately sought closure to the enigma that had been the focus of their conscience for so long and had been praying their psychopathic nemesis would come out of hiding, make a mistake, and leave a clue to reveal himself. *Just one damn clue.*

"I will share with you something about the Green River Killer that we have not shared with the press or anyone else. It needs to stay in this room."

Garrity took a deep breath. "We believe he returns to dead corpses and has sex with them. The sick bastard props their eyes open with sticks when he does it, too."

A hush hung heavy over the room. Hargrove closed his eyes and gritted his teeth. Nizzi hadn't mentioned that detail to him.

"After we found the first two victims fully clothed and face down, I puzzled over that too," Nick finally answered. "But then with Kathy Simmons..."

"Your observations are correct, detective," Johnson interrupted. "Her crime *does* appear to be sexually motivated. The vaginal swab we took was inconclusive, but the underwear found in her mouth *did* contain sperm. We were unable to retrieve any evidence of that kind from the first two victims, but of course, they were in the elements for much longer."

"There's another thing bothering me," Garrity continued. "What was the one thing missing from all the Green River victims?"

Nizzi responded. "Blood. All those years we studied those bodies in the woods, I always had the feeling the Duwamish River Man had an aversion to the sight of blood. Look at those photos. There's no shortage of it on any of the victims up here."

Garrity picked up one of the photos, nodding his head in agreement.

"Have you ever heard the name Warrens? Lev Warrens? Has that name ever been mentioned to you in connection with the Green River case?"

Nick waited for Garrity to process it and shake his head no.

Livingston stood up, addressing the group. "After digesting these reports and listening to your findings, I do *not* think it is the Green River Killer. I don't think he'd move to a new hunting ground and change his M-O so drastically. And as you so accurately observed, stranglers don't suddenly flip a switch and become blood-thirsty slashers. Your victims are not street walkers, and he didn't return to them with necrophilia intentions. The fact that your first two were found face down and fully clothed suggests to me that sex wasn't the motive for those crimes at all. I think it is more likely we have a second serial killer. And given the state of your last victim, it's highly probable he's trying to be a Green River copycat. Lord knows there has been enough press coverage on that case. I want to hear more about the evidence found on Kathy Simmons. Dr. Johnson, you said you retrieved testable fluids?"

"Yes, we recovered a suitable amount from the underwear that was so unceremoniously stuffed in her mouth. It has been submitted to my lab for DNA fingerprinting, and for the first time in the state of Washington, we think we will be able to identify it ... produce a profile."

"You have a lab equipped to process DNA?"

Dr. Johnson's smile revealed the pride he'd been saving for this moment. "I do. Over the past few months, I've been assembling a small panel of scientists who are trained in biotechnology. You've all probably read DNA evidence was used in a Florida rape case last year, the news coverage was pretty hard to miss. But it's never been done here. Until now. My team is confident they can extract DNA from Kathy Simmons's underwear."

"That's a most welcome development, Dr. Johnson. DNA labs are something the Bureau is looking into as well. You can count on the FBI to provide you with all the backing and additional support you need."

Cat now fully out of the bag, Dr. Johnson strutted to the front of the room. His enthusiasm bubbled from every word. "My scientists have found the missing piece of this puzzle. They're going to extract DNA and it will be the key for you to solve it and make an arrest. This case will be the first. The landmark. We're talking about a scientific break-through of global importance, but of course we can't do it without *you*."

"Without us?" Hargrove scoffed, gesturing with an open palm to the table full of cops. "What are *we* supposed to know about DNA?"

Johnson gave him a baited smile. "It's simple, really. DNA is a molecule found in the chromosomes of every living object. Every single person has them in their genes. And every single one is unique. They can identify people *better* than fingerprints. For us to solve this crime with DNA, two things must happen. First, my scientists need to get a DNA fingerprint from the underwear you recovered, but equally important, we need a DNA profile to match it to, which means, *you* need to collect DNA for us from your suspects."

Hargrove got excited. "I see. If we can get DNA from the killer, you can match it with the DNA found on Kathy Simmons—and it will solve the Vallesteros murders too?"

Johnson raised his eyebrows and pointed at him like he was a star student. "Bingo."

"Holy shit. What's the best way to get it?" another detective asked. "Have our suspects donate blood?"

"Actually, it can be done with saliva samples. And my team is making up kits as we speak. You get the killer's DNA, we'll positively match it to the DNA found on the victim's underwear, and you'll have your match. And as the brilliant Lieutenant Hargrove alluded, we'll solve three crimes at once."

The officers murmured amongst themselves. A little bit of spit was all they needed to identify their killer? Would it really work? Most had seen the national news shows about the Florida case, and the future promise of DNA forensics, but still they were skeptical. Could a murderer really be positively identified through microscopic molecules? Could Johnson's scientists really extract it? Would DNA stand up in court? Doubts lingered, but hope rose.

"Let's get on it," ordered the Chief. "We need to collect saliva samples from everyone on the Dragline list. And everyone she encountered that night at the bar."

The men groaned. It wouldn't be easy to get that many DNA samples. Workers on the Dragline list had proven to be young and mobile, many lived in other states. Livingston agreed to call law enforcement as far away as New York, California, Arizona, Colorado, and Texas to assist. With a plan now in motion, Livingston packed his briefcase and promised he would begin working on a new psychological profile, for another Seattle area serial killer, when he returned home to Virginia the next day.

"Now we know we have a second killer working in Snohomish County. It's not the Green River and we need to make that clear with the press, so they don't continue conflating the two. And the best news is we have DNA science on our side and a solid strategy to catch him."

"I'll call another press conference," offered the Chief.

## CHAPTER 26

# SECOND PRESS CONFERENCE

The Everett Police Department's second press conference of the summer had to be held in a much larger room than the first, for the media frenzy simmering the past two weeks had now boiled over into a full-blown circus. Reporters from as far away as Idaho, Oregon, and California mingled out front, exchanged business cards, and slyly tried to determine what the others knew that they didn't. A reporter from the *Los Angeles Times* received pats on the back for being a finalist for the previous year's Pulitzer Prize for Investigative Journalism Excellence. Thick with make-up and pressed designer clothes, television personalities jostled to secure live-shot positions. Cameramen followed anyone who looked even remotely official.

While the police team detested the attention, they also knew this much publicity was their best bet to get a tip that could lead them to their killer. With only the short-list of Dragline leads, scant witnesses, conflicting theories, and unprocessed evidence to guide them so far, they either needed a breakthrough from the medical examiner's DNA scientists or help from the public. And as the Chief reminded them every morning, noon, and night, time was ticking. The killer was active—and bound to strike again.

"Good afternoon everyone. I want to thank you all for coming on such short notice," Chief Wagner opened. "We've called this press conference to give you details of another homicide we are investigating, our third this summer."

The crowd hushed. Wagner cleared his throat.

"Sunday afternoon at approximately ten after twelve, a body was found at Lowell Rotary Park, southeast of town. The deceased was a female, a nurse here at a local hospital, thirty-two years old, and a long-time Everett resident. The coroner has positively identified her as Kathy Simmons."

The crowd groaned. Wagner waited until the room once again grew silent before continuing. "The coroner has ruled her death deliberate homicide. She suffered severe wounds to the head, almost identical to those found on the Vallesteros sisters. We believe the same person killed all three victims."

Several hands from the press shot up.

"Let me finish, please. Kathy Simmons was last seen Saturday night leaving the Lighthouse Pub on Hewitt Avenue around eleven o'clock. That bar was busy that night. Kathy Simmons didn't just disappear. She was taken. There must be someone out there who saw her leave, maybe even spoke with her as she left. We're asking for the public's assistance and have set up a special phone number for tips and information. Now, we'll open it up for questions."

One young television reporter from KOMO News blurted out, "How confident are you this murder *is* connected to the murders of the two Filipino sisters?"

"We are still processing evidence, but we *do* have strong reasons to believe all three victims in Everett this summer *were* killed by the same person."

Another reporter cut straight to the chase, "Is it the Green River Killer?"

Hargrove snapped back a quick answer, "We do not believe this is the work of the serial killer down south, but we are moving forward under the notion that our crimes were committed by the same man."

"So, there is a second serial killer working the north end?"

Nick nodded. "We met with both the Green River Task Force and the FBI. We all came to agreement on that."

"Why don't you think these murders were committed by the Green River Killer?"

Nick frowned. "The two biggest reasons our crimes differ are the way they were killed and the victims themselves. As you know, the Green River Killer is a strangler. Our victims were not strangled. Also, our three victims in Everett were not prostitutes, his were. Both are big differences. We have other crucial evidence suggesting the existence of a second serial killer as well, but we are not prepared to share that with you today. I can only tell you what we believe at this point. He may have copied some of the Green River's attributes, but it's not him."

Throughout the press conference, Julian had been trying to process the possibility that Lev could have killed Kathy. *Lev is a serial killer now? And he came looking for me? They really need to find this guy.* From the back of the room where he was seated next to Lindsay Fiori and Francis Bernard, he raised his hand and called out, "Detective Nizzi, are you using DNA forensic science to help solve these crimes?"

Nick squinted through the lights. Whose voice was that? It was familiar somehow. All eyes turned to Julian. When he was in college, he had been introduced to the emerging possibilities of DNA forensics and had been fascinated with their potential to someday help solve crimes. He had been a part of many heated classroom debates discussing the merits, potential ethical issues, and drawbacks of the new science.

"Interesting question. I can share with you that we retrieved from the body of Kathy Simmons what we believe to be suitable evidence for DNA testing. With assistance from the FBI, our medical examiner is currently processing it, and we are hopeful that DNA forensic science will help us get this crime solved. But he warned us, and I want to caution you, in the state of Washington there has never been a crime solved with DNA, and so far, only one in the United States, and that one wasn't a murder. It's new to all of us, so we are cautiously optimistic. But I assure you, we are doing everything we can to solve these crimes quickly and get the killer off the streets."

After a few more follow-up questions, the press stampeded the door. An undeterred news machine waited outside, impatiently waiting to be fed. After all, the most discussed story of the year had just gotten much bigger. Neither Kathy Simmons nor the Vallesteros had been murdered by the Green River Killer. There were two serial killers on the loose. And one was a copycat. The Northend Copycat. And he had just struck again.

∽᙮∾

The *Seattle Post-Register* investigations team gathered that evening and watched the local television news media air story-after-story-after-story. Every newscast featured interviews with either Wagner, Nizzi, Hargrove, or Garrity. Breaking news trumped regular programming. Television producers couldn't contain the news until ten. A steady stream of video feeds showed sleepy Everett side streets lit up from news truck camera lights like a Major League baseball stadium during playoffs. Television news played up the notion that there were two serial killers on the loose. The Northend Copycat Killer was active while the Green River Killer lay dormant. It made for good ratings. Bernard turned the TV off.

"Fiori, you've got our main story," Bernard walked to the head of the room. "Talk to the Task Force detectives again. I want their take on why they don't think it's the Green River Killer. Get quotes."

The editor-in-chief scribbled on his whiteboard without pause. "Harold, write up an exposé on Kathy Simmons. What can you find out about her life? We know she was a nurse. Interview her co-workers. Get some pictures. Do her friends think she was targeted by an enemy or was she simply in the wrong place at the wrong time?"

Bernard pointed to the far end of the table. "Hopkins, you get your own assignment this time. I want you to write up a background piece on DNA forensics. Most of our readers don't know what DNA is, let alone that it can be used to help solve a crime like this one. How was it discovered? Where did it all begin? What does it mean? Interview Medical Examiner Johnson. Provide background and tie it to these cases. If you can pull it off, you'll get your first published byline in our paper. See if you can have it done in time for Sunday's edition."

Julian's eyes grew wide. He couldn't have concealed his grin if he tried. Finally! Was he really getting his shot? A major story featuring a new way to identify an uncaught serial killer with possible ties to a second? He flew back to his desk and immediately arranged an interview with the Snohomish County medical examiner. Then he brewed a fresh pot of coffee and began a long night of research.

❧

News tips rolled in almost immediately after the press conference. One tipper reported he remembered a woman who resembled Kathy walking up the hill outside the bar the night she disappeared and getting into a truck. There had been no struggle. In fact, she acted like she knew the driver. However, the man cautioned that he and his two friends had been drunk. Very drunk. It had been hard to see detail through the rain. His description of the driver, who might have been black, or at least dressed in black, and the vehicle were generic. When questioned further, he admitted he didn't get a clear glimpse of the man, for his eyes had been glued on Kathy. He couldn't remember the color of the pickup truck or give any more useful clues. But he was sure the woman had climbed in on her own accord.

Another caller remembered seeing a man in a pickup truck parked in an alcove of the gravel lot across the street from the Lighthouse Pub intently watching the front door. The driver had avoided eye contact when the man walked past. He thought the driver was dark-skinned with dark hair. He too was drunk, but recalled the truck being beige, light brown, or white. He couldn't guess the age of the mysterious driver or remember enough detail for a sketch. But the driver had been so focused on watching people coming and going from the bar it had given the man the chills.

A woman telephoned and said she had been approached by a strange man, creepy in both action and appearance, a week before as she left a different bar on the other side of town. She recounted the man had asked her if she needed a ride home, but he came on too strong, almost desperate, so she declined. She described him as a white man with charming but deadly brown eyes. He had shown her a picture of his child. She too had been drinking heavily but thought his hair had been dark grey, almost black. Slicked-back and oily. He had been driving a white truck with a canopy on the back. The detectives had her to come down to the station and later drew a composite sketch of both the suspect and the pickup truck with her help.

The detectives grew frustrated. The only thing all accounts had in common was that a black, white, or brown man in a white, brown, or beige pickup truck, picked up a woman who looked like Kathy close to the Lighthouse Pub the night of the murder. They did get a pair of rough composite sketches out of it for what was probably an unrelated incident. But beyond that, they felt like the whole effort had been a big waste of time.

"I'm going to swing by Hopkin's house again," Hargrove muttered on his way out. "Has he returned the message you left for him at the newspaper?"

Nick looked up and shook his head.

# CHAPTER 27

# DISCOVERY

As Julian was escorted into the office of Dr. Richard Johnson at his lab, his eyes were immediately drawn to the chief medical examiner's panel-wood wall covered with diplomas from Ivy League universities. On a shelf behind his desk were framed pictures of the doctor standing next to what appeared to be FBI agents and other prestigious-looking uniformed men and women.

"So, I understand you're writing an article on DNA and forensic science. It's about time the *Post-Register* took an interest."

Julian nodded. "Actually, I studied it in college, so I have a bit of knowledge. In his press conference, Chief Wagner said you are using it to help solve the Everett murders and catch the Northend Copycat Killer. What can you tell me about that?"

It quickly became obvious DNA science was the doctor's favorite subject. For over an hour he explained how miniscule amounts of saliva, skin, blood, hair, or semen could be used to extract unique profiles and reliably link criminals to crimes. It could be used both to secure convictions, and to exonerate innocent suspects who might be falsely charged or wrongfully convicted. The doctor reiterated they had collected evidence on the body of Kathy Simmons he believed could be used to extract a DNA profile. His scientists, with new expanded resources from the FBI, were working on it. He wouldn't provide specifics on what the evidence was, however. To Julian, it sounded like the medical examiner was one hundred percent convinced DNA fingerprinting was the way they'd identify their serial killer.

"If you're so confident, why isn't it used more often?"

"Well, it's still not a slam dunk by any means. The evidence will take at least a week to analyze and could take much longer than that. It's possible we might not be able to get a DNA profile at all. And even if we do, we still need to match it to the DNA of the killer. That's the biggest problem. We don't have many DNA fingerprints of bad guys on file yet. I'm hoping someday we will have a massive data bank to compare crime samples with. If we had that, we would solve more crimes. Many, many more."

"Has the Green River Killer Task Force tried using DNA technology in their investigation? You'd think they would have lots of DNA."

"You would think that," Johnson took off his glasses and rubbed the sides of his nose. He'd been watching every word Julian had been writing down, pausing to give him time at the places he wanted him to emphasize. "But really, they don't. And like everyone else, they are waiting for the first case ... the breakthrough. The *one trial* that demonstrates how effective the technology has become. The *one pivotal ruling* that uses DNA to indisputably convict a killer. After it happens, I guarantee it will have a domino effect for hundreds of other unsolved crimes in this state and others, including the Green River Killer. I'm telling you, we're on the verge of a crime-fighting revolution. And I'm going to lead it. Feel free to use that direct quote in your article."

Julian sat captivated and had filled almost an entire legal pad with notes. The science had advanced so incredibly much since he first heard about it in j-school just a year before. He thanked Johnson for the interview and sped back to the newsroom. Originally, he had planned to stop by his apartment and grab some clothes, but in his excitement, he'd forgotten his gun. He dreaded the thought of meeting Lev without it. Plus, he was on assignment.

The imminent use of DNA forensics to solve violent crimes expanded far beyond the Everett murders. He was convinced by Dr. Johnson's belief in the accuracy of DNA forensic science and the pressing need for a national DNA data bank. The more he researched, the more high-profile unsolved cases he uncovered. Most had crime scene evidence that probably contained DNA, but little of it had been scientifically processed and if it had, there wasn't a DNA profile of a bad guy to match it with. If there was only a way to easily match DNA with the DNA of killers, these mysteries would probably *all* be solved. He worked deep into the silent recess of the night. Case-after-case he uncovered, and piece-by-piece his story came together.

∽✦∾

On the same Thursday afternoon Julian was interviewing Dr. Johnson, Nizzi and Hargrove knocked on the front door of Julian's house on Kromer Street for the third time in as many days. They were getting ready to leave when Ellen Brown answered. The detectives were quick to flash badges.

"Good afternoon, ma'am. Does Julian Hopkins live here?"

"Why, yes. Yes, he does," the old lady put her hands on her sides. She'd recently grown cool towards Julian after correctly sensing he was trying to avoid her. "He rents the efficiency apartment downstairs. But I don't think he's here. His truck's not. I just got back from visiting my daughter and grandkids in Spokane. They're two and four and are so darn cute! He might be working. He's a reporter for the *Seattle Post-Register*, you know. That boy is always working. Why? Why are you looking for him?"

"Would it be okay if we knocked on his door to see if he's here?" Nick cajoled. "Can we come in?"

"I suppose so. He has his own door downstairs. But you can get down there through here as well. Is he in trouble? He doesn't seem like the type to be in trouble."

Nick answered with a calming smile, "No, ma'am, he's not in trouble. We have a few questions for him concerning an investigation we're working, that's all."

Mrs. Brown unlocked the door at the top of the stairs and pointed them down to Julian's basement apartment.

"He doesn't use the front door very often. In fact, I don't think he's used it since the day he moved in. Down there he has his own bathroom, kitchen, and entryway," she explained. "I rarely see him anymore."

Hargrove knocked on Julian's door, listened for movement, and mumbled something to himself.

Nick questioned Mrs. Brown at the top of the stairs.

"Do you know if he's had any visitors lately?

"I don't think so. Whenever I see him, he's always alone."

"Has anyone come to your door looking for him?"

Mrs. Brown sifted through the haziness of her senescent memory. "Not that I remember."

"A guy named Lev Warrens, maybe?"

The old lady strained to remember, desperately reaching for something just beyond her grasp, but eventually gave up and on the verge of tears over her failing memory, shook her head.

Hargrove wedged his business card in the crack by the door handle. "We'll try again later, without bothering you next time, ma'am. But if you see him, please tell him to give us a call any time of the day or night."

In the kitchen, the shrill ring of a phone offered her escape. "That's probably my daughter calling to make sure I made it home safely. I need to take that. Please let yourself out when you're through," she motioned down the short hall leading to a side door.

On their way out, the detectives paused next to a stack of fishing and camping gear in the hall. "Whoa. Would you look at that." Nick pointed at a clear-topped tackle box sitting on the top of the pile with the name 'Hopkins' written in black permanent marker, filled with shiny Pixie lures with pink centers. He popped it open for better inspection. Most of the lures had two black dots clearly drawn in the dimples. He grabbed his partner by the arm.

"Do you see what I see?"

"Oh yeah, I see them. I fish with Pixie lures all the time and those are the only ones I've ever seen marked with black dots like that..." He turned wide-eyed and gasped, "except for the one we found in the bushes five feet away from the dead body of poor Kathy Simmons."

∽✕∾

Nick snapped the door shut firmly behind him as he and Hargrove barged into the office of Chief Wagner. At first, the commander was annoyed by the sudden interruption but quickly changed his tune.

"Okay. Slow down. You're sure it was the same kind of fishing lure?" he verified as he held up the one discovered on the ground in Lowell Rotary Park. "You're sure the one you saw at Hopkins' house matched this one? Black marks and all?"

"One hundred percent positive," Hargrove pumped his arms in the air and punched his fist. "The Pixies at Hopkins' house are all marked with black dots just like that one. And the tackle box even has his name written on it. As I was telling Nick, I'm a salmon fisherman myself, and I've never seen them with markings like that before. Hopkin's got a bunch of them."

"This is a major twist, for sure," agreed the chief. "But I'm glad you left them there. We'll need a search warrant to retrieve them. I'll call the prosecuting attorney and get him over here right away."

It didn't take long for Snohomish County Prosecutor Adam Lee Hayes to arrive. He was acutely aware of Nizzi's reputation and experience on the Green River Task Force and had worked with Hargrove many times before. As he listened, he double-checked Julian Hopkins name on the Dragline employee short list and reviewed the photo of his pickup truck parked in the Dragline lot on the day the detectives first interviewed Clayton and Elvin at the bunkhouse.

"The Dragline HR manager checked his flight dates for me too," added Hargrove, so anxious to make an arrest he couldn't sit down. "Hopkins flew to Alaska on June seventh. Three days *after* the Vallesteros girls were murdered."

The prosecutor carefully examined the fishing lure from the crime scene and agreed it was unique. And if there was indeed an identical one in Julian's possession, it was significant. He concurred a search warrant was supported and phoned the district court judge, adding a special request that DNA retrieval be added to the warrant.

Mrs. Brown was shocked to see four detectives back at her house, three hours later, this time holding a search warrant. She let them right in. Hargrove rushed straight to the pile of gear in the hall and ordered one of the officers to seize the whole tackle box. As he sifted through the rest of Julian's gear, Mrs. Brown gave Nick a key to Julian's locked apartment.

"Don, get in here, you have got to witness this," Nick called out a short time later from the bedroom. He pointed to a thin gold chain necklace with a salmon pendant, two small diamonds for eyes, dangling from a lamp next to Julian's bed.

"Recognize that?"

Hargrove lit it up with his flashlight. "I sure as hell do. It's identical to the ones the Vallesteros sisters were wearing in that photograph."

Both detectives had spent many hours staring at the picture of the two girls.

"Do you know what this means?"

"Yeah. I do. It means Julian Hopkins has some serious explaining to do."

# CHAPTER 28

# JULIAN'S FIRST BYLINE

It was after midnight when Julian returned to Lindsay's eleventh floor Second Avenue apartment, just a stone's throw away from the Pike Place Market. Downhill on the wharf, tied up for the night, the Washington ferries had ceased their all day, back-and-forth trips to Bainbridge Island. Most of the windows in the tall-glass office buildings rising out of the mist of the city streets were dark. Except for loud bar music over a block away, downtown Seattle was weeknight quiet.

"Did you finish it yet?" Lindsay murmured as he climbed into bed. "You've been working on that article for two days straight. Francis gave you all week, you know."

"Yeah. But there's a lot riding on this case. DNA forensics is advancing rapidly. Dr. Johnson is convinced the science is on the verge of a crime-fighting revolution. This is a much bigger story than I originally thought it would be."

"You just want to see your name in print," she cooed.

"Next to yours."

Julian was gone by the time Lindsay woke, and was in fact sitting in a chair outside Francis Bernard's office when he arrived in the morning.

The head honcho chuckled, "Either big news is breaking, or someone is eager."

Julian handed him a draft of his article. Other than the stories he had submitted with his resume, this was the first time he had shown Bernard his work. Excited, nervous, yet feeling strangely confident, Julian followed the newsman's eyes as he read, an unbridled attempt to connect facial expressions and reactions to points in the story he had written. The seasoned veteran finished without revealing any emotion, then read it again, this time out loud.

## KILLERS BEWARE, DNA IS COMING

*By Julian Hopkins*

*On a Thursday afternoon in the summer of 1986, 15-year-old schoolgirl, Dawn Ashworth took a shortcut home. Ten Pound Lane had always been a safe footpath from her Leicestershire, England school, but not today. When her body was found raped and strangled two days later, police immediately connected it to another unsolved crime. They were dealing with a serial murderer. But this would be the monster's last kill. With the help of a revolutionary new science known as DNA fingerprinting, police captured their predator and prevented a miscarriage of justice at the same time.*

*Here's how that landmark investigation went down: Under intense pressure, police quickly arrested a 17-year-old classmate. Under questioning, he confessed to Dawn's murder but adamantly denied the second. Convinced the two girls were killed by the same man and certain the boy was lying, police charged him with both murders and threw him in jail.*

*Meanwhile, at nearby Leicester University, Professor Alec Jeffreys had made a remarkable discovery. While in his lab studying inherited illnesses, he extracted DNA from cells and attached it to photographic film. When it unexpectedly displayed as a sequence of bars, the geneticist realized he was onto something big. He could identify every individual in his experiment with unique precision. Shortly after, he publicized his findings and was soon asked by local police: Can your new science prove our suspect murdered not only Dawn, but both girls?*

*DNA fingerprinting had never been used in a criminal investigation before, but Jeffreys was confident. He tested the suspect's blood and semen taken from the dead girls' bodies and determined they had indeed been raped by the same man. But positively not the one they had in custody. Reluctantly, police set the innocent boy free, then gathered DNA from 5,000 males in the area. One of those samples led to the arrest, confession, and conviction of the true killer. And a new era of solving crime was born.*

*So why aren't more law enforcement agencies employing this new technique? Snohomish County Chief Medical Examiner Dr. Richard Johnson believes he knows the answer. "There is great promise in this emerging science, no question about that. But in the United States, prosecutors are hesitant because DNA was not actually tried by a court in the Ashworth case. Her killer pleaded guilty, so the prosecutor didn't rely on DNA to get the conviction. But I believe it would have held. And I also believe DNA will be the most significant breakthrough to solve serious crimes since fingerprinting was adopted in 1910. We just need one murderer in this country to successfully be tried and convicted in a court of law by DNA. Once we get that, we'll be well on our way to a new crime-fighting revolution."*

*And Johnson is not the only one embracing DNA's potential. In Florida last year, a circuit court judge convicted a rapist after tests matched his DNA from a blood sample with that of semen traces found on his rape victim. Now, authorities across the country are looking at old cases in a new light and with new hope. But they still need the first murder conviction to pave the way. The recent discovery of Everett native, Kathy Simmons's body in Lowell Rotary Park over the weekend, may just be the one for which authorities have been waiting.*

*In a press conference Friday afternoon, Detective Nick Nizzi of the Major Crimes Unit of the Everett Police Department announced, "We retrieved from the body ... what we believe to be suitable evidence for DNA testing. The medical examiner is currently working on it, and we are cautiously optimistic that DNA forensic science will help us get this crime solved quickly."*

*So why are Dr. Johnson and the Everett PD so convinced? "The blueprint to life, DNA, is found in your genes," Johnson explained. "And it only takes a miniscule amount of saliva, skin, blood, hair, or semen for us to reliably test and produce a profile. Every person's DNA matches ninety-nine percent of everyone else's on earth. It's that remaining one percent, called microsatellites, that makes each of us unique. Microsatellites have the power to identify killers, link criminals to crimes, and set innocent men free."*

*Sound easy? Johnson explained why it is not. "Even if we extract a perfect profile, we still need to match it to the DNA of the killer. Because we don't have many DNA fingerprints of bad guys on file yet, it's our biggest hurdle. I'm hoping someday we will have a national databank to compare DNA samples with. If we had that, we would solve more crimes. Many, many more. And high-profile ones too."*

*Like the Green River case? "Yes. The Green River Task Force has collected samples from his victims, but they don't have a lot of material to work with. Until DNA is proven in a murder conviction, they don't want to risk it. And given the magnitude of that case, I can't say I blame them. Law enforcement in Washington seems to be waiting for the first conviction ... the breakthrough that will pave the way. Once it happens, we believe it will have a domino effect for thousands of other unsolved crimes coast to coast ... including the Green River Killer and Northend Copycat. DNA technology is what law enforcement investigators have needed for the past hundred years. If they would have had it, along with a complete data bank of DNA profiles, I believe it would have changed legal history. I'm certain it will change the future. And it will all start in Everett with Kathy Simmons."*

Bernard set the article on his desk, took off his glasses and stared at Julian in a new light. Finally, he grinned and slowly nodded in appreciation.

# CHAPTER 29

# INTERROGATION

It was a picture-perfect summer morning in Seattle. Short-sleeve warm and surreally clear, this was the type of day residents longed for during winter months of drizzle and saved sick days all year to enjoy. A fully visible Mount Rainier grandstanded south of the city. Both the Cascades and Olympics were framed with water east and west. Nick Nizzi called the *Seattle Post-Register* and sat back in surprise when he reached Julian at his desk.

"Hopkins, glad you picked up. I need to ask you a few questions about Lev Warrens," he lied. "Can you come to the station to meet with my partner and I this afternoon?"

Hallelujah! The news Julian had been hoping to hear. The cops were finally taking his lead seriously. He'd do just about anything to help authorities catch the bastard. His dreams had been getting worse. Because he had finished his article well before his given deadline, he had time to burn and agreed to drive to Everett and meet them that afternoon.

"I'd sure like to go with you," Lindsay carped when Julian told her where he was going. "But if I do, there's no way I'll get this assignment done on time. And I'd really like to do something fun this weekend, outside in this incredible weather. With you."

He gave her a wink. "I'll be fine. After I speak with the detectives I'll swing by my house and grab a few things. I'll be back at your apartment by the time you're off work."

"Your house? Julian ... be careful."

"Always."

When Julian arrived, Nick came out to greet him at the reception desk. As the two shuffled through the station's Friday afternoon bustle, he probed. "So, what do you do at the Post-Register?"

"I'm a reporter. I started there a few weeks ago when I got back from Alaska."

"And where were you in Alaska, again?"

"Dillingham. I worked for Dragline Fisheries. The money I made up there put me through college."

Nick ushered him into a sparse room with three metal chairs and a small table in the center. Other than a large mirror, there was nothing hanging on the white cement block walls. Hargrove was already seated. Suddenly suspicious, Julian raised his eyebrows.

"Julian, thanks for coming in so freely. As you know, we're investigating three homicides. You called me last week and told me about a man named Lev Warrens. You said you worked together in Alaska and think he may have known the Vallesteros girls. And he may have had something to do with their murders. Tell us once again why you think that."

"Lev worked on the Filipino laundry crew. The one the Vallesteros sisters were supposed to be on. In fact, I was told the only reason he was on that crew is because they didn't show up."

"So, what are you saying?" Hargrove butted in. "That he killed two people to take their laundry jobs at a remote Alaska fish camp? That doesn't seem to be a very compelling reason to commit double homicide to me."

Julian shrugged. Nick interjected, "Julian, tell me. How did you know the two girls were on their way to work at Dragline? Or that they were on their way to Alaska for that matter?"

Julian paused. There was something hidden in the detective's tone. Was this a conversation? Or an interrogation? "Well, I didn't know it when I was up there. I only learned of it last week after one of our reporters called Mr. Vallesteros in Manila."

Nick turned to Hargrove with raised brows, before focusing his attention back on Julian. "So, what can you tell us about him? About Lev Warrens?"

"Really not much," Julian looked around and studied the room. "You'd think after two years I'd know more, but I don't. Nobody does."

"Two years?" Hargrove erupted.

"Yep. He came up there the year before too. He came up that season with Reuben Martinez and the Mexican crew. He worked for my friend Chris as a glazer. Chris didn't like him much."

The older detective turned red with anger. "Lev Warrens was an employee of Dragline, not one, but two years? You're sure of that?"

Nick held up his hand. Hargrove retreated and flipped through the pages of the stapled Dragline packet.

"Okay. Go on. You worked with him for two fish seasons."

Julian told the detectives everything he could remember about Lev Warrens. How he struggled on Chris's crew the first season because he was older and slower than the others. How Julian felt sorry for him in year two and put him on the slime line until he eventually got reassigned to laundry duty full-time. He told them how Lev had dyed his hair and described what he looked like the best he could. He recounted the conversation on the Agulowak when Lev revealed he lived in a cabin on a Reservation near a salmon lake in the mountains. The fight with Charlie. Hannah. And the unsettled-foreboding feeling Julian had all season that something wasn't quite right with Lev Warrens.

"The day he got caught stealing, the day Mike kicked him out of camp, he was vicious. I mean *really* violent. He made wicked threats. Everyone in the plant heard him and some of those threats were at me. That's why I got so nervous when he showed up at my house in Everett. That's why I keep my pistol loaded. And that's why I called you."

Visibly frustrated, Hargrove waved in the air his stack of papers. "Can you tell me why the name Lev Warrens does not appear on this list that Dragline gave us of all their employees? You're on it, all the other names you've mentioned so far are on it, but Lev Warrens isn't. We talked to Bob Clayton and he said he doesn't know anyone by that name."

"What the hell? I have no idea," Julian slid back his chair. "Ask anyone who was up there, and they'll repeat the same stories I just told you. Venju del Prado crewed him. Mike Matthews fired him. He bit Reuben Martinez, his boss from the year before. He gave his co-workers nightmares. He was there all right and he came looking for me at my house. The old lady upstairs spoke with him! I'm telling you, you need to catch this guy, and you need to catch him now!"

Neither Nizzi nor Hargrove were expecting such a tale. They had assumed Julian had made up the name Lev Warrens to throw them off *his* trail. But this story sounded credible. And if it was, dozens of people could corroborate.

"Julian, we went to your house and asked Ellen Brown if Lev Warrens had been there. If she had spoken with him."

"And she didn't," growled Hargrove. "She didn't remember anyone by that name."

"Ellen Brown sometimes doesn't remember her own name! She's eighty-one and forgets things all the time!"

"Can you excuse us for a second?" Nick retreated.

The two detectives left the room. When they returned, Hargrove carried a box. He pulled out a tape recorder. "Mind if we record this?"

Julian shrugged.

Nick reached in and pulled out the pink Pixie fishing lure with two black dots seized from Julian's tackle box. He set it on the table. The mood in the room instantly changed.

"Is this yours?"

"Yeah, sure, that could be mine," Julian admitted. "I draw black dots on all of my lures. My uncle once told me big fish like to eat things with eyes. Wait. Why? Where did you get that?"

The detectives looked at each other. They both noted he used the word "my."

Hargrove's eyes flared as he put a matching lure next to it. "Because this one we found next to Kathy Simmons at her murder scene. That's why!"

"Hold on to your horses there, Don," Nick restrained. He turned back to a gasping Julian.

"Julian, Dragline Fisheries gave us their employee list and of course your name was on it. We have pictures of your pickup truck parked in the Dragline lot right after we found the bodies of the Vallesteros sisters. In our efforts to eliminate suspects, we visited your apartment and saw your tackle box. Your lures are curious to us, so we need to ask you a few questions before we send you on your way. Can you help us out?"

Questions were pouring into Julian's mind so fast he had trouble sorting them out. None of this made any sense. Trying to elevate himself out of his confused daze, Julian was incredulous, "Suspects? I'm a suspect?"

"Have you gone fishing in the Snohomish River around Lowell Rotary Park lately? Is it possible you could have dropped one of your lures on the ground?"

Julian took several deep breaths before replying. "No. I've never been there."

"Have you loaned your tackle box to anyone, or given any of your lures to other people? Anything been stolen?"

Julian continued to shake his head, then stopped. "Hey wait a minute. The day I took Lev Warrens fishing he used my stuff. I bet he stole a lure. He *is* a known thief you know."

Nick wrote it down. Hargrove scooted a picture of Kathy Simmons across the table. "Do you know this woman?"

"Ah … of course I know who she is. We've been writing about her all week. But I never personally met her."

"Where were you the night she was murdered?" Hargrove growled. "Last Saturday night around eleven thirty?"

"What?" Julian stammered. "Wait a minute. What the hell is going on here? Why are you asking me these questions? I thought you were looking for Lev Warrens. Am I seriously a suspect?"

Hargrove leaned in close, almost touching Julian's face with his own. "Answer the damn question, Hopkins. Where were you last Saturday at midnight?"

"I was looking for Lev Warrens," Julian said softly. "Out on the Olympic Peninsula. At Lakes Ozette and Quinault. The only lakes out there with wild Sockeye runs. I camped near Forks Saturday night and got back Sunday to my house around nine."

Nick interjected in a calm voice. "Julian, we found this fishing lure five feet away from Kathy Simmons in Lowell Rotary Park. It sure looks like the ones we found in your tackle box, doesn't it? And didn't you just call it yours?"

Horrified, Julian stared at the plastic evidence bag with the lure inside. The one sitting next to it from his tackle box was identical. He knew it was his. The black eyes seemed to stare back at him, even mock him.

"We also found this in your apartment." Nick held up the salmon necklace, also sealed in an evidence bag. "Does this look familiar to you?"

"You were in my apartment?" Now petrified, Julian nodded and whispered, "Yes. I got that from a friend. A girl I know at Dragline gave it to me."

Nick placed the gold chain and fish on the table next to the lures. The pile of evidence was mounting. Hargrove showed him the picture of the two Filipino girls who were both clearly wearing the same jewelry. "Doesn't your necklace look like the ones these girls are wearing?"

Julian studied the photo, took another peek at the one Hannah had given him, swallowed hard and nodded. "Yes."

"Why was this necklace in your room, Hopkins? Did you take it from one of the Vallesteros sisters? As a trophy?"

Julian stammered, "Like I said, I ... I got it from a friend in Alaska. A girl ... a girl I worked with up there named Hannah Miller gave it to me."

Hargrove opened a manila envelope and produced more graphic crime scene photos. Several were of the bloody body of Kathy Simmons sitting upright against the tree, legs spread wide and posed, underwear stuffed in her mouth. Others showed the partially decomposed bodies of the Vallesteros sisters. He waved them in Julian's face, then slapped them down on the table. The horrific images of death snapped Julian's memory back to the grotesquely deformed body of Eddie Chiklak on the Dragline dock. His face paled. He started to shake, resisting the urge to vomit. Both detectives noted his reaction.

"So, you knew these girls, huh?" Hargrove unleashed. "They worked for Dragline Fisheries ... just like you."

"No, I told you. I've never seen them before. I never met them. Lev Warrens killed them. It had to have been him. Why don't you believe me?"

Julian took a few deep breaths to regain his composure. "Look, we've been covering this story at the P-R and I didn't know they were employees of Dragline until one of our reporters called and talked to their father. I didn't know them. I didn't know Kathy Simmons either. And I sure as hell didn't *kill* anybody."

"And I don't believe you!" Hargrove shouted.

Julian turned to Nick. "I ... you have to believe me ... I didn't kill anyone. I'm an innocent man."

"We believe those girls were killed on their way to Alaska this year, just like you said. In fact, on their way to Dillingham, where you worked. On Friday evening, June third, when you were admittedly in the area. According to your airline ticket, you didn't arrive in Dillingham until Tuesday, June seventh. Were you staying in the Dragline bunkhouse that weekend? In Room 203, perhaps?"

Julian stared at the wall. There was no way he would let himself get emotional in front of these detectives. "I interviewed with Francis Bernard for my job at the *Seattle Post-Register* that Friday and spent the weekend camping. I knew I was moving here and wanted to see what the country around here felt like."

"Do you remember where you camped? That's a busy time of the year and there aren't a lot of open camp sites. If you stayed at one of the county campgrounds, they would probably have a record of it. That would help us clear you."

"I stayed in the back of my truck. In my camper shell. Just like I always do. The first two nights in the mountains near Gold Bar I parked by the side of the Skykomish River. There were a couple of others there too, but I didn't get their names. We drank beer together, so they might remember me if you can find them. The second two nights I went north and camped by the Skagit River. I left my truck at Dragline Tuesday morning, talked to Bob Clayton for a few minutes, jumped on the shuttle to the airport and flew straight to Alaska. I never stepped foot in the Everett bunkhouse."

"What about last Saturday night? The night you say you were camping near Forks. Was anyone with you? Anyone who can provide you with an airtight alibi?"

Julian fought back feelings of defeat. "Unfortunately, not. I went alone. But I spoke with at least half a dozen people in Taholah and Ozette. They'll remember me."

"Do you have their names?"

Julian shook his head. Hargrove scoffed and slid back in his chair.

Julian leaned in toward both detectives, making eye contact with them one at a time. "Look ... I didn't kill anyone, I swear! I have never met any of those women. A girl named Hannah Miller gave me that necklace in Dillingham this summer. Call her and she'll tell you it's true. Call my friend Boone Davis too. He'll vouch for me. Look, I didn't commit any of these murders. I didn't kill *anyone*. You have the wrong guy. It's Lev Warrens, for god's sake! He's your goddam serial killer."

Nick Nizzi looked deep into Julian's eyes. Julian didn't waver or blink. Finally, he backpedaled, "Okay, Hopkins, you are free to go. For now. Expect another call. And we'll keep searching for Lev Warrens."

Julian breathed a sigh of relief almost knocking over his chair as he got up to leave.

"Oh, one last thing. We need to collect a saliva sample from you for DNA testing."

"And we need to measure your shoes," growled Hargrove.

## CHAPTER 30

# FORGOTTEN CREEK

By the time Julian arrived at his house on Kromer, the western sun had slipped behind the Olympic mountains, leaving them awash in an orange-fiery glow. He'd been stuck at the police station for most of the afternoon waiting for a DNA tech to arrive and take his saliva sample. *Four goddam hours!* He was tired, hungry, and extremely irritated. What the *fuck* is going on anyway? He still couldn't believe the questions the detectives asked. The accusations they made. The evidence they produced. Of course, he hadn't killed anyone. But they seemed to think so. Especially Hargrove. What a prick. Thank god, they requested his DNA. That will get them off his tail. Prove his innocence. Make them finally focus on Lev. Were they even looking for him? He had his doubts.

Ruger drawn, chambered and ready, Julian eased open the door of his apartment and froze. Drawers were pulled out. The clothes he had so neatly folded were haphazardly stuffed back in. Somebody had been sitting in his kitchen chair and the cushions on his couch were upside down. They'd tried to conceal it, tried to put it back, but his place had obviously been ransacked. Police had been here all right, bastards.

"Is that you down there, Julian?"

Mrs. Brown, upstairs. *Damn this day.*

"Yes. Hello, Mrs. Brown. I'm just grabbing a few of my things."

"The police were here yesterday, Julian. They were looking for you. They had a search warrant, so I let them in."

"I see that."

Julian slammed the door behind him and tucked his pistol back in his belt. The last thing he wanted to do right now was have a long, useless conversation with old and senile Mrs. Brown. What the heck was Hannah doing with a necklace that looked like the ones the Vallesteros were wearing in their picture? Wait... she said Lev gave it to her. Could it have belonged to one of the sisters and he took it? And Kathy Simmons. Jesus. What a cruel and grisly sight. Lev had stolen one of his lures, he must have. But why did he kill *her*? Why did he plant his lure next to her body? The attempt to get into the man's mind gave him a chill to the soul. It had to be Lev. He'd probably taken it the day they fished together on the Agulowak. But why? What had he ever done to that crazy son of a bitch anyway? What had Dave done to him? And why the hell did Bob Clayton deny knowing the man? Screw it. He'd pick this shithole up later. He stuffed a few shirts in a gym bag and fumbled for the key to lock his door. *Oh, what's the use?* What would he say to Lindsay? Or Francis Bernard? Those detectives need to find that prick, Lev. And if they wouldn't do it, he would. Just wait until he got his hands on that son of a bitch.

"What's going on, Julian? What were the police looking for? Why were they here?"

Mrs. Brown again. Dammit. He turned. She was still standing at the top of the stairs.

"A ghost, Mrs. Brown. Everyone is looking for a goddam ghost. Boo!"

⌒✕⌒

After the cops released Julian and he left the station, they met. The entire group of officers who had been assigned to the case had been watching the interview through the two-way mirror. Chief Wagner had been taking notes in the corner. The lead detectives knew the evidence they had collected so far was mostly circumstantial, but it all seemed so strong. Even so, Julian looked nothing like the composite sketch that had been drawn up after the Kathy Simmons press conference, and he'd confessed nothing damning in his interview with detectives. Opinions were split. They replayed the tape recording again and again. They argued. Finally, Hargrove stood up and recapped his suspicions.

"Here's what we have on Hopkins so far. He admitted he was in the area the nights all three murders were committed, and he has no alibis. He was an employee of Dragline Fisheries and we have a photo of his pickup truck parked in the company's long-term lot. He denies staying in the bunkhouse, in Room 203, but I think he's lying. And he knew the Vallesteros sisters were employed by Dragline Fisheries in Dillingham, even though we withheld that information. Most damning, a uniquely marked fishing lure was found next to the brutally murdered body of Kathy Simmons, which he admitted was his, *and* we discovered jewelry hanging from a lamp next to his bed identical to the necklaces the Filipino girls were wearing. A twisted trophy he was keeping, I'm sure. Guys, his shoes look to be the same size as the footprints in the mud! What are we waiting for? Let's arrest this asshole!"

"Not so fast," Nick scoffed. "We're not doing anything until we check Hopkins' story out. The prosecutor will require us to build a much tighter case than this if we are going to push for an arrest. We don't have a plausible motive. He said nothing that even remotely resembled a confession, and we have no murder weapon."

He pointed to one of the young officers. "Call the folks on the Dragline list again. Ask them about Lev Warrens. And ask them if Hopkins ever displayed any violent behavior. What's this guy like? How does he treat women? Do any of his co-workers think he is capable of rape and murder? And let's get Bob Clayton back in here. If Lev Warrens truly was a Dragline employee, for two seasons no less, why doesn't he know about him?"

"I already called Dragline," Hargrove interrupted. "Clayton is traveling around Alaska until next Friday. But believe you me, I'll be waiting for him outside his office when he gets back."

"Before then, get back over there and talk to the janitor again. Show him Hopkins' picture ... and the composite sketch too. Press him to remember who stayed in Room 203. And speak with that HR manager again."

Nick walked out of the room, stopped, and turned to Chief Wagner. "I left a message for the plant manager, Mike Matthews, in Bethel. Both Clayton and Hopkins mentioned his name. He should be able to tell me more about Lev Warrens and he'll certainly be able to corroborate the story Hopkins told us. Or not. I'll speak with Hannah Miller too. If they don't call me back for whatever reason, I may need to fly up there."

Wagner immediately shook his head. "There is no way you are flying to Alaska right now. As soon as we get the DNA analysis back, I'll need you here in town."

Nick winced. "Okay. But someone should. It's important we track these people down pronto. As suspicious as this evidence appears, my gut tells me Julian Hopkins is *not* our serial killer."

"I disagree. My gut says it's him," Hargrove argued.

"Keep your guts to yourself." Wagner interjected. "When the DNA analysis comes back, it will clearly reveal which one of you is right."

❧

The family market on Forgotten Creek sat next to the trailhead of a meandering gravel path. Popular with families, dog owners, and weekend photographers, the track featured sharp switchbacks cut into mossy hillsides choked by a thick bramble of ferns and snowberry bushes. A series of wooden walk bridges snaked back and forth over a wild, maple-wooded ravine that slithered downhill and eventually melted into the shore of Puget Sound. At the bottom, a single outlet, Pidgeon Creek Road, marked the hike's end a half mile away.

By the time Julian pulled into the market parking lot, his emotions had cooled. He needed a beer. Or three. He'd grab a bottle of Merlot for Lindsay too. He hadn't spoken with her since he left the newsroom at lunch and at this rate it would be after eight before he made it back downtown to her apartment. He had a lot of explaining to do. Good grief. What should he say? Should he tell her about his conversation with the Everett PD? Would she believe him? Would she turn against him or stand by his side?

As he plodded out of the store, mind racing in wild and confusing thought, arms loaded with bottles, another car pulled in and parked. Its headlights swept through the lot, briefly illuminating a hooded figure standing by Julian's truck. Startled by the interference, the man turned and ran.

What's that guy doing by my truck? Is that …?

Julian dropped his bags and reached for his Ruger as bottles shattered. He gave chase.

"Hey. Hey, Lev. Lev Warrens!"

The man didn't turn. Julian raised his gun but didn't shoot as the blurred, hurrying figure found shelter in the shadows and disappeared into the thick undergrowth of Forgotten Creek trail. It sure looked like Lev. A lot. Jesus. He was losing his fucking mind.

∞

In Julian's dream he was a Redfish swimming effortlessly through an open-azure sea. His powerful tail propelled him. Food was wherever he wanted it to be. With his beak he cut the water like a sword. He was free. Seals and Orcas chased him, but he was far too quick and darted safely out of their way. Ahead in an estuary guarding a river's mouth, a net appeared. He easily swam around it and found himself in the middle of a large, teeming school. They all had faces. He saw his family, his child-hood friends, Dave, Boone, Chris, Hannah, Charlie, Josie, and Lindsay. They gained strength from each other and together swam upstream into a strong river current. But one-by-one they vanished, swiped away by an invisible force in the air above. Suddenly, his body slammed sideways, pierced through the side with a wooden spear. He was lifted into the air. Teeth bared, Lev Warrens pulled him from the water. Julian thrashed and fought, causing Lev to emit a maniacal shrieking laugh.

With a sudden jolt, Julian sat up in bed, dripping with sweat, choking for air.

"You okay?" Lindsay whispered. "Gracious. It looked like you were having quite the vivid dream. Are they getting worse?"

Panting heavily, Julian looked around the bedroom, then at her with a sigh of relief.

"Yeah. And I need to find Lev. Before he finds me."

# CHAPTER 31

# DNA RESULTS

When Julian's article appeared in the Sunday edition of the *Seattle Post-Register*, it created an immediate uproar. By the time television news aired that evening, everyone in the Emerald City was calling for a local DNA data bank to be created and questioning why investigators weren't collecting more DNA from crime suspects. Finally, it sounded like there was a way to catch the elusive serial killers who had terrorized their community for far too long.

Over the next few days, the medical examiner's office in Everett was flooded with calls. So was the Green River Killer Task Force and Everett PD. National media organizations picked up on the story and the DNA data bank cry gained momentum across the country. Dr. Johnson reveled in the limelight. He granted a nonstop parade of interviews both in person and on the phone, eventually even being featured on *60 Minutes*.

"DNA is the future of crime fighting and with the help of the FBI, I'm going to show you how it's done. Give us a national DNA data bank, and we'll show you how to put these killers behind bars."

Hargrove brought a copy of Hopkin's article to the station and showed it to everyone. The team had finally made it through the Dragline employee list and had collected dozens of saliva samples, which they had sent to Johnson's lab. There was still no trace of Lev Warrens, but they were still looking.

"I spoke with Hannah Miller in Fairbanks," Nick reported. "She corroborated Hopkin's story about Lev Warrens getting fired and making violent threats when he was thrown out of camp. Warrens went after her too and stole some of her things before he left. Hopkins' story checked out on that. But she wouldn't talk about the salmon pendant necklace. When I pressed her, she said she couldn't remember? I think she's lying."

"I met with Elvin at the Dragline bunkhouse again," Hargrove scratched his head. "He's known Hopkins for several years and was positive he didn't give him a key back in June. He doesn't think Hopkins could possibly be a killer, nor does anyone else I spoke with over there either. But of course, they're going to say that. He was a likable guy. Some serial killers are. Unfortunately, the HR manager is out sick, and Bob Clayton is 'who knows where' in Alaska until Friday. Even without them, we've got the evidence we need to arrest him, and I'm still convinced he's guilty. Hopkins drives a pickup truck and his timeline fits the movements of our culprit. He's our killer. I don't care what anyone else thinks … he's our guy."

"I can see how you might think that," Nick reluctantly conceded, still unconvinced. "But isn't it possible someone else marked up a fishing lure like that, or even planted it, like Hopkins says? There's no motive I want to swear on. And there's no murder weapon we can find. I realize he doesn't have good alibis for the nights of these crimes, but real killers tend to make up good alibis, you know that. Camping by himself? If he is the killer, he'd be smart enough not to use the same flimsy alibi twice, don't you think? My gut tells me it's someone else. But I got nothing on Lev Warrens. Just stories and rumors. It's almost as if we're tracking an apparition."

Chief Wagner shrugged. "I guess we'll know soon enough. Johnson called this morning and said his team has analyzed over a hundred of the saliva samples we've sent him. He said things are looking promising on his end. Ironic that DNA may solve this case after Hopkins published a newspaper article on the topic, huh?"

❧

Julian was so focused on finding Lev Warrens he barely heard the praise sung to him all week for his celebrated debut article. His co-workers treated him like the resident authority for all things pertaining to the topic of DNA forensic science and clamored to take him to lunch. Normally, reporters loved to bask in the attention after a big article, but he barely heard their compliments. He was on a sleepless mission to find Lev. That upcoming weekend he and Lindsay were planning to scour Wenatchee and Baker Lakes. Both had made endless phone calls with little more than hope to go on. All Julian could tell her was what Lev had told him on their fishing trip. He felt helpless for knowing so little about the man as Lindsay prodded him to remember something more.

"He's Native American. He lives in a cabin on a Reservation by a lake that has a wild Sockeye salmon run."

"And that's all you remember? How old is he?"

"I don't know. Fifties, late forties maybe. The guy looked different every time I saw him. He even dyed his hair black last season. It was grayish brown the year before. The guy was a loner. I feel stupid for not knowing more, but that's all I can remember, and he didn't talk much … to anyone. I'm starting to think Lev Warrens isn't even his real name. Not one of these state agencies I've been calling have any record of him, or if they do, they're not telling me."

With a frustrated sigh, Lindsay alphabetically phoned the Native American tribes in the Northwest, starting with the Makah, Puyallup, Quinault, and Tulalip. After none of them claimed a tribal member named Warrens, she expanded her search up and down the coast and to other states. Midweek, Mike Matthews finally returned from his Arctic caribou hunt and responded to Julian's message.

"Julian, how are you? I hope you're enjoying the house and your new job too."

"Mike, I'm in some trouble down here. I could sure use your help. What can you tell me about Lev Warrens?"

"Lev Warrens? Has that fucking thief resurfaced again? I wondered where he went after he left Dillingham."

"I think he's more than a thief, Mike. I think he's a killer too. A serial killer. And he's trying to frame me for his crimes."

"He's doing what?"

Julian told Mike about all the events that had transpired. About the Vallesteros sisters, Kathy Simmons, Lev visiting his house, and his fishing lure found at the crime scene.

"Julian, I don't know any more about Lev Warrens than you do. But Jesus. Get the fuck out of there. He's dangerous. Where's Boone and Chris? Have you called the cops? They left a message for me here, but I wanted to call you first."

"Yeah. The cops think *I* committed these crimes. They interrogated me and I told them all about Lev. But I don't think they're listening. I don't think they're even looking for the prick. So, I'm hunting for him myself."

"Have you spoken with Venju del Prado? Or Reuben Martinez? They both hired Lev and brought him up here on their crews. They might know where he lives or at least where you can find him."

"I can't get ahold of either."

"How about Bob Clayton? He might know more than we do."

"I've tried. He's up in Seward until Friday. He told the cops he doesn't even know Lev Warrens. And he hasn't returned any of my calls."

"He told the police he doesn't know Lev? Seward? Okay. Let me see if I can reach him. I'll get back to you."

◈

In Julian's nightmare, Charlie's face was desperate. So determined, so horrified, so pained. From *Proud Mary* he pulled and strained. A storm raged around him. He fought for control, searched for his knife, and screamed at the sky. Beneath the turbulent waters off Kanulik Beach, Lev Warrens had a death grip on Dave's feet, and he wasn't letting go. Lev waved Charlie's knife in his face, just beyond his reach, and laughed a maniacal, sinister shriek. He pulled Dave deeper and deeper into the waves. Dave reached his arms up for Charlie. He fought for his life, gasping for air, desperately trying to kick the heavy weight of Lev off. He didn't want to die. Not now. Not like this. Not ever! But Charlie was no match for the strength of the force below. The harder he pulled; the lower Dave slipped. As Lev dragged Dave's head under the surface for the final tragic time, Julian woke up gasping.

"The same nightmare again?" Lindsay whispered.

As he gulped for breath and tried to regain his composure, all Julian could do was nod his head. He pushed his hands into the sides of his temples. The deafening wails of Eddie Chiklak's grieving Yup'ik mother from that sorrowful day on the Dragline dock blared in his ears.

୬୶ଚ

On Thursday morning, Medical Examiner Johnson called Chief Wagner with unbridled excitement and announced he was on his way over. His chemists had done it! They had successfully extracted DNA from Kathy Simmons' underwear and linked it to the DNA of a suspect. It was a perfect match; of that he had no doubt. Along with Snohomish County Prosecuting Attorney Adam Lee Hayes, the entire detective team was assembled when Johnson strutted in.

"We did it. From hundreds of samples we've identified your killer! We've got the Northend Copycat Killer dead to rights!" Johnson slapped several copies of his official DNA analysis report on the table and tapped on a name. "The DNA found on Kathy Simmons' underwear perfectly matches the DNA fingerprint of this suspect. I didn't believe it at first, so we tested both the underwear and the suspect's sample four separate times. The FBI verified it every step of the way."

The medical examiner threw his hands in the air in victory celebration and paced to the far end of the room, impatiently waiting for the group to finish digesting his findings. He traced the lines on the wall map with his finger, pretending not to watch the detectives read. The prosecuting attorney examined each page, each paragraph, each word, and number on the report. He'd been under heavy media pressure all week but knew that to push for an arrest, he'd need to provide to a judge information that would lead a reasonable person to conclude the suspect had unequivocally committed the crime. DNA was new to him, so promising, and he was eager to put it to test. But was this evidence indisputable? Would it stand up in court? In a case as high profile as this one, he needed everything to be perfectly in order. Finally, he finished reading and scrutinized, "You're sure? One thousand percent positive? You'd be willing to place your hand on a Bible and defend this in front of a judge and jury?"

"A stack of Bibles," Johnson replied without hesitation.

Chief Wagner turned to his detectives, "Can you make this arrest without a shootout?"

"Yes, we can," growled Hargrove. "I've got the perfect plan."

# CHAPTER 32

# THE ARREST

The next afternoon, the Everett PD held its third press conference in a month to an even bigger reception. Residents of Everett were getting weary of the attention. After all, they lived in the small town to avoid big-city drama, not be the center of it. They wanted the media circus to go away almost as badly as they wanted the Northend Copycat Killer caught. Chief Wagner addressed the packed room with his same well-practiced formalities.

"We have called today's press conference on short notice to announce that the Snohomish County Medical Examiner, Dr. Richard Johnson, and his forensics crime lab have made a major scientific breakthrough. For the first time ever in the state of Washington, DNA found on a homicide victim has been positively matched to the DNA of a suspect. In this case, our killer has been identified by DNA evidence found on the body of Kathy Simmons."

Sounds of surprise whistled across the room. This was big. A dozen conversations started at once. As though someone had suddenly turned the heat on the stove to high, the energy of the attending media began to bubble over. Wagner waited unsuccessfully for the crowd to calm. "As we announced in our last press conference, we do not believe the murders committed this summer in Everett, the two Vallesteros sisters and Kathy

Simmons, are the work of the Green River Killer. But we do believe all three were committed by the same man. A serial killer. A serial killer hiding in plain sight."

Wagner motioned for Detective Nizzi to join him at the podium. The tension in the room was felt by all. "Today our officers will be making an arrest."

Nick bellowed in a loud clear voice. "In fact, we're making an arrest, RIGHT NOW!"

He pointed to the back of the room. "Julian Hopkins, you are under arrest for the murders of Kathy Simmons and Dari and Jesiree Vallesteros."

Hargrove had been waiting by the rear door. He quickly strode over and stood Julian up by his shirt. Julian's notebook flew off his lap. The detective spun him around and snapped a handcuff on his wrist. Using more force than needed, Hargrove yanked his other arm around to finish the cuffing. The loud snap broke the tense air. People gasped. Francis Bernard sprang out of the way, spilling his coffee on the reporter in front of him. The room erupted.

Lindsay Fiori jumped up and screamed, "NO!"

"What are you talking about?" Julian cried. "You're making a terrible mistake. I haven't killed anybody. You have the wrong guy! You *know* you have the wrong guy!"

With great theatrics, Hargrove held Julian up and paraded him out the back door. Cameras rolled. Light bulbs flashed. In an instant, the room turned to chaos as reporters jostled to get their cameras positioned for a better shot. For the first time in her fifteen-year career as a hard news reporter, Callie Calloway from KOMO-TV fainted.

The detective half-marched, half-shoved Julian down the hall and pushed him into the same small interrogation room he had been in before. Hargrove read him his Miranda rights, and forced him down into a hard metal chair. It was as cold as the officer's tone.

"You stay right there. You … you, murderous asshole. I knew it was you all along."

He stomped to the door, yanked it open, and slammed it shut as he left. Julian pinched his nose between closed eyes and pressed hard, trying to stop the loud ringing in his inner ear. Was this really happening? What the fuck is going on here? His DNA? How?

A short time later, after the press room had emptied, Nizzi and Hargrove walked in together and sat across from Julian. Nick, in seeming disbelief, mandated, "Julian Hopkins, you are under arrest for three counts of aggravated murder in the first degree. We tried to arrest you at your house on Kromer last night, but you weren't there. We knew you owned a pistol, you told us that, and we were worried you might try to use it. So, we figured this would be the safest way for everyone. A press conference at the station after you were checked by security. And it worked. We've got you now. It's time to come clean."

Hargrove tossed on the table an evidence bag. Inside were a pair of dandelion-yellow panties with dancing bunnies on them. Julian choked. He immediately remembered them as the ones Hannah Miller had been wearing that fateful, stormy night in Dillingham.

"Recognize those, huh? You of all people should have known the DNA on those would perfectly match yours. You ... sick bastard. We just read your article on DNA this week! You thought you were smarter than us, didn't you?"

Julian shook his head, incapable of speaking.

Hargrove hissed, "Well, you're NOT! You'll burn for this, you son of a bitch. We've got you now. You'll probably get the death penalty for this. And I hope you DO!"

Julian felt something treacherous, something frightful, something sinister attack his core. His heart missed a beat then raced out of control. Sweat poured from his brow and the pits of his arms. His face and neck grew hot. The realization that he was a victim of complete deception overpowered all rational thought. He wanted to cry out and run, take flight in any direction, get away. Uncontrollable waves of panic swept over him.

"I didn't do it," he pleaded, voice cracking. "I didn't kill them. I've been framed."

Hargrove slammed his fist on the table. "Let me guess. Lev Warrens?"

"Yes! Lev Warrens. He worked in the laundry. I bet he took those. They're Hannah Miller's, I think. He had access to them, it must be him.

*He* killed Kathy Simmons and must have planted Hannah's underwear to frame me for it. I'm not a murderer. You *have* to believe me!"

"Well, I *don't* believe you," Hargrove bellowed. "YOU killed Kathy Simmons. YOU killed the Filipino sisters. DNA doesn't lie, you son of a bitch. We've got you dead to rights and now you're gonna pay."

His words exploded in Julian's head like a cherry bomb. The same words Lev used. You're gonna pay *bad* for this, Julian Hopkins. You're gonna pay!

"Hold on. Hold on," Nick reeled Hargrove back. He was skeptical of Julian's excuses, but still wanted to give him the benefit of the doubt.

"Hopkins, why is your DNA on Kathy's underwear?"

"Hannah Miller and I had sex. Once. It was a mistake. I … I've been framed. I didn't kill anybody. And I'm not saying another word until I get a lawyer."

Frustrated, the detectives peppered Julian with more questions, but he remained silent. Eventually, they left the room. In complete despair, Julian put his head on the table. Lev's final threat echoed in his head. You'll pay *bad* for this, Julian Hopkins. You're gonna pay. *What the fuck did I do to deserve this? Does Lev think I ratted him out for stealing? I bet that's it. Does he think I'm the reason he got fired?* But Lev had also tried to attack Hannah. And Boone. And Archie. And Reuben. He must hate them too. *Maybe he just hates everyone?* Julian's body began to shake. He slammed his fist on the table. The loud sound echoed off the walls. He yelled and kicked a chair across the room, pacing like a caged wolf.

"Find Lev Warrens, you dumb fuckin' jackasses!"

"He's lying," Hargrove sneered from behind the two-way mirror. "He knows we've got him red-handed and now he's grasping for straws. There's our serial killer right there having a fit."

"You may be right. But still none of this sits well with me," Nick answered. "We're probably looking at a capital case here and we positively need to get it right. A man's life is at stake. So just to be sure, we *do* need to track down Lev Warrens. In the meantime, Julian Hopkins will have plenty of time to sit and think about things in the county jail."

"He can rot in prison for all I care," Hargrove growled. "Listen to him. He's a goddam wild animal in there. At least he's behind bars where he belongs."

# CHAPTER 33

# BRADLEY K. JAMISON

W hispers. From the far end of the corridor he heard whispers. Muddled by the cold, cement confines of the Snohomish County jail, Julian couldn't make out the words. He pressed his ear through the bars. There they were again. Were they whispering about him? Of course, they were. He hadn't slept since he'd been pushed into this tight, empty dungeon, and the jumble of his thoughts—combined with a body-gripping, one-piece orange suit—made it hard for him to breathe. What time was it anyway? Through the blur of uncertainty, he struggled to make sense of what had happened. Jesus. The press conference. His job at the newspaper. Francis Bernard. Lindsay. He shuddered at the vision of her anguished face as he was being led out by Detective Hargrove. Did all that truly happen? Three counts of murder? Serial Killer? The death penalty? TV news must be having a heyday. Julian laid down on his bunk and covered his head with his pillow. He didn't want to hear the muffled sounds of freedom outside. The distant whistle of a train. The honk of a horn. A lid dropping on a dumpster. And the whispers.

"Hopkins, you have a visitor."

Julian said nothing. He didn't move. He couldn't distinguish real from illusion anymore.

"Hopkins?"

Julian rolled over as the man jangled his keys in search for the one to open his cell door.

"Who?"

"Come with me and find out."

The jailer snapped on a pair of handcuffs and led Julian down a desolate hall, eventually pushing him into a small room. As if produced by a phone booth, a tall energetic gentleman in an expensive blue suit and crisp-red tie stepped forward to greet him. In one rhythmic motion he popped open a briefcase and flashed Julian his business card: Bradley K. Jamison, Attorney at Law.

"Mr. Hopkins, I'm here to offer you my services."

"It's Julian," he mumbled.

"Julian. That's good. Julian, I've been following your drama very closely. For lord's sake son, who hasn't? Didn't you get the memo about keeping a low profile? You're the top thing on the news right now. In any regard, there are many rights we can assert for you, even more than the ones provided by the U.S. Constitution. You're protected by the rules of self-incrimination, illegal search and seizures, and the Miranda Law. We'll explore them all … and more, to get your charges reduced. Or dropped altogether at your arraignment hearing when you plead 'not guilty.' You are 'not guilty,' aren't you?"

Julian's eyes brimmed with skepticism.

"I've worked on quite a few murder cases through the years and I'm good at what I do, son. That is, of course, if you want my help."

Julian swallowed away the dryness in his throat.

"Why?" he stammered. "Why are you helping me?"

"Let's just say Bob Clayton and I are old friends. I've been handling all the Dragline business since his Old Man put out the company shingle many years ago. Bob returned from Alaska last night and told me all about you. Mike Matthews set him straight and Bob feels responsible for allowing Lev Warrens into the Dillingham camp. They both know you didn't commit these crimes, and he's ridden with guilt for not telling the detectives about Lev early on in their investigation. Bob's prepared to post your bail."

Julian looked down at the card again. He breathed deeply. Maybe there was a way out of this after all. He tried to think of something clever to say, couldn't, and simply nodded.

"Alright. I'll consider that a successful job interview. I get the feeling there is more to your story than meets the eye. Much more. Let's hear it. And please start at the very beginning, son. I've got all day."

∽⚬∾

Francis Bernard felt like he had been kicked in the stomach by a Missouri mule. An Associated Press videographer had caught the arrest on camera and the stunning footage had been played and replayed on every news station ever since. Never in his twenty-eight years as a professional journalist had he been blindsided like he had been in that press conference. And the story Lindsay Fiori was telling him now? It sounded so wild and unbelievable it almost had to be true.

"Julian didn't do it," she cried. "There's a killer running loose named Lev Warrens and he's framing Julian for his crimes. Julian said they worked together last summer in Alaska."

"And you believe him?"

"YES!"

Lindsay recounted for Bernard everything she knew—the vague tidbits of information Julian had shared with her. How she had called Native American tribal centers throughout the Northwest, especially the ones close to rivers that had returning wild Sockeye salmon populations. How Julian had been hunting for him up and down coastal rivers and lakes. The elder newsman listened intently before speaking.

"Why would this person want to frame Julian?"

"That, I don't know. Julian doesn't either. The man is a maniac. A homicidal maniac."

"Do the police know about him?"

"Yes! Julian spoke with Detectives Nizzi and Hargrove last week. They met. Even before he told me. They told Julian they'd track Lev down, but obviously that hasn't happened. We've been trying to locate him too, but there's nothing."

"Have you tried the Department of Motor Vehicles, the Social Security Administration, and the IRS? They won't give you Warrens' information, but they might tell you if they have record of him and they would certainly turn those over to homicide investigators. *If* the man exists, of course."

"We've called all those places. Julian questions whether Lev Warrens is even his real name."

Bernard locked eyes with his star reporter and shook his head, she'd given him that look before. She wanted something from him, and he knew he wasn't going to like it. "What are you asking me to do, Fiori?"

"Nothing. I just need more time. I'm going to find Lev Warrens myself."

"No. You are not. And I'm afraid time is something I don't control."

Bernard stared into the afflicted-crying eyes of Lindsay Fiori. He grew silent and gazed at the framed Pulitzers on the wall before sitting and putting his head in his hands. The editor had seen a story like this one play out before. Two years earlier, the Seattle media had nearly ruined an innocent man's life while covering the Green River Killer investigation. The P-R had been a part of it too, at his discretion. Desperate for closure, the Task Force had notified the media they had a prime suspect in custody, the man had failed a lie detector test, and they were offering him psychiatric treatment in exchange for a confession. But after no evidence was found connecting the man to any of the crimes, he was released without charges or an arrest, but not before having his reputation permanently crucified by news coverage implicating him of being the notorious serial killer. Bernard looked up at Lindsay.

"Look, I'll make some calls to see what I can find out. Police Chief Wagner owes me a favor or two, but don't get your hopes up. I doubt he'll tell me anything we don't already know. If Julian really is being framed by some mystery co-worker named Lev Warrens, or whoever he is, and if the man is culpable like you say, this is a huge miscarriage of justice. But right now, it *is* my responsibility to ensure the P-R covers the facts as we know them fairly and accurately. There was, after all, an arrest, and a very public one at that. We can't just ignore the facts. No matter how we might feel about it."

The next morning the front-page headline of the *Seattle Post-Register* read: P-R REPORTER ARRESTED FOR MURDER.

∽✤∾

Dragline Human Resources Manager, Jane Ellis, sat in a corner chair trying to look inconspicuous behind a magazine when Nick arrived in the Everett PD lobby to welcome her. Outside it was overcast and rainy. She was hiding behind dark sunglasses, a wide-brimmed hat, and an overcoat.

"Can we go somewhere more private?" she stammered in a hushed voice, barely daring to breathe. "I have something I need to get off my conscience. Something I need to tell you. Alone."

Puzzled, the detective led her back to his office and closed the door.

"I quit my job and I'm moving away. The shame is unbearable, and I just can't hold it in anymore. Bob Clayton hasn't been telling you the whole truth. Lev Warrens *was* an employee, kind of, and he *was* at our Dragline Dillingham processing facility both this summer and last. He flew up with Venju del Prado's Filipino laundry crew and was probably at the bunkhouse the weekend the Vallesteros sisters were murdered. The weekend of June third."

The detective nearly choked on his coffee. "Can I call my partner in for this? This is something he needs to hear."

She nodded. Nick left the room and returned with Hargrove.

"Go on, Jane. Please finish."

"Dragline uses illegal hiring methods. We're not the only ones. Many in the Alaska fishing industry do. So do the fruit pickers up and down the West Coast. It's been going on for years, for as long as I've worked in this business."

"What do you mean by illegal hiring methods?"

"It's not easy to hire hundreds of workers all at once for seasonal jobs that last only a couple of months. We try to advertise in college newspapers, and we do get a bunch of people that way, but hiring is still a wild scramble. I can never seem to keep up. No matter how hard I try, it always seems like we're short most seasons and always at the times we need labor the most."

Hargrove started to ask a question. Nick silenced him.

"So, each year we form business arrangements with Mexican, Filipino, and sometimes Japanese crew bosses to have them do some of the hiring for us. Rather than deal with the headache of having each of their individual workers on our payroll, Dragline hires the boss, LLC. They then hire as many workers as we need. It's his responsibility to handle problems as they arise and make sure they show up on time, work hard, and do their jobs. He buys them airline tickets which we then reimburse. We pay him, and he pays his workers. In return, the crew bosses keep a cut of each worker's pay. I know they do. We don't know what deals they make with their workers. We don't know their names, where they came from, or even if they are legal to work in this country. Other than the bosses, most of them don't even speak English."

Jane welled up, overcome by the confession of her long-hidden mendacity. "I know it's dirty, but it's the only way we can fill our production crews some years."

Nick sensed Hargrove's rage erupting and shushed him with a finger over his lips. She regained her composure. "That's why Bob didn't tell you Lev Warrens was a Dragline employee. And technically, he wasn't. He wasn't on our payroll. I tried to explain it to you earlier, the last time I was here. *I did.* But Bob told me not to. He said, 'Zip your lips.' But I had to tell you. I can't sleep. I feel responsible. Lev Warrens was up there in Alaska this summer. And when his co-workers spoke with me as they got back from Dillingham, they all admitted to being scared of him. Scared to freaking death."

⌘

Snohomish County Prosecutor Adam Lee Hayes had never lost a case. Divinely driven and dog determined, he had the reputation for doing whatever it took to win. For years, people said he had his eyes on the prize of one day being state governor. When questioned about it periodically by the press, he always laughed, but never denied it. Along with

Medical Examiner Johnson, Hayes was convinced the DNA evidence was indisputable and made their argument a slam dunk. In interviews with reporters after the arrest, both men boldly touted the big picture ramifications of the trial and how it was going to be the catalyst case to get a national DNA data bank established and DNA labs created in every major city. Police departments, commentators, and television viewers across the country were captivated. Forensic science needed a guilty verdict. There could be no doubt of its certainty. As he poured unlimited resources into building his strategy, the prosecutor boasted time-and-time again, this would be the one.

While Johnson and Hayes oozed confidence, behind the scenes, Nizzi was wracked with doubt. Hargrove was no help… he'd jumped on the DNA bandwagon too. Divers who were sent to locate the murder weapon in the Snohomish River returned empty-handed. Hayes promptly sent them back to dive it again. The wooded knoll where the Vallesteros sisters were found was scoured so many times it was now beaten down like a park. Potential witnesses were interviewed, re-interviewed, and reluctantly released. Motive was still a guess. Jane Ellis had confirmed for them that Lev Warrens truly *did* exist. Lev *had* worked at the Dragline Dillingham laundry, and he *had* been in Everett the weekend of the Vallesteros murders. And then she skipped town. But nobody wanted to talk about that, nobody seemed to listen. Was Julian Hopkins truly innocent? Why was he the only one concerned they had arrested the wrong man?

Nick carried his concerns to Chief Wagner who for a while listened intently, but in the end said it was out of his hands. The excitement and potential of DNA science had infiltrated his department too deeply and besides, all his resources had been allocated to strengthening the case against Hopkins. They were a band fully committed to finishing the song they'd started, the only option was forward, and it was far too late to change the tune now.

"I'm sick and tired of hearing about Lev Warrens, or whoever he is," Hayes castigated him. "You've called every state agency you can think of and the federal ones too. No one has a record of issuing him a driver's license. Either that's not his real name, or you're looking for an invisible man. And even if he *does* exist, it doesn't make him our killer. We have no evidence against him. Stay focused on the hard evidence, detective! DNA points directly at Julian Hopkins. And DNA doesn't lie. Keep looking for that murder weapon. And when this goes to trial, we'll let a jury decide."

# CHAPTER 34

# PRELIMINARY HEARING

At the heart of Everett on a meticulously raked and manicured grassy hill, ancient oak trees guarded the pillared-white historic Snohomish County courthouse like sentry. From Rockefeller Avenue, an exhausting stack of white-bleached steps stretched up to open doors where they turned to shiny-waxed wood. Inside, lavish halls led to expensively decorated offices and meeting rooms. Like a bread-crumb trail, dusty framed black-and-white pictures of prestigious judges from the past hundred years led visitors to the center of the second floor, where a grand courtroom hosted the county's biggest trials. And in this room, the much-anticipated preliminary hearing of Julian Hopkins' triple murder case began on a Tuesday morning in early October.

Judge Elizabeth Rollins had been watching the Julian Hopkins drama unfold all summer, it was impossible not to. She knew he worked as a reporter for the *Seattle Post-Register* and was acutely aware how pivotal these proceedings could be for the future of DNA forensic science. Hearings didn't get more high profile than this one, and like everyone else in the region, she had been glued to the news. But even so, in her seventeen years on the bench, she had never been swayed by outside influences and she wasn't going to let that start now. Today she would not rule guilt or innocence, but simply whether or not the State had strong enough evidence against Hopkins to move forward with a jury trial.

Even though the hearing was simply a "trial before the trial," the event did not go unnoticed. Far from it. Over the past few weeks, DNA had been discussed on every news show on every channel. Was Julian Hopkins the Northend Copycat Killer? Would DNA convince the judge to allow for a jury trial? Would this become the benchmark conviction authorities had been waiting to find? If so, would DNA forensics be used to capture the Green River Killer and solve countless other unsolved tragedies nationwide? Amid such media interest, Judge Rollins agreed to let cameras in the courtroom, under the condition no civilian witness faces would be shown.

"Today the court will hear the case People versus Julian Hopkins," opened the judge. "The defendant is charged with three counts of Aggravated Murder in the First Degree and has already entered a plea of Not Guilty. The Snohomish County prosecuting attorney will be presenting his argument with the aid of two sequestered witnesses. The Defense will have a chance to cross-examine and are scheduled to present three witnesses of their own. Prosecutor Hayes, it's your courtroom."

Before he delivered his opening statement, Hayes eyed the gallery. In addition to the media and dozens of curious Everett residents, Kathy Simmons' family and many of her friends were in attendance. The Vallesteros would not be there until the jury trial began, but Venju del Prado had flown back to represent the Filipino community. Preliminary hearings didn't usually draw crowds this big, but on that day, every seat in the open court was filled and some members of the media spilled out into the hall.

In the three weeks since Julian had been arrested, his office had cut no corners and spared no expense. Hayes had bolstered the detective squad and requested extra manpower from the FBI. Today was a formality. He was saving his best show for a jury. Hayes had spent most of his career working on cases involving violent criminals and had stood in front of dozens of judges and juries in murder trials. But this one was like no other. He was convinced the State's facts and his carefully organized evidence was strong enough to make the judge rule for a jury trial for all three crimes. And this time he had DNA. Perhaps this would be the catalyst that would jettison his career into politics like a rocket. At least that's what he hoped as he looked out confidently across the room.

"Your Honor, I'm going to prove to you with indisputable evidence and compelling witness testimony, the defendant, Julian Hopkins, committed three counts of Aggravated Murder in the First Degree. The State is convinced Hopkins is guilty of these extremely cruel and violent, premeditated, cold-blooded acts of violence. Justice must be served. A jury must be selected, and we must take this to trial. Julian Hopkins is a serial killer. And he needs to *pay* for what he has done."

Seated next to Attorney Jamison at the defense table with a fresh haircut and fitted blue suit, Julian closed his eyes and cringed when he heard those words.

"On the night of August twentieth, Julian Hopkins left his workplace, the *Seattle Post-Register* newspaper office in downtown Seattle around ten thirty. We have a witness who will testify speaking with him as he left. On his way home, we believe Hopkins encountered Kathy Simmons outside the Lighthouse Pub, which is nine blocks from where he lives. Witnesses reported seeing a man in a pickup truck, possibly the same make, model, and color as the defendant's, outside the bar. The victim was visibly drunk, walking home alone in the rain and vulnerable. An easy target for a man motivated by sex. We believe Hopkins coerced Kathy Simmons to get into his truck with the intent of propositioning her to take part in lascivious deeds. When she refused his advances, Hopkins got angry and hit her on the back of the head with the tire iron we found under his seat. After she was knocked unconscious, he raped her."

Hayes turned to the crowd to make sure his dramatics were having their intended effect. They were. Kathy Simmons' family cried. Cameras rolled. Reporters were scribbling notes. All eyes were riveted on him as intended.

"Hopkins panicked when he realized how bad her injury was, or maybe he feared she would recognize him and turn him in for rape, in either case, we believe he drove her to the first wooded area he came to, Rotary Park in Lowell, where he killed her by cutting her throat. Hopkins then tried to mask his crime. He made several trips back to his truck to get what he needed to pose her suggestively to make it look like a Green River Killer crime. As a newspaper journalist, he would have had access to Task Force files and probably thought he could use the Green River Killer's signature to lead us away from his own trail. Hopkins *knew* how the Green River serial killer left *his* victims. And his plan may have worked ... except for two crucial details. First, he dropped one of his belongings near the body. Detectives at the crime scene recovered a uniquely marked fishing lure the defendant admitted in a documented police interview belonged to him. It was drawn on with his own hand with a black permanent marker. But most damning, and the crux of State's evidence, Julian Hopkins left his DNA on the underwear he so vilely stuffed in Kathy Simmons mouth. And we can prove it positively matches DNA he provided with his saliva sample to detectives under a condition of a legal search warrant."

Hayes paused, removed his glasses and made eye contact with the judge. He turned to look at Kathy Simmons' family again, before continuing solemnly. "I'm prepared to show photographs of all his heinous crimes. I have witness testimony to prove Hopkins was in the area on both fatal nights our three victims were killed, and we have physical evidence that proves his guilt. He had the means. He had the motive. And he had the opportunity."

The judge spoke for the first time. "And the murdered Vallesteros sisters from the Philippines? Jesiree and Dari? Do you have DNA evidence for them as well?"

"We do not, Your Honor. Their bodies were so decomposed that no usable DNA from the killer was recovered on their clothes or bodies. But we do know the cause and manner of their deaths were identical to that of Kathy Simmons. It was unique. We can prove it. You'll soon hear from our medical examiner who is prepared to show that the same weapons, a tire iron and knife, were used in all three murders, and the same injuries were made on all three victims. We believe the motive, sex, was the same in that crime. Hopkins was in town at the time they were killed, with no strong alibis for his whereabouts. Once again, we believe he had the means to kill the Vallesteros sisters, and we have this..."

Hayes held up the gold salmon necklace found in Julian's apartment.

"This belonged to one of the victims, either Jesiree or Dari, made in the Philippines and presented as a gift to each girl by their parents before they left. Their mother positively identified it. Both girls were wearing those necklaces when they left for America the day before they were so brutally murdered. We only recovered one. Hopkins had it hanging in his apartment next to his bed. He's your killer, Your Honor. We believe we can convict him of these unconscionable murders, positively and unequivocally. We plan to seek the death penalty."

The courtroom sat spellbound. The judge raised her eyebrows.

"With your permission, Your Honor, I'd first like to call to the stand Snohomish County medical examiner, Dr. Richard Johnson. Doctor, please share with us why you believe the weapons used were the same on all three victims."

Through autopsy and crime scene photos, Johnson described for the judge in meticulous detail how he found identical, unique wounds on the base of the skulls of all three victims. He produced photographs of the tire iron measurements compared to the victim's trauma wounds. "The same weapon made these three wounds, Your Honor. We believe that weapon was Julian Hopkins' tire iron."

Satisfied, Hayes produced several blown-up pictures of the underwear stuffed in Kathy Simmons' mouth. The victim's sister screamed and was led out of court. As the audience settled, Hayes continued. "Tell us about the victim's panties, Dr. Johnson. Were you able to extract a DNA finger-print from them?"

"As a matter of fact, we were," Johnson straightened his shoulders and spoke in his signature booming voice loud enough for the reporters sitting in the back of the room to hear. "There was sperm on her under-wear and my scientists, and I were able to extract DNA from it. From there, our lab positively identified it as belonging to Julian Hopkins from DNA on the saliva sample obtained by detectives. It was a perfect match. The FBI confirmed. We are one in twenty million times positive."

More courtroom murmurings. The judge silenced them with her gavel. On further questioning, Johnson explained in fastidious detail how DNA testing was done and how DNA had successfully been used as the lynchpin to convict a serial rapist in Florida.

"DNA is a precise science that will change the entire legal system as we know it," he boasted. "Unsolved cases across the country can now be solved using DNA to link killers to crimes."

He turned dramatically to the judge. "The future for using DNA in Washington State and across the country starts today, here in this courtroom, Your Honor."

More whispers from the audience. Julian shuddered and closed his eyes. Judge Rollins turned to Julian's lawyer, Bradley Jamison.

"Your witness," she directed.

"Dr. Johnson, during your thorough testing, were you able to determine how old the semen on the underwear was? How long it had been there?"

Johnson shuffled uncomfortably in his chair. "No, we did not test the age of the semen. Just the origin."

"Then is it possible, it could have been two months old?"

"I guess. I mean I don't know how to answer that," Johnson grew tense. He was not used to being questioned like this. Everyone else accepted his word as the gospel truth. How dare this lawyer doubt him. What did he know about forensic science anyway?

"And if it is possible that the evidence was two months old, is it also possible that the evidence was planted, to frame my client?"

"Objection, Your Honor," Hayes yelled.

But Dr. Johnson had already taken the bait. Before the judge could stop him, he shot back, "It's a new science. I suppose anything is possible, Attorney Jamison."

"No further questions, Your Honor," Jamison concealed a smile as he marched back to his seat.

Next to the stand, Hayes called Detective Nick Nizzi. As the lead officer was being sworn in and seated, Hayes placed on easels blown-up graphic crime scene photographs of both Kathy Simmons and the Vallesteros sisters. The crowd groaned. A few left. Some cried. As bloody and gruesome as the photographs were, the judge ruled them admissible because their probative value outweighed their prejudicial effect.

"Lieutenant Nizzi, please walk us through the discovery and crime scenes of each of the three victims, starting with the most recent, Kathy Simmons."

Nick gave a painstaking account of the day her body was discovered. He told the judge how they had ruled out the owner of the Blazer, searched Kathy's apartment, spoke with those close to the victim including the ex-husband, and drove the route from the Lighthouse Pub to the crime scene. He pointed to the photos of the underwear in her mouth, stating they were immediately turned over to the medical examiner for DNA testing. He recounted the press conference, heavy media coverage, and viewer tips that came in afterward.

"We initially thought we were dealing with the Green River Killer, an investigation I had worked on for years," Nick explained. "But after speaking with the FBI and Task Force, we unanimously ruled that out."

The judge quizzed him over what was said in that meeting and who was in attendance. She made him describe his process and walk through the chain of custody for evidence found at the scene, especially the underwear. Seeing she was satisfied, Hayes approached Nizzi on the stand.

"Your Honor, I would like to introduce another crucial piece of evidence," Hayes held up the pink Pixie fishing lure with black dots still sealed in an evidence bag. He handed it to Nick. "Detective, what can you tell us about this?"

"My partner and I found that in Julian Hopkins' tackle box during our first search of his home. The box had his name on it written in his own writing. That one exactly matches the one we found in the weeds five feet away from the body of Kathy Simmons."

Hayes tapped on the blown-up photos of the two lures side by side. Onlookers ribbed each other and whispered amongst themselves. The judge nodded. No doubt about it. They indeed matched.

"Those black dots were unmistakably drawn with the same technique and were done by the same person. We have spoken with over a dozen different sports fishermen and none of them have ever seen these types of lures altered like this before. This is unique to Julian Hopkins, and he has admitted that he marks his like that. He also admitted that the lure was his in a recorded interview at the station."

The judge took more notes before turning to Nick. "That evidence does seem convincing, detective. Have you located the murder weapon as well?"

"We recovered the tire iron in his truck that we believe he used to knock out each of his three victims, but we have not yet recovered the blade that made the fatal wounds. Knives are sometimes hard to find, and easy to dispose. So, no, we have not, but we're still looking. We have had divers go in the river on three separate occasions, and we've searched the defendant's apartment and vehicle thoroughly. Hopefully, we'll find it before the trial."

The prosecutor knew this was a huge weakness in his case but was so confident in the strength of the DNA, he was banking on the hope that the judge would look past it.

She continued, "Detective Nizzi, have you spoken with any witnesses who can place Hopkins at the scene of the crime, or gotten any form of confession?"

"Several callers after our press conference reported seeing a pickup truck outside the Lighthouse Pub that night driven by a male who could easily have been Hopkins. But unfortunately, none of them could pick him out of a photo lineup."

The judge took notes on a pad of paper before turning to Jamison. "Defense Attorney Jamison, it's your turn to cross-examine the witness."

Jamison stood up and calmly approached the stand. "Detective Nizzi, why would Julian Hopkins leave a fishing lure at the crime scene? If those markings are as unique as you say, doesn't that seem a bit odd—like pointing a finger at yourself in the mirror?"

"Every murder scene is odd," Nick responded. "Why he left it there, we can only speculate. It's possible he dropped it there by accident. My partner thinks he left it as a calling card."

Jamison took several steps toward the audience and startled the judge when he suddenly twirled back to Nizzi and demanded in a commanding voice, "Detective, is it possible someone else left it there to make it look like Julian Hopkins was the killer?"

"Anything is possible, I guess," Nick spared a glance at the judge. "But in my experience, that would be quite a stretch."

Bradley Jamison took off his glasses and pointed them toward the stand. He had spent many hours readying himself to cross-examine each of the witnesses for the prosecution. With his staff he had diagrammed tactics to challenge the credibility of each. He had especially been waiting for Nizzi, an honest man he knew was haunted by the unsolved Green River murders. "Isn't it true that you tried to find a man named Lev Warrens regarding this murder *after* Julian Hopkins was arrested and sitting in jail?"

"Yes, that's true." Nick sighed. "Hopkins and several others implicated a man named Lev Warrens as a potential suspect and we wanted to make sure we explored every possibility. Unfortunately, there was no record of him, and he couldn't be found. Believe me, we tried. As far as we can prove, Lev Warrens is a man who has learned to be invisible– a ghost if you will."

Jamison pounced. "And in your opinion, is that type of man devious?"

"Sure."

"Maybe capable of killing and getting away with it, scot free?"

"Possibly."

"Yes, Detective Nizzi—quite possibly, maybe even probably. Tell us, do you personally believe Julian Hopkins is responsible for these three murders? Or do you think it was Lev Warrens? A man you just admitted is devious and you can't find?"

Nick Nizzi closed his eyes and sighed. Jamison was right. His failure to catch the Green River Killer had cost him his job, two wives, his ability to sleep, his sanity. And now another serial murderer he couldn't seem to catch was eluding him too. *He needed closure! But only if it was the right man.* He shifted uncomfortably in his seat but did not reply.

"I object, Your Honor!" yelled Hayes.

"Objection granted. Do you have any other questions, Attorney Jamison?"

"I have no further questions, Your Honor. Thank you, Lieutenant Nizzi."

As he traipsed back to his seat, Jamison gave Julian a sly wink. He took a drink of water. Murmurs broke out in the courtroom. The damage was done. The lead investigator on the case had clearly displayed a seed of doubt to Julian's guilt … and confirmed the existence of a mystery man. Hayes asked for and was granted a recess for lunch.

# CHAPTER 35

# DEFENSE WITNESSES

After a one-hour recess, a time that every television reporter in attendance used to send live shots back to their noonday news shows, Bradley K. Jamison stood and approached the bench.

"Your Honor, Julian Hopkins is innocent of these crimes and we will prove it. He has a sparkling-clean record and no history of deviant behavior of any kind. There's no proof that he knew any of these victims at all. The prosecutor has no witnesses he can produce who can show otherwise. The sex motive suggested by the State is ridiculous and no murder weapon has ever been found. The DNA found at the scene with Kathy Simmons was planted, as was the fishing lure. And the necklace was given to him by a friend in Alaska who will corroborate that fact. If it weren't for planted DNA, false evidence, and this case's high profile, it would have been thrown out long ago."

"Go on, Attorney Jamison. Tell me why you think evidence was planted."

Jamison glanced across the courtroom and approached the judge. "Your Honor, I want to tell you the story of an angry man. A spiteful man. A vicious man. A murderous man. His name is Lev Warrens, or at least that's what he told everyone his name was. He worked for two summers with Julian Hopkins at Dragline Fisheries in Dillingham and threatened to do him harm in an extremely violent and vicious way when he was fired for being a thief back in July. We have sequestered witnesses—who we expect to arrive any minute now—who will corroborate hearing those threats. Lev Warrens is the real killer and he framed the defendant for reasons only a psychopath could understand. Like us, the Everett PD have been trying to find him. But the man is still on the loose. This afternoon, through reason, logic, and witness testimony, I'll show you that Julian Hopkins did not commit these crimes and there is no evidence or testimony strong enough to put in front of a jury. The killer of these women is still out there. Julian Hopkins is an innocent victim and he must be set free!"

The judge raised her eyes at Hayes, before refocusing on Jamison. "Then it is your courtroom, Mr. Jamison. Please introduce your witnesses."

Jamison looked at his watch and whispered in Julian's ear. Julian nodded. "Your Honor, our first witness is Boone Davis, who worked with the defendant in Alaska, and has flown in from Colorado. Mr. Davis, please share with the court your experience the day you went fishing with the defendant and Lev Warrens."

Boone explained how he and Julian fished together often and gave the history of why Julian drew eyes on his lures. He relived the day of the Agulowak fishing trip, leaving out the part where Chris had been demeaning to Lev, and told everyone how Julian had shared his gear with the older man.

"Lev Warrens fished with Julian's gear all day. He could have easily pocketed that lure."

Jamison approached the bench, holding up the police composite sketch created by the Kathy Simmons tipster blown-up to poster size. He turned so everyone in the courtroom could see it before placing it on an easel in front of Boone.

"Mr. Davis, can you please tell me who the man in this sketch resembles?"

"Lev Warrens. That picture is a dead ringer for Lev Warrens."

As the courtroom reacted to the revelation and slowly settled down, Jamison walked over and whispered in Julian's ear, "They're late. They're not going to make it."

"Boone likes to talk," Julian replied in desperation.

Seemingly reinvigorated, Jamison asked a series of other questions as he kept a mindful eye on his watch. For over an hour, he prompted Boone to talk about the fish season, the summer, the storm, Dave's drowning, finding Eddie Chiklak under the dock, the Dragline plant, Pete's cooking. The courtroom audience lost interest and began fidgeting in their seats. The judge finally stopped the shenanigans. "Mr. Jamison, I fail to see how anything you have asked in the last hour has anything to do with this case. Prosecutor Hayes, do you want to cross examine the witness?"

Jamison nervously eyed his watch as Hayes rolled his eyes and declined. Suddenly, the courtroom doors popped open, Mike Matthews and Hannah Miller burst in, escorted by Bob Clayton who had just sped them straight there after picking them up at SeaTac airport. Hayes threw his arms up in exasperation. Jamison glared at Clayton, calmed his nerves with a loud nose breath, and turned to the judge with a virtuous smile.

"Your Honor, I'd like to call to the stand, Dragline Fisheries Dillingham plant manager, Mike Matthews."

Mike, still dressed in flannel and jeans after a long flight, was seated and quickly sworn in.

"Mr. Matthews, was a man named Lev Warrens an employee at Dragline Dillingham last summer?"

"Yes. He was a contract employee with the Filipino laundry crew."

"Please explain to the judge what a contract employee means."

Mike had briefed with Clayton and Jamison on the phone the day before and the three had settled on their defense strategy. Reluctantly, Clayton had agreed that Dragline's illegal hiring methods needed to be shared with the court, for Julian's sake. Mike explained it to the judge. Visibly upset, both Prosecutor Hayes and Judge Rollins took notes and silently vowed to pursue that legal issue with Dragline at a future date. Jamison continued his line of questioning.

"Mr. Matthews, is it true, Lev Warrens left under, let's say, not so happy terms?"

"That's an understatement."

Mike recounted the complete story of how the room-to-room search was conducted and how stolen items were found in Lev's possession, including several pairs of women's underwear. He then relived the incident in the breakroom along with the threats and violence that ensued.

"Mr. Matthews, do you remember if Lev spoke with the defendant on that day?"

"Oh yeah. Lev screamed and swore at Julian as he was being taken out of the plant to the airport. He had to be restrained and carried. The last thing I remember Lev saying was how he would make Julian pay."

"Make him pay? Pay for what? Did the defendant owe him money?"

"I interpreted it as a threat of revenge. For what, I do not know. It was a heated situation. One of my employees got bit and later had to be taken to the hospital. I was worried Lev would hurt others as well."

"Did you think Lev was going to kill someone?"

"Yes."

"How about Julian? Do you think he has the capacity to kill a person?"

"Absolutely no way. Julian has been a witness to many violent situations, like fights, through the years in Alaska and has always showed great sanity and restraint."

"So, you've never seen Julian Hopkins in a fit of rage?"

"No, I have not," answered Mike Matthews. "In fact, Julian is the leader who I rely on to break fights up, not start them."

"And Mr. Warrens?"

"I'll never forget the look in Lev's eyes the day he left. I don't know where Lev Warrens went after he left Dillingham, but judging from the way he was acting, I certainly wouldn't put it past him to do something like this. I can easily imagine him committing murder and trying to frame Julian Hopkins for his crimes. I always suspected he was a whole lot smarter than he let on."

Hayes declined cross examination and Mike was excused by the judge.

The final witness for the Defense was Hannah Miller. At first, she had refused to fly to Washington to help Julian, but after Jamison explained the severity of the charges against him, and how the police would close the book and stop looking for Lev if Julian was convicted, she agreed.

Because of midterm tests at her college, the defense attorney had flown her in that morning and scheduled her to leave right after she testified.

"Miss Miller, when you were in Alaska last summer did you present Julian Hopkins a gift?"

She lifted her eyes and peeked at Julian. He smiled back, hopeful.

"Yes. I gave him a friendship necklace."

Julian sighed in relief.

"Did it look like this?" Jamison handed her a gold chain necklace with a dangling, diamond-eyed salmon charm.

She inspected it closely and nodded. "Yes. That's the one."

"Miss Miller, do you remember where you got that friendship necklace?"

"Yes. Lev Warrens gave it to me."

Murmuring spread across the courtroom. Hayes dropped his head and shook it in disbelief.

"Miss Miller, do you recognize these panties?"

Hannah held the evidence bag in her hand for just a second before setting it down. "Yes. They're mine. They were stolen from my dirty laundry by Lev Warrens."

Hayes was desperate now. He looked at Medical Examiner Johnson, then at the judge. Incredulously, his airtight DNA case was slipping away before his eyes. He leaped out of his chair, knocking it over.

"Miss Miller. That pair of underwear was found in the mouth of murder victim Kathy Simmons. It was scientifically proven to contain the DNA of Julian Hopkins. Can you tell me how that could possibly be?"

Hannah looked out at the crowd. The room was coiled in silent suspense. She glanced at Julian, then Clayton, then at Judge Rollins. She dropped her eyes, squirmed in her chair, and in a soft voice she wished wasn't hers revealed, "Because Julian and I had sex."

The audience exploded. Venju del Prado stormed out of the room and kicked a trash can in the hall. It took flight and smashed into a far door. Because the Vallesteros family was holding him personally responsible for their daughters' murders, he had flown back from Manila and offered to be a witness against Julian for Prosecutor Hayes after it went to a jury.

He left the courthouse in tears of frustration. Judge Rollins smashed her gavel. "Order! Order in the court!"

Hayes knew his case was dismantled, especially when Judge Rollins left for her chambers and returned just ten minutes later.

"While the medical examiner's DNA forensic science is quite compelling, and the prosecutor has shown an elevated level of suspicion, the rest of the State's evidence is insufficient for charges of Aggravated Murder in the First Degree. There is no believable motive, Mr. Hayes, and until you present more evidence, it is my ruling that this case is not strong enough to take to a jury. Find the murder weapon, Prosecutor. And find Lev Warrens. Until you do, all charges against Julian Hopkins are hereby dismissed."

The courtroom was an unstoppable volcano, second eruption bigger than its first. The judge disappeared through her chamber's door. Julian tried to stand but collapsed back in his chair.

Shawna Owens screamed. "No! No! Don't set him free. He's a murderer!"

Lindsay rushed to Julian and threw her arms around him. Bradley Jamison swept his papers into his briefcase and turned to the pair. "Congratulations, young man. My work here is done. You are as free as a bird."

Julian hugged him, then Lindsay again. Around them, the mass of people paraded slowly toward the exit to the main hall. Julian turned to Lindsay. It was so loud he couldn't hear the words her lips were saying. Jamison motioned them to follow.

"Come with me, out the attorney's exit," he yelled. "You'll never make it out that way. It's a mob scene."

As Julian and Lindsay moved briskly behind the lawyer, a frenzied throng of reporters and television cameras converged on Hayes and Johnson in the hall.

One reporter yelled, "Prosecutor, if you find the murder weapon will you be prosecuting Julian Hopkins again for these murders?"

A jumble of cameramen and reporters holding microphones rushed forward. For the first time in his career, Hayes resented the limelight. "We are disappointed in today's ruling. But I assure you we will keep searching for the physical evidence that will support our claims against Julian Hopkins. Until then, these investigations will remain open and these murders will stay officially unsolved."

Other reporters called out to Medical Examiner Johnson, "How disappointed are you that your DNA evidence won't be used in a murder trial? What's it going to take to allow DNA to be used to convict a murderer successfully in Washington? Will they try it now on other forensic cases like the Green River?"

Like Hayes, Johnson was sorely frustrated he did not get his day in high court or chance to prove the power of DNA science in a murder trial, but at the same time he was ecstatic that so much publicity had made both the public and law enforcement agencies across the country aware of the possibilities. Ironically, Julian Hopkins and the article he wrote had played a pivotal role.

"We'll keep trying. We know DNA is the Rosetta Stone to solving violent crime. I promise you it will be used to put murderers and rapists behind bars. It won't be long before we use it to get a conviction, I'm sure of that. And once that happens the science will spread quickly across the globe. Violent criminals beware. The first conviction might just be closer than you think."

Johnson's words would prove to be prophetic. Shortly after the Hopkins hearing, Detective Nick Nizzi left the Everett PD, married a fellow officer, and rejoined Hank Garrity on the Green River Killer Task Force. Now armed with the knowledge of DNA forensics, he scoured old evidence, worked closely with Johnson's FBI lab, and several years later, snapped his cold gray cuffs on Gary Ridgway, the true Green River Killer. While Ridgway was never connected to the murders of Kathy Simmons or the Vallesteros sisters, his DNA and grim confession following his arrest convicted him of forty-nine other brutal homicides. As part of a plea deal to avoid the death penalty he admitted to murdering seventy-one.

As Hannah was leaving the courtroom to catch her flight back to Anchorage, trailing behind Bob, Mike, and Boone, Chris Fitzpatrick approached her.

"Hi, Hannah. I'm sorry things got so crazy last summer, with Lev and all. I'm sorry how it ended. And I don't care that you dated Jules. Hey, I've been meaning to call and ask, are you going back out to Dillingham next summer?"

"Oh, hi Chris. I ah, I'm not sure, especially after all this happened," she stammered. "Why?"

He flashed her a coy grin. "Because I'll go back if you do."

Hannah Miller's face heated as she dropped her eyes to the floor. Finally, she stood up straight and tall, nodded, and with a sanguine smile breathed, "Okay."

Suddenly lost in conversation, neither of them paid any attention to a white-haired old man sitting motionless in the crowd, intently watching Hannah. As they filed past, he got up and followed, gaining ground through the congestion until the pair abruptly reunited with Bob, Mike, and Boone waiting outside. Frustrated, the old man turned the other way and pounded his cane down the steep stack of courthouse steps, anger mounting with each reverberating clop. As he rounded a corner in the sidewalk, his gait steadied and quickened. When he got to Rockefeller Avenue, he stopped using his cane. Finally, as he entered a side alley, Lev Warrens looked back, confirmed no one was watching, hopped into his truck and took off a neck brace, wig, glasses, and hat. He reached under his seat for his Colt revolver, popped it open, rolled the cylinder to confirm it was loaded, snapped it shut, and placed it gently on his lap.

# CHAPTER 36

# NATAL WATERS

Outside the courthouse it was overcast and crisp, the cutting breeze blowing off Puget Sound stark contrast to the warmth radiating from Julian and Lindsay's embrace.

"I know we're as opposite as the north and south poles, Lindsay ... but, ah ... have you been feeling what I'm feeling?"

Lindsay had fallen hard for Julian. She couldn't explain it but felt it sharp and deep. It was almost as if they each had half the pieces necessary to make a full person. She blushed and nodded.

He kissed her again and took her by the hand. "Can I take you out to dinner later to celebrate, maybe to that quiet little Italian joint on Lake Union?"

Lindsay had carefully considered their potential for a future together. She couldn't help it. While it cut completely against her calm and cautious grain, she appreciated his energy, buoyant personality, and humor. His impulsiveness and sense of adventure charmed her. The fact that they were total opposites added to her sense of arousal. He made her happy. He was fun. God, he'd been treated unfairly by the cops, the press, and everybody else. She could not deny she was hopelessly in love.

"I would like that very much," she relinquished.

Julian bent down and kissed her deeply. Lindsay had stood by him throughout this whole affair, never once doubting his innocence. In that moment he felt natural, happy, complete. She made him feel safe and soothed, like the relief bare feet experiences as it uncovers wet sand on a scorching hot day at the beach. They belonged together. Neither could deny it.

"I love you," he whispered. "I love you, Lindsay Fiori."

Inside him, emotions stirred foreign and beautiful. Intense and confusing, yet safe and secure. A feeling like he was finally home after an endless journey. Such esoteric words. He'd never expressed them to a woman before and meant them like that. Julian closed his eyes to soak in the moment and exhaled. So, this was what true love felt like. Now he could see why people sought after it so much.

Lindsay laughed and playfully pushed him away. "I need to get downtown to the newsroom and make sure they don't screw *this* story up. And *you* need to get back there and talk to those television reporters. I'm sure they're looking for you, after all you are their lead story, again … and mine too. You and I will continue this conversation soon. Very, very soon."

She giggled. "And I love you back, Julian Hopkins."

He lingered longer before reluctantly letting her go, thoughts racing with all the things he needed to do. Thank Bob Clayton for bailing him out and hiring Bradley Jamison. Call Boone, Chris, and Mike. Apologize once again to Hannah and befriend her properly. Meet with Francis Bernard. Find his truck. Go back to his house and pack his things so he could move in with Lindsay and get away from Mrs. Brown for good. But first, he needed to return to the courthouse and talk to those damn reporters. He'd give them a piece of his mind, *damn them*, and oh did he have some things to say. He kissed Lindsay again, on the forehead this time, then quickly spun away.

"I'm free!"

He skipped into the autumn breeze, tip-tapping a two-step. He jumped in the air and clicked his heels together like an uncoordinated Fred Astaire.

"I'm Free!"

Julian disappeared around the corner. Lindsay laughed and shook her head as she heard him yell again, louder this time, "I'm FREE ... and I'm in LOVE!"

As Lindsay bounced her purse to find her car keys, her jangling was overpowered by the loud crack of a gunshot. Then another. She dropped her bag, sprinted around the corner, and screamed.

"JULIAN!"

A scarlet pool spread out from underneath him. He tried to get up, couldn't, and fell back down on the sidewalk. She helped him roll over on his back as a truck burned rubber and sped away. The autumn wind rustled through the branches of ancient oaks. Down the hill on the waterfront sprawled the Naval base where Julian was born. Dragline Fisheries was visible in the distance beyond that. An oak leaf released overhead and floated down lazily in the breeze. Hesitating in mid-air, momentarily resisting the pull of gravity, grasping to stay aloft, it finally succumbed to it's final, inevitable fall to freedom. Julian took a deep wheezing breath and exhaled flecks of blood. He tried to smile.

"I almost made it," he labored. "I almost made it home ... to you."

A red trickle drained from the corner of his mouth.

"You'll get there, Lindsay. You will ... keep swimming upstream ... against the current."

He gasped for breath. "Good ..."

"Don't you say it," she cut him off. "Don't you say good-bye."

"But I ... need to."

"Not this time, you don't. I won't allow it."

His eyes resisted resignation as they danced with hers in silence. As sirens approached, they conceded and closed.

❧

By the time Lev Warrens turned off I-5 onto Highway 20 in route to his far-away cabin to the east, the veins on the side of his neck pulsated with such wild adrenaline they looked ready to burst. Emitting a maniacal, sinister shriek of glee, he reached out and flicked Dari's Nerka charm necklace, swinging it sideways on his rear-view mirror. He had pulled it off and made Julian pay. Sitting on the seat beside him was a crewman's knife with a red handle. One side of the blade was serrated, the other, straight and sharp like a shave razor. Burned into its handle, still smudged with Kathy Simmons' dried blood, were the initials C.S.

Hours later, near a tiny mountain town outside Winthrop, he tapped his brakes and slowed down to a sudden crawl. A teenage girl was walking along the side of the road. Straining under the weight of a heavy backpack, she wore a denim jacket over a bright, dandelion-yellow print sundress, hair pulled back in a ponytail. She turned toward him and popped up her thumb. *Is that Hannah?* Lev eased over and stretched across his bench to roll down the passenger window.

"Need a ride? I'm headin' east."

Even though she had been hitching for hours and was desperate for a lift, she hesitated. Something didn't feel right to her. He sensed it.

"It's okay. I got some'n for ya," he drawled with an innocent grin. "I got this for my kid, but you kin' have it if you want."

He waved in the air Hannah's small, pink stuffed bunny and flopped its ears to point at the picture of a young boy taped to his dash. The hitchhiker relaxed. She exhaled a nervous breath and let her young-trusting eyes glimmer and flirt. Almost unable to contain himself, the subdued face of a demon grinned back.

"Hold on a sec. Let me move some things around for ya."

Lev looked both ways. No houses were in view. The highway was empty, the two completely alone. He glanced at the short-handled stone club strapped snugly to the back of his seat, acknowledging its presence with a sneer. But as he reached over to push the neck brace, wig, glasses, and hat to the floor, his hand came to rest on Charlie Steven's fishing knife. Hot memories flashed through him like an electrical current, an epiphany piercing his heart. Dave had been such a good guy. He'd always been so kind. Dave had taken him fishing once, had even offered to take him again. Dave had stuck up for him when others had not. He hadn't tried to kill Dave. *He hadn't.* It was Charlie he'd been after. Lev gasped. Warm emotions he'd never felt before swept through him in unwanted waves. Face flushed and fumbling for breath, he tried to overpower the moist sensations, shake them off like they were spiders, but was helpless to their fervor.

"Should I put my pack in the back, mister?"

"Just you wait," Lev hissed. "Wait right there."

Levon Cameahwar peered desperately into his rear-view mirror. The gentle brown eyes of his mother gazed back. Sad. Loving. Forgiving? The swaying Nerka totem glowed an intense-golden aura. Brilliant light reflected off its hand-etched scales and diamond eyes, momentarily leaving him blind. He blinked to repel the vision, convulsing his head from side-to-side. The image of the only person to ever truly love him wouldn't go away.

"I didn't mean for Dave to die," he choked, ripping the necklace down. With an impetuous heave he threw it, then Charlie's knife out his window into the far ditch. A moment later he hurled his stone club. "I didn't kill him. Not Dave. *I didn't.*"

"Mister? Are you gonna give me a ride, or not?"

The rusty-white pickup truck with a canopy on back and stolen Washington plates peeled out in the gravel, leaving her standing by the side of the empty highway, alone.

# CHAPTER 37

# REDFISH LAKE

Nestled at the base of Idaho's Sawtooth Mountains, nine hundred miles inland from the Pacific Ocean and sixty-five hundred feet above it, lies the clear-cold alpine waters of Redfish Lake. While the deep natural basin is just a few miles long and three-quarters of a mile wide, it is an evolutionarily significant place. A mystical destination. A spiritual Eden revered by the nearby Shoshone and Bannock tribes. For one unique strain of wild endangered Snake River Sockeye, the natal freshwaters of Redfish Lake are their beginning. Their essence. Their being. Their end.

For as far back as ancestral Native American legends could recall, the region's nomadic tribes journeyed there each autumn to derive subsistence from the anadromous schools of Nerka. Once, the Redfish returned in such massive number legend says one could walk across water, on their backs, to the other side of the lake. In those days the massive crimson glow of so many spawning adults dying into new life gave the lake its name.

A few mountain miles from Redfish Lake's closest town, on a narrow highway tracing the sharp bends of the Salmon River, a hard-ridden jeep with oversized tires and two sets of skis strapped in a top rack pulled out of the gravel parking lot of the General Store. Signs for ice, firewood, gas, and propane—that backcountry's no-frills essentials—reflected in its headlights. Tourist season was long since over. No one else was awake. A sliver of dawn piercing the eastern sky provided hope for the upcoming day.

After turning on a forest service road on the north shore, the Jeep slowly pulled up next to a rusty-white pickup truck with Idaho plates and a camper shell. The dimly lit campground was surrounded by thin, dry timber. A dirt-smashed square created by a season of tourist tents lay vacant. In a steel-grated fire pit, branded with welded lines Site 17, smoldered a tired fire, starving for wood, that had been lazily burning through the night. On the other side of a picnic table, hunched over on a log at water's edge, smoking a Salem Menthol, a still figure stared into the morning ripples. Other than a lonely raven cawing for another that had not yet come, the campground was silent and empty. The man by the lake did not look up as the door of the Jeep opened and slammed firmly shut.

"Finally. I was beginning to think this day would never come."

A frost-bearded Julian stepped to the front of his Jeep with a .30-30 lever-action varmint rifle crooked in the bend of his arm. He was in his late thirties now, but still dressed the same as always. His ripped jeans were pulled over worn cowboy boots and a weathered green-felt mountain man hat was molded to his head. He was shielded from the crisp October morning by a red-and-black checkered wool shirt. Ever since Lev had told him years before that he lived in a mountain cabin on a Reservation near a high-alpine lake where wild Sockeye still returned to spawn, Julian had been tirelessly searching.

With one hand in his pocket, the other clenching a sharp, hand-whittled spear, the figure got up slowly and turned. A deliberate, methodical, confused smile stretched his lips thin as he recognized Julian, but still, he said nothing.

"I've been hunting you for a long time, Lev. Every autumn I've followed the runs of Sockeye from the ocean all the way inland to the lakes. I've scoured every Reservation in every state on the West Coast, and Canada too. I almost gave up, until I heard a few Redfish still make it up the Snake to spawn in this one lake in Idaho."

Stunned, Levon Cameahwar gazed back in emotionless silence devoid of human sentiment, uninhibited by moral obligations. Now in his late sixties, he hadn't known affection since the day he had watched his father beat his Shoshone mother to death. A lifetime of atrocities and lengthy list of wrathful acts of violence confirmed his soul was glacier cold.

"When I was a papoose, the Redfish here were so many they'd turn this water the color of blood." Lev motioned to the shallow-pooling waters at the mouth of the creek. Floating belly-up, with a spear hole in its side, noosed with twine to a rock, was a single large Sockeye. "You could get one with every throw. This year, only one came back."

Julian bristled, clicked the safety off his Winchester, flipped it to his left hand, and took a step away from his Jeep, creating a clear shooting lane between he and Lev.

"Put down the spear, you vile son of a bitch. I know you murdered Kathy Simmons. And the Vallesteros sisters too. But tell me right here and now, were you responsible for Dave?"

The raven glided down from its perch and landed by the edge of the lake. It cawed again. Unable to keep eye contact, Lev winced and looked away, silently studying the bird.

"Goddam you. I knew you were somehow. I dreamt it many times, you soulless bastard. Why did you do it? Why did you kill Dave?"

Inwardly pushing back against empathy and remorse, Lev didn't look up. Julian's anger mounted.

"How about the Chiklak boys? Did you pull the plug on their skiff?"

Lev bobbed his head, back turned.

"Jesus Lev. They were just kids. Face me, motherfucker."

Lev turned around coolly. Pure evil pulsed through his veins; soul permanently scarred by a lifetime of savagery.

"Speak up, Lev. This is your last fuckin' chance. Why did you kill all those people? And why did you try to peg it on me?"

Lev closed his vicious-prideful eyes and thought back to the two young Filipino sisters, Dave Stevens, Kathy Simmons, the Chiklak boys, the uncountable list of unpunished murders he had committed before them. No curable mental illness stepped forward to claim responsibility for his long procession of hideous crimes.

"None of them loved me. No one has ever loved me. And I never loved no one. They all deserved to die."

"What about me, Lev? I always showed you kindness."

Lev's anger came quick, wicked and unfathomable desires flickered, dark-devilish pupils locking on Julian once again. "'Cept for Hannah. Hannah loved me. I was bringin' her with me to my cabin, 'til you stole her. I saw you coming out of her room. I saw her sheets ... what you did to her."

Julian chambered a shell with a loud *cha-chink* and bristled with rage. "What in the FUCK are you talking about? *That's* what this was about? You shot me for *that*? You really are a deranged son of a BITCH."

He lowered his barrel and took a step forward with gritted teeth. "Guess, what? Hannah *never* loved *you*. She didn't even fuckin' like—"

A shot from a revolver hidden inside Lev's coat shattered the still. Julian was spun sideways, falling backward into the picnic table before hitting the ground. Shoulder bleeding, he stretched for his rifle.

With startling quickness, Lev rushed across the small beach, grabbed Julian by the hair, pressed his knee in his spine, and exposed the white of his neck.

"You're a liar! Hannah loved me. And I loved her. I made you *pay* once. Now I'm gonna make you *pay* again!"

Lev slid a double-edged knife out of a hidden sheath inside his boot. The bone handle glistened cruelly, as vile as its wielder, both murderous to the core. Obsidian eyes flared. Deeply rooted evil intent flushed his face. He raised the blade.

"LEV!"

Startled, the demon whipped around. Julian broke free and rolled for his gun. From the other side of the Jeep, Lindsay stepped out and fired a sixteen gauge. Lev stumbled back and grabbed his torn, bleeding stomach.

"Leave us alone!" she screamed, pumping another shotgun shell and firing again. Bewildered, Lev fell back against the stump and looked down at the deep-oozing hole in his side. Losing consciousness while trying to twist his lips into words, his ripped-lacerated body hit the ground and rolled down the hill toward the lake. Blood trickled across the sand into the calm-clear pool, clouding it smoky crimson.

"You're done killing, Lev Warrens. It's over. You're done murdering people for *good*."

Smoke danced from the end of Lindsay's barrel like the wisp of a departing soul. She dropped her firearm on the ground.

"Holy shit, Lindsay," Julian gasped, fighting through sharp pain with a forced grin. "You're a better shot than I thought."

She dashed to Julian and helped him to his feet and away from the fire pit. As she lifted his good arm and draped it over her shoulder a diamond wedding ring, studded with sapphires, flashed on her finger. "Omigod, you're bleeding bad. Let's get you some help."

Julian paused to gaze over his shoulder. The morning sun had now fully risen. In the distance, majestic Thompson Peak welcomed the new day. Golden sunbeams bounced off the Sawtooth's and Grand Mogal projecting mirror images into calm waters.

"What now? He'll die if we don't do something."

Julian eyed the phantom who had terrorized his psyche for so long, the beast who had dispassionately served death to kinship and peace. Crumpled at water's edge, letting blood, barely breathing, Lev now seemed so primal, fragile, extinct.

"I don't know. Give me a sec."

Reverently, Julian laid down his rifle and limped down to the beach, eyes shifting to the speared Redfish gently being caressed by the waters that had produced it. With a contemplative grimace he bent over, and with the whittled point of Lev's crude spear scratched in the frosty-cold sand, SAVE THE SALMON.

THE END

To read the Afterword, Unpublished Backstories, and Book Club Questions visit: www.conradjungmann.com

# conrad Jungmann jr.

AUTHOR & SCREENWRITER

Conrad Jungmann Jr. earned his Master's in Journalism at the University of Missouri before embarking on a twenty-year career in journalism and digital marketing. While working at BELO, KTVB-TV, KING-TV, Microsoft/ MSNBC and his own company that he founded in 2006, LION Digital Media, on advertising campaigns for some of the world's most prestigious brands, his mind often wandered to the Alaska adventures of his youth and he vowed to someday share those stories with others. EDGE OF REDFISH LAKE is Conrad's debut novel and first feature screenplay. Conrad lives in Lynnwood, WA. with his wife and three children. He is an avid fisherman and outdoorsman.

If you enjoyed this book, please consider giving it a Review on Amazon and Barnes & Noble so others can more easily find it. You can also be among the first to hear about my future books and be eligible for upcoming giveaways by signing up for my email list at:

**www.conradjungmann.com**

CPSIA information can be obtained
at www.ICGtesting.com
Printed in the USA
LVHW092158150721
692648LV00011B/232